Borrowed Time

A story of Hong Kong

STEVE LANGLEY

Copyright © 2018 Steve Langley

All rights reserved.

ISBN 978-1-7291-1984-6

PART 1

I keep a map on the wall to remind me where I am. It is a map of the world that has been my only constant travelling companion for 40 years. It is my only companion now. Everywhere I have lived and worked is marked with a cross in red Biro. Childish, I know. But each cross shows that my life has been a success. I've been places. I've come a long way.

It used to be a comfort. It used to be a pictorial diary I could glance at, proud as the little red crosses spread, focusing on one and thinking about my life and work at the point it marked. It used to tell me where I had been and, I liked to think, where I was going. Now it upsets me. I still keep it on the wall but its boasts are barbs, not aids. It reminds me where I am. And it is tired, like me, and not going anywhere any longer. It says there will be no more red crosses across that stained, torn, worn, Sellotaped paper.

I can't remember where I bought it, or why. In those days, I had not been much further out of London than the Norfolk coast. But I do remember pulling the map out of the cardboard tube and spreading it out on the counterpane. I remember gazing, as if hypnotised, at those muted pastel blocks of countries and continents and thinking that one day I would have markers in each and every one. Places I had been. I tacked the map on the wall in my bedsit – a clean room, as I *recall, not one where it was necessary to hide mould and damp stains – and let my eye wander over the tracts of land and the blue in between. And I wondered.*

I don't know how many evenings I wondered. It could have been one, it could have been a hundred, a hundred quiet, lonely evenings in that small room with the big wooden wireless set next to the bed singing softly to me. I was eager to mark the chart, eager to make it, and what it represented, mine. It seemed to be virgin for so long. And then it was no longer. I had been somewhere and felt the urgent need to pinpoint it. It was Liverpool, I think. It seemed so important at the time, so grand. But I can't remember a thing about Liverpool. I have never been back

I had landed a job as a travelling salesman, one of those greasy individuals – and there seemed to be armies of us in those days – selling spoons or soap or scrubbing brushes and going all over the country with a pair of heavy cases. I would stay a couple of nights here, a couple of nights there, always in dank, dark bed-and-breakfast places, always on a busy high road or within sound of a railway line. And always in the rain. My memories are flooded with rain. Wherever I went, it seemed to be drizzling. That is unlikely but it was a grey decade.

Whatever, the rain did not dampen my spirit. I would load those two rattling cases of cutlery into the boot of a coach at Victoria Station – it was so much cheaper than the train – and set off northwards in search of a new profitable pitch. I would disembark at what was usually a bombsite, big Leyland buses scattered around a pitted yard with tufts of grass sticking out of low walls, the clouds building up, shabby people milling around, looking lost with their luggage, and I would drink in the view. Like a captain sighting land, like a conquistador finding El Dorado. Ridiculous, I would have cut a ridiculous figure to anybody who had cared to notice. Every town looked the same. But they weren't, of course, not to me: they were points on the map, different points, and I would collect them like they were stamps or rare butterflies, not grey, blasted urban piles of depressing uniformity.

I would pause by the coach and scan the slate-tiled roofs and broken buildings, unhealed wounds from the war a decade or so earlier, then head to the gates on to the road. Without fail, a travellers' hotel would be planted opposite those gates and I would check in for one, two nights, maybe a week. I would store the cases in the bottom of a big walnut wardrobe in my room and before I had even unpacked my toiletries I would carefully pull the map from its tube, unfurl it, mark it, smile at it, then repack it.

I made it a rule – one of many I have followed through life – to work hard on that first day and go to bed early. Only from the second day would I give myself any time for anything other than the job, food and sleep. On the second evening, I would venture into the hotel bar or the nearest pub, hoping to team up with other salesmen. When they weren't working they did not like to travel far and the nearest place selling a pint of stout, no matter how uninviting an establishment, would be their berth until the last bell.

I was prototype fat then, waiting for the flesh to fall on me from my larger, older, wiser compatriots, along with their bad-breath overconfidence and gems of wit and tales of sexual conquest and tips for making the big one – the sale that would set you up for life.

But apart from a weight problem during my National Service in Belgium, a weight problem long since burned away, I was imbued with none of their characteristics. My confidence was of the quiet, determined kind, my wit and imagination were flat, my ability to make the big one was almost crushed by one slammed front door too many.

So I got out of selling spoons. I looked at the map one night after a particularly unfruitful day and burst into bitter laughter. My conquering tracks through the world were reduced to a pathetic shuffle of crosses in the northern provinces. I returned to London and resigned. I took evening classes in business studies and stopped drinking, for a while. I found a job selling insurance, London-based, better commission, a better class of salesman, I thought. But I soon realised that what I was doing was even more demeaning than my previous job. I was not even satisfying a customer's need any more: I was exploiting a fear. And I felt penned in, traipsing the same streets in the same boroughs, day after day, month after month. There were no longer any crosses to put on the map. It was too large-scale to recognise such petty achievements.

It was the girl I was courting at the time who helped release me from the cage. Her brother found me an office job with a big components firm. "Stick with this and you'll go places," he said unwittingly. I did. I worked my way up and worked my way out – from that office, from the surrounding streets, from the town, from the country that had contained me all my life. I worked my way up through office manager, sales team leader, head of sales, area manager, products and promotions deputy director, regional sales director all the way to running the entire Far East and Australasia division.

From that first office in London's Surrey Docks to the last in Hong Kong I travelled via Singapore, Manila, Tokyo, Bangkok and Melbourne. Each one marked with a cross. Each one telling a story. And the most recent marker will be the last story to tell.

1

The teargas had cleared, the bruises healed, the questions pushed away, the fear subdued to another day. The riot was just another point in the history of the camp. Soon, the camp itself would be history. It would be cleared and razed and rebuilt as something else. The Vietnamese boat people who lived within its confines would be sent back to their own land after their bitter shop-window experience of Hong Kong.

They had been picked up in their fishing boats and their leaking sampans, south and west of the territory, in their lost search for a new life. They had been plucked from their vessels and dropped into barrack dormitories, remote from the glamorous cityscape of their dreams, kept as prisoners in tin-roofed huts, uncooled in the summer and unheated in the winter. They were never allowed to feel at home: this place was not their home, nor would it ever be. It was a land of opportunity only to a certain type of refugee – not to any chancer from the region. Money or the promise to make money were the only recognised passports.

On this suffocating day, the camp was heavy with the stench of lethargy. Adults sat on steps in shaded corners, slicing paths through unmoving air with makeshift fans, and children played in short, de-energised bursts between lines of washing. Guards from the Correctional Services Department meandered from alley to alley between the huts.

For a month after the riot, the camp had been closed to outsiders. The volunteer agencies were barred; the press were denied access. The place became invisible again, an embarrassment. "There is no story here," reporters were told. "The riot is over. You will get a copy of the inquiry report."

The injured returned. Vendettas were played out in quiet corners. But defiance and provocation were too hard in the sapping heat of that early summer. They faded away, just as the memory of the riot faded. The camp shuffled into its normal lethargic rhythm. When the inmates had been lulled into sleepwalking again, the camp was reopened to visitors.

A stifling Saturday morning was crawling towards noon when the first group of aid workers arrived at the gates of the compound. A dozen people, local and expatriate, had volunteered to take a select group of children out of the camp for the day. The brakes of their coach hissed and the guards at the entry post looked up with the same dumb insouciance they always affected as a man stepped from the vehicle and walked towards them. His face glowed and his feet dragged through the gravel. In this hollow, shielded by thick vegetation from the staring towers of the neighbouring new town but not from the unblinking sun, the air was thick enough to swim through.

The man forced a smile and pulled out a laminated card as he looked unwaveringly at the guards. He tried not to see them as the enemy. The taller guard flicked his eye over the card and gestured the man towards the reception hut on the other side of twin fences.

Aboard the coach the volunteers, the liberal, the wealthy and the bored, watched him as he disappeared behind metal. They were like tourists, protected by glass from an exotic but disturbing sight. The poverty and the hopelessness, the huts and the razor wire, were snapshot glimpses of a world that would cease to be as soon as the coach went back up the hill.

It was the first time that Alice Bradshaw had seen the scarred underbelly of the city. It was a repulsive sight, strong enough almost to nauseate. She had a sudden urge to run from the bus and escape back to her unbothered life in her plush apartment high up on the hill, away from all this. She wanted to be far away and drown the miserable image of the barracks with a gin and tonic and a piece of Rachmaninov. She wanted to look through different windows at a nicer view. The sweeping valley of trees and towers all the way to the harbour would soothe her and deny this grubby intrusion of a poorer, more desperate, world. She could be safe and comfortable and selfish.

"This is terrible," she said to the man sitting next to her. He was half her age and was called Wayne or Sean or something. He had muttered his name as if it embarrassed him, introducing himself like an afterthought. He was wiry and attractive and throughout the journey she had repeatedly checked herself looking at his bare legs in ragged shorts. She had managed to strike up a brief rapport with him early on but had lapsed into silence, the heat sapping his enthusiasm, the suspense hers.

He glanced sideways at her and his eyes shimmered in indignation. "Yes," he muttered.

The team leader came out of the reception hut scratching his head and blinked up at the sky while he squeezed his ID back into his wallet. He smiled from the coach steps. "Everybody got bags?" he said. He grinned and a flicker of relief passed through the coach. His light tone reassured them, made them blank out the stunned, helpless rage they felt.

"This is the bit I've been dreading," smiled Alice as she flustered with plastic bags.

The driver, who had been standing at the door sipping on his cigarette like a last drink, threw the tab into the gravel and climbed back into his seat. The engine roared and the coach eased through the gates, through alleys of wire and huts and washing and defeated people. The volunteers fell back into silence.

The coach stopped by another guardhouse where a group of children were marshalled. Of a thousand children in the camp, 30 would be allowed a day's escape and they stood regimented in line, their eyes fixed on their unknown rescuers. Many of them born in this jail, the kids could get past the wire once or twice a year before they were ushered on to a plane with their parents and a few toys and flown back to Vietnam. Their temporary reprieve from the camp was by lottery. Their permanent exclusion from the city was by executive decision. They were all choiceless.

"They look so thin," cried Alice. Bright clothes and brighter faces could not disguise their emaciated frames. "They look terrible. Don't they feed them here? How old are they?"

The man next to her gave her a resigned smile.

"I think they're between eight and 12," he said.

"None of them looks more than six. What are these people doing to them?"

"Looking after them. At least they can't be accused of giving them an easy life."

"I thought this place was civilised."

"Depends who you are." He walked to the front of the bus and ruffled the hair of a girl waiting uncertainly on the bottom step. She touched him on his hip, a shy, sad movement, then got into the coach, her wary eyes drawing a smile from Alice as she passed. Other children followed, singly and in pairs, holding hands or clutching belongings, giggling or silent, and scattered to random seats. As they boarded, small brown hands the length of the line reached out to touch the strangers and cries of "Hello!" erupted in well-rehearsed English. The man who had been sitting next to Alice trotted to a grey-faced boy at the back, holding open a bag like a gift. The driver gunned the engine.

The coach moved up the hill on to a main road, through the heartless new town, past hills colourless in the white glaze of the sky, and into the old part of the city, the ass-end of clogged streets and buildings filthy with their own sweat. In the crawling heat of afternoon traffic, the euphoria on the coach wore off. The children were bored. A few sketchy friendships had been struck up with the white strangers but the language barrier allowed few breaches. The interpreter had fallen asleep in the seat behind the driver.

Alice was petting the head of a girl. It was not the words, which she could not understand, that had won the girl over, but the voice, which was soft, like her mother singing. The smile, too, had an echo of home. It was a smile that spread slowly and pulled back to expose two large, white teeth. But the eyes were sad.

Alice wound the girl's black hair in her fingers, spreading it like cloth over her lap, and daydreamed. The girl eased into sleep. The woman looked at the traffic, busy and thick, directionless yet going somewhere, and at the dense mass of people on the pavements with that same deceptive nomadism, and thought about her husband. George had not wanted to join her. Too busy. Saturday afternoon and too busy. She could not understand it – still – but years of the same excuse had worn away her protests. Silently, she had watched him leave the apartment for work that morning and she had nodded blankly when he called a cheery "Enjoy yourself" from the doorway. His indifference made her feel small, unimportant. He would show an interest when she related the story of her day but it would be the interest of an impartial observer, of someone reading a feature in a magazine, superficially absorbed. To him it did not really matter. He would not belittle her, not consciously, but overshadowed by his towering detachment she would belittle herself.

Beside him, her life was small.

He was always active, always busy, never consumed by the doubts and ennui that sank into her. He never had enough time to do all that he wanted; she had too much. It was boredom and the fear of it that had driven her to put her name down for this trip. To find some meaning, to establish some worth, alongside the meaning and worth her husband had found. The predictable routine of her life was choking her. Another Saturday afternoon in the apartment, alone, pretending to balance her time between phone calls and shopping trips and planning dinner and social activities and barking orders at the amah who really wasn't worth the money. Reminiscing about life in England when everything had had a point and her husband was more loving and children and friends were never too far away.

Then was real. Real life. Real children, real friends, not the superficial ciphers she leant on out of a barely repressed desperation here, their shared lethargy their only link. She remembered an article she had read when she first arrived four years earlier. She had been excited, then, anticipatory, everything was new and fresh and a challenge. The article, a lightweight piece of lay psychology, had appealed because it seemed to be speaking directly to her, the newcomer. It was about the stages of adjustment the expatriate had to go through when moving to another country. The first stage, which she was still savouring as she pored over those words, was excitement. Then, warned the article, came disappointment and rejection. Many expats could not break through that stage. They were homesick; the alien culture which had been so exotic had revealed its imperfections. They got impatient with the way things were done and focused on the bad points of the life all around them, exaggerating the differences, always contrasting them unfavorably with home. The brusqueness of the people, the ugliness of the language, the clearing of throats in the streets, the indifference of taxi drivers, the bad television. The noise, the smell, the congestion. Even the weather was not as good as it was at home.

Sensible people stuck in that stage recognised their difficulties and left. Others withdrew into the almost exclusive company of their own compatriots, unhappy guests in an unwelcoming land. Others persevered and tried to fight, to win through to the next stages of assimilation and integration.

The memory of that article, so long buried, shocked Alice. She was stuck in the second stage, she now realised, had been for years, while her husband was moving blithely on to the fourth.

She was stuck in her empty, easy lifestyle and ached to get away, to return to a reality that this could never become. But the one thing preventing her leaving *was* the one thing she could not give up. Her husband. She could leave everything else behind: the wealth, the spectacle, the gossip. Even her friends, her transient friends. They were fun, they were interesting, but they were just shipwrecks like herself. Just refugees. She and her circle had nothing in common other than their homelessness.

She looked down at the girl and, caressing her face, her pity was transferred. She fell asleep.

*** *** *** *** *** ***

A jolt and a hiss of airbrakes brought her to. The girl was gone from her lap. She shook her head and looked around. Behind a clump of trees and a plastic tower of soft drink crates she could see the glow of the beach and the water beyond.

Excited children were rushing for the door, ignoring the half-hearted efforts of the volunteers to keep them in order. The earlier regimentation had gone. They were away from the cod-military lifestyle of the camp, free of its wire and its walls, its incomprehensible regulations and its unnatural order. Their excitement stirred the stagnant pool of Alice's feelings.

She was last off the coach and made her way to the adults clustering around the team leader who was splitting them into small groups – some to play at the water's edge, some to prepare food, some to watch. Alice volunteered to watch. It was the obvious choice for her.

She found a bench and squinted her eyes against the sparkle off the water. Now and again she would be dragged from her reverie by a child showing off a shell or pointing out a sandcastle. They wanted her to participate, but she was comfortable making noises of approval and flashing encouraging smiles. She was aloof from it all and glad that she was aloof.

In the far corner of the beach she caught sight of three or four children scrambling up the rocks at the base of a low cliff. A wave slapped the jagged rocks and splashed the group who shrieked with joy. Alice stood.

A click distracted her. She turned. Behind the bench, a young woman lowered a camera. Her pretty, rounded face was burnt by the sun and the spray. Her forehead looked scalded under a fringe of blonde. Alice had seen her on the coach but they had not spoken.

"Sorry," said the stranger. "Couldn't resist." She waved the camera.

"Oh. That's all right," said Alice.

"Camera freak. That should be a good shot. I'll let you have a copy if you want." There was a trace of American in her accent. "Didn't mean to startle you."

Alice replied with a smile.

"Isn't this great?" said the woman, coming round the bench. There was a slow sensuality about her. "I'm Carol. Is this your first time out with the boatkids?"

"It is," Alice smiled again, then slipped behind formality and stuck out her hand to introduce herself.

"Mine too. It's such a shame that we can't bring them out more often," said Carol as she scanned the figures on the waterline. "Poor kids. Well..." Their conversation seemed to dry up in the heat and Carol moved away. "I'm going back into the water," she said. "It's too hot here. Nice to meet you."

"And you," Alice called at the receding back.

She returned to the bench. The children she had been watching before she was interrupted were forgotten. Out of sight, they were getting braver with each step. The waves crashing over the knife-cut rocks exhilarated them and they challenged each other with screams every time the water boomed against the stone and threw its tangy spray into their faces. The rockpools fascinated them; the shellfish stuck fast were prizes to pull loose; it was fun sliding feet along polished planes of grey and black slate and edging past jagged outcrops. And there were no adults around, no one telling them what to do, no silly men and women pretending to be children. They were truly by themselves for the first time in their lives. This was their adventure, this edging along the treacherous tumbledown of flint, slipping in the moisture, gasping as the waves came over, getting further and further away from their captors.

The eldest boy was at the front. His companions were happy to let him lead as they skirted the edge of the cliff and the beach was sliced bit by bit from view. He was already bleeding from the knee and his hands were grazed. The terrain and the roaring water did not worry him. He kept going.

He turned, giggling, to his friends. A boulder blocked their path. He said they would have to hang on to it and lean out over the sea to get to the other side. The girl at the back of the line baulked and shook her head; she let out a tiny sob and began to whimper. A wave erupted in a funnel and broke over their heads. She screamed and stepped back.

"Come on," he shouted over the noise of the sea. She shook her head and her fear enveloped the two children in the middle, dragging them towards her. They began the panicked scramble back to safety with the sneer of the eldest boy frozen in futility. He made a soft final gesture of pleading, then edged towards the boulder. His fingers were shaking as they splayed out to grab the slippery rock. The girl screamed again, a piercing call that echoed over the beach. The boy's determination hardened. He wrapped his arms around the boulder and pushed himself out, a wave cracking in the air behind him. The sound startled him and he slipped, his ankle twisting. He span, lunging awkwardly for the rock but his flapping hands missed and he fell, and the water bounced up to meet him. All he could see was the girl's round, screaming face floating in the air, and that huge boulder, wedded to the cliff. The two images merged; the face became the boulder and then split into two boulders, then four, reduplicating itself with each part rotating until there was nothing but a spinning blur of stone in front of him. All he could hear were her screams sucked beneath the thump of the water. Then there was the shock of hitting the sea and his breath being torn from his body and the violent drag of the current and the crack of something against his head. He was twisted and pushed away from the cliff as the water held on and took him away.

Alice heard the screams and ran at an ungainly lope towards the cliff. She stopped short, panting, unable to run further in the unyielding sand and called to the nearest group of volunteers. "I think there's someone in the water," she cried. Carol ran into the sea and leapt and seemed to run through the waves with powerful strokes sending up sparkles of spray around the strobe flashes of flailing arms. Other volunteers followed her, or ran to the cliff or herded children to the concrete apron at the side of the road. Alice stood alone at the water's edge, looking anxiously towards the rocks, wondering how she could help.

Carol reached the edge of the cliff and disappeared. She bobbed up, clenching something to her chest. The boy's head was thrown back over her shoulder as if broken, spewing seawater, his feeble arms dangling behind him.

Carol turned the body, holding the limp head, and dragged herself towards the shore. The beach, rising and falling with a sickly motion against the waves but never coming closer, teased her with its unreachable distance. Then she was staggering into the sand and laying the boy down. As she pressed her interlocked hands into his bony chest and pumped a desperate rhythm of life into it, volunteers gathered around. Alice pushed through them.

"Oh don't say, don't say …. is he alive?"

"I think so." Carol pressed down harder into the boy and stared pleadingly at his swollen eyelids. Water frothed at the mouth and trickled into the sand.

"I saw them. I saw them on the rocks. I should have been quicker. I should have thought."

An ugly sound ruptured the boy's mouth and a gush of bloodied water spurted out. He shook his head and coughed, a long, endless fit of choking that shook his weedy frame from head to toe. His eyes flickered rapidly like a silent movie at the wrong speed.

Carol pressed her lips to the child's and breathed a slow thread of life into his lungs. She pulled her head back, her hands massaging the chest, and bent forward again with a new breath. The boy's eyes opened and stared, no longer flickering but frozen on the sky.

"Thank God," she mumbled.

"We'd better get an ambulance," said Alice.

"They should have been watched properly. Someone should have stopped them going to the cliffs," growled Carol. Her breath rasped as she turned burning eyes on Alice.

She could think of no defence. It was her fault. She had been too slow, too preoccupied, too passive to act at the right time.

"Do you think he'll be all right?"

"I think so. I don't know. I'm not a doctor."

"You saved his life."

Carol's eyes shut as if in pain and opened again. She stroked the boy's fine black hair. "It wasn't your fault," she said. The boy's eyes locked on hers.

"You're an excellent swimmer," Alice said. She felt the need to reciprocate the other's generosity. And she wanted to prolong the conversation, out of shock, out of sadness and loneliness and fear.

The team leader, panting with the exertion of running up to the road and back, said that the ambulance was on its way and lifted the boy from the ground. The body was still limp but there was a determined vitality in the eyes. As the volunteers trooped after him through the sand, Alice fell back to Carol and began chatting awkwardly. The tension faded. By the time they reached the coach they had innocently gone through the cliched litany of first-time questions and answers, both uncaring of their staleness. How long have you been here? Will you stay after the handover? Do you like it? What do you do?

Nothing at the moment, said Carol. She had just arrived with her boyfriend, who had found work as an English-language teacher, after extended backpacking through Asia. She was looking for a marketing job.

"I'll have a word with my husband," said Alice. "He might be able to help you."

The old bird isn't as stiff as she seems, thought Carol.

2

When he lost the game 9-6 he knew it was time to quit. George Bradshaw and his partner had been evenly matched. But after 30 minutes he felt that desperate twinge in his heart and his knees were throbbing and his strength was drained. He could not complete the set.

"That's me out, Wilson," he said, gasping as he stooped over, putting all his weight on his squash racquet. He gave his partner a pained grimace.

"Young man's game," he sighed. "Young man's game."

He straightened himself and with a final whack smashed the ball into the wall. He felt the power slip from his forearm as he brought it back. The rubber ball cracked against the concrete. With a casual flick, his partner caught the ball in his small palm as if it were an insect.

"You're getting too good at this." He was wheezing and eyed Wilson enviously. They were both the same age yet the differences were startling to Bradshaw. Not just in physical stamina but in physiognomy. Bradshaw was a big man, solid; his partner small and lithe. Where Bradshaw's face was crumpled and cragged with age, Wilson Chan's was smooth. Where Bradshaw had body hair from his hard brush-bristle moustache to the black wisps curling out of his sneaker tops,

Chan was shaved clean. The hair on his head was black and silk-like; Bradshaw's was wiry and grey.

"Still. A good game," said Wilson.

"Yes. Very good." Bradshaw gave him a friendly punch on the arm.

They eased through the door in the glass wall of the court and made their way to the changing room. The banter was all about the game: this serve, that return, those missed chances, that sudden display of excellence or luck. The inquest was over by the time they reached the lockers. Outside the room, they could hear the crack of balls against walls and the car brake squeal of sneakers on the floor.

"Lunch?" said Bradshaw, hunched over on the bench and rubbing his red-glowing knees. The ache in his chest beat like a warning drum.

"I should really be getting back."

"Everything's under control. And it's Saturday, man."

"You're encouraging me to malinger. Maybe because you've cleared all your work this morning." Wilson smiled. "And a stressed executive is not productive, eh? Not good for the company, you've told me many, many times. All work and no play makes Jack a dull boy." He beamed at his partner, pleased with his grasp of idiom. He collected them like badges, badges of progress, happy when he heard a new colloquialism and proud when he could use it in the right context. Bradshaw could speak Cantonese better than most Westerners whose lazy attempts were limited to asking for the bill and ordering a taxi to stop, but he could not ease his Chinese conversation along with slang. It was dry, textbook stuff, his chat, as stilted and lifeless as a weather report and belying the energy of everything else he did.

"So how is Mrs Bradshaw?" Wilson called over the hiss of the shower.

"Not too bad. A bit down. And Mrs Chan?"

"She was fine last night. She's still in Shanghai, visiting with her mother. One more week."

"We'll take a break soon. Mrs Bradshaw needs a break. She's working too hard."

Wilson was puzzled. Mrs Bradshaw did not work, she did not go out to work. There were no children to look after.

"Phuket, I think," Bradshaw continued. "Haven't been there for a few years."

He yanked the faucet to shut down the water. He put too much energy into even the simplest of tasks but he was never aware of it; only those who saw him knew that he wasted strength. There was too much energy within him and he never tried to harness it. He did everything well and felt that there was power to spare. The truncated game of squash only made him more determined to exert himself elsewhere. He lived for the day, hurling energy at everything as though it were his last chance.

Every movement was a gesture of defiance, an exaggeration. Stepping from the shower cubicle he whipped the towel into the air and started furiously rubbing his head. It was not anger, it was desperation, an anguish with time. Everything was at speed.

"Thai or dim sum? What do you fancy?" he asked as Wilson stepped gracefully from his cubicle.

They ran across a road treacherous with traffic to reach the restaurant. Thick shadows thrown by the sun which had finally burst through the glowering sky had left this side of the street wrapped in darkness and all the lights were on as they pushed through the doors. The roar of voices and clattering plates greeted them and Bradshaw felt invigorated. He used to hate these restaurants. They were like huge, chaotic warehouses, frantic, overlit, public, with no ambience and no privacy. But now the sheer, good-hearted throb of life, the excitement of something as basic as eating, the emphasised gratification, stirred him.

They took a table in the middle of the floor, surrounded by moving mouths and flashing chopsticks, and Wilson banged the table with a cup to alert a waitress.

With the bowl just below his mouth, Bradshaw shovelled in the rice, scattering white flecks across the table like confetti. In this environment it was not considered graceless. He leaned towards the rotating dais in the centre of the table and plucked a shrimp from its bed of grease, cramming it into his mouth and talking through the food. They had moved from the family and holidays to business talk: sales, targets, staff, problems.

It was a dialogue of numbers, an arcane code of figures and numerals, the lingua franca that linked their two disparate cultures. Even personalities were reduced to sums: how much someone cost, how much they earned. Dollars, percentages, fractions and points were thrown across the table with the briskness of gossip. There was no emotion and no sentiment. The talk was of business. Around them, mobile phones screamed.

An informal sales plan was drawn up, a purchasing trip pencilled in for Wilson, a decision reached on a promising but troublesome new salesman. The conference ended as the meal did.

Bradshaw pushed himself back from his chair and looked around the emptying restaurant. He called for the bill and slapped his credit card on to the salver, waving away Wilson's protests. He brushed imaginary dust from his grey slacks and reached for his sports bag under the table.

"You're going back now?" he said.

Wilson, mining his mouth with a toothpick behind coyly cupped hands, looked up.

"Of course."

"I'll see you Monday. I'll do that Berlin call from home."

On the corner he caught a taxi and rode to a quiet street above the city. The air had loosened some of its clamminess at this altitude and the sparsity of people gave him a sense of liberation from the choking density below. Aloof colonial architecture imposed a respectable quiet. This was his favourite area for walking, where he could saunter without the need for dancing and bumping through a press of pedestrians, and where he could drink in the artistry of the buildings and the beauty of the greenery. It was a siesta from the city.

He stopped by the window of a small craft and jewellery store and examined the display. Among the Tibetan knickknacks and Indian figurines he saw a tiny pendant of a Buddha, its arms raised, its face smiling, its belly stuck out in vulgar pride. It was crudely cut in pinkish-brown wood and from it snaked a fine gold chain.

A present, he thought, breaking into a smile. It was cute. An ideal present. Flowers indicated a love not necessary to articulate or a guilt he had no reason to feel. This little token would be an innocent gesture of fondness, nothing more. He bought the trinket, not bothering to argue the price with the salesman.

He stepped on to the pavement and turned towards home. Past the ubiquitous construction sites and the roadworks, past restaurants and shops and opulent apartment blocks and past the old civic buildings that maintained their alien dignity. In a place with no respect for history it was a surprise to him that any of them were still standing. This city, driven by the constant need to reinvent itself, to be brand new every day, like a product or a marketing strategy, had no room for sentimentality. Old product was unsellable product.

He stopped by a gap in the vegetation that allowed a view over the entire business district. In the solar glare, the glass and concrete towers shone with money, with success and with purpose.

This is mine, he thought.

3

The tie, yanked down, pink and floral, was knotted as tight as a ligature but the knot was not where it should be. It hung a button down from the throat. His collar was stained with yellow patches. He held his jacket by the shoulders crumpled into a ball and his trousers were damp and creased. His face was bruised with drink and fatigue and the pain of the rising sun made him squint as he contemplated his nausea.

Phil was drunk. Again. And again he was getting home after dawn, weaving up the long hill from the ferry in pantomime staggers. He lurched from one side of the pavement to the other, balancing on the kerb and thrusting his body forward and sideways to stop himself from falling into the road.

It was quiet except for a few birds twittering in the hill of bushes to his left. He was glad there was nobody about; he was still aware, even in this state, of how contemptible he looked. His shame would burn at a single disparaging glance from the first person skirting him in amplified anxiety. The burn would flare into rage and self-contempt. He would curse the passer-by and then himself. With weariness pulling and nausea pushing, he would swear that he would never get drunk again.

Of course not. He knew he was lying to himself. He enjoyed the drinking. It was an after-work relief, a way out of depression and exhaustion, a good laugh. He and his girlfriend, Carol, had flown to Asia a year earlier for a fresh adventure and this was the end result. She was hostage to the same drive that had pushed her out of Connecticut to find answers in England when she was 22 years old. They were not there. "We will never win the car," he had said. "Maybe we'll get the right answers if we go travelling, start a new life." She laughed it off.

And this was not a new life, he knew; it was the old life with all its faults and disappointments dislocated and magnified. But here he had the chance to think his way out of that. There was such a buzz to this place that it demanded excess in everything. He was only too willing to oblige.

In England, they were a couple, established in routine and companionship. Occasionally, one of them would struggle for breath, suffocating in the airless box they had built around themselves; but these were passing fears. Deep down they knew they were suited for life, but life as they lived it did not seem to suit them. They swept away dissatisfaction with a nice meal out or a weekend away in a country hotel.

One day they were both suddenly aware that the box was shrinking. Panic swept through them. Nothing had happened, nothing had been said, but they were claustrophobic. Both had returned from bland, uneventful days at work, had eaten almost in silence and while she sat in the lounge with one eye on the television and the other on a magazine, he shut himself in the spare room playing music and video games. They were turning into strangers. There were things missing, but they did not know what, too many compromises, no challenges any more. They were not sharing their lives, they were sharing their space.

He had pulled open the door of the spare room just as she was reaching for the handle on the other side. Their eyes met and blazed with realisation. They had come so close to destruction but had seen, simultaneously, that there was no more time.

"Are you ready to go for the car?" he said. "It's tonight's star prize."

Yes, she said. Something had to be done. They had to escape, not from each other, but from their own lives. There was enough money in the bank to go travelling, lost and searching and hoping and found. Asia was the most exotic place on their map.

But the money, abused because it had trapped them in the first place, ran out quicker than expected. Thailand, Malaysia, the Philippines, Indonesia all cheap and cheerful destinations in their travel guides, but not in reality when every bottle of water had to be paid for. In less than six months, a second decision had to be made about their future. While travelling, things just happened and they just accepted them – they were part of the experience. Now, stuck in a rundown hotel in an unsavoury town in Mindoro, they saw that the answer they were seeking was just as evasive as when they had set out. But still they did not want to go their separate ways. They had grown too much into each other.

The only thing they had learned was that they did not want to return to Britain and their sedentary, predictable life. They could do that when they were older.

Phil and Carol wondered for days. Hong Kong called to them, the great, shining edifice of concrete and civilisation in an interminable vista of jungle and shanty towns. It was a place full of promises and lies. It was where they could find protection against insects and pickpockets and poverty and the sapping heat of the tropics. It was a place, they thought, where everyone spoke English and there were plenty of jobs and good money to be made, and an endless supply of spectacle and entertainment. The maximum city – just what they were looking for.

They had travelled the world and seen the sights and were ready for a few home comforts. But not his of Little England or hers of Smalltown USA. They had tasted escape from limits and routine and would live for each day, always something new, but protected. Within six weeks of their arrival they had worn grooves into different patterns of habit.

And Phil's habit was drinking till he dropped.

He flopped, exhausted, on to a low fence. He could see the top of the tower block that was his borrowed home and thought he could never reach it. He wanted to roll over the fence on to the manicured lawn of the communal garden and sleep. But now there were people about. He could not stand their looks – the gweilo lush asleep on the grass, drunk, just like they always were. Even though he would sleep through their derision he would not let himself be humiliated. At least here, perched on this fence, he could present himself as sober; tired but respectable. Just taking a rest.

Just out of reach on the pavement in front of him was a $20 bill. He leant forward to pick it up, then resisted. Twenty bucks. What's that? he thought. Barely enough for half a pint or a packet of paracetamol.

A woman passed, towed up the hill by two Afghan hounds. She spotted the money and hesitated.

"You take it," he smiled, catching her uncertainty. "Go on, it's yours." He waved at it and nodded his head encouragingly but she suspected a trick. "Have it. I don't want it. I'm a pervert, missus. What's the definition of a pervert in this town? Someone who prefers women over money. Good morning." He laughed and she blanched, bemused, tugging at the dog leads and moving quickly on.

He watched her receding figure and thought of Carol, thought of her curled up asleep in the bed of their three-room flat, of her getting out of the bed and pulling off her T-shirt. He thought of her soft white shoulders and her tits bouncing free of the cloth as she removed the garment. Pervert.

It aroused him, there on that bench in the brightening day, and he got up to walk on. He had the drinker's urge for quick, uncomplicated sex. She had told him, early on, that if they put a pea in a jar every time they made love in their first year together and removed a pea every time they did it afterwards, they would never empty that jar. She had said it so seriously, with such knowingness, and that had made it funnier. But it now seemed to be true.

"Time to take another pea out of the pot," he said and stooped to pick up the $20 bill.

The rush of water from the shower met him as he let himself into the flat and leant back against the door. He sighed deeply and lurched to the sofa, falling into the plump, grey cushions on the shining rattan.

The noise of water stopped. Carol entered the room, drying her hair. Her face was hidden by the towel.

"You made it then?" she said, sweeping the towel from her face like a curtain.

"Hmm," he replied, ginning stupidly.

Her lips curled.

'What?" he said.

"You. Look at you."

"What about me?"

"You're pissed. Again. Must be the third time this week" She hurled the towel at the chair and went back to the bedroom.

"Second time, actually." The grin had dropped from his face.

She returned, zipping a short lilac skirt at her hip and smoothing the material over the small bulb of her belly. "Second time, third time what's the difference?"

"Lots."

"Drunk and incapable. Drunk and missing from bed. Drunk and preferring a good night out with the boys. Yet another good old night with the good old boys. Rather than spending some time with me. Drunk again. And pathetic."

"I'm not pathetic."

"Must be me, then." She sighed, looking at the floor. Then she slowly turned her head sideways to look at him slouched across the cushions as though his back were broken. "I must have got the wrong idea about all this," she continued softly. "I thought we were going to be together, at least while we were here. I thought that our time in this apartment – out of that fucking slum we landed in and have got to go back to in three fucking weeks – was supposed to be like a holiday. You know: relaxing a bit more, enjoying ourselves. Spending time together. Being happy again. That's part of the reason Dirk and Philippe offered us this place to look after while they're away. They're not blind: they can see we've got problems but they put them down to the fact that we live in a shitty shoebox in Wan Chai you can barely swing a cat in."

"A holiday?" he sneered slowly. "What are you talking about? I've still got to go to work, haven't I? And while we're in this wonderful place, I'm spending more time travelling to get there. And back. What time is there for a bloody holiday?"

"The same time you've got to go out and get pissed up every night."

"It's not every fucking night."

"It feels like it." She leant past him and reached for her handbag on the lower deck of the coffee table. Yanking at it, angry at being just a breath from his stubborn, stinking body, she dislodged a packet of cigarettes. It clattered to the floor.

He grinned.

"Knew it," he jeered. "How many's that? Twenty? Thirty?"

"Oh, shut up. It's nothing to do with it. Don't change the subject." She swept the carton into her hand and put it on the table.

"You said you were going to give up. You promised."

"Well, I've broken my promise, haven't I? Is it any wonder?"

"Excuses."

"Look, Phil, you stop drinking and I'll stop smoking. Okay? You never used to be this bad."

"Another promise."

She stormed from the flat. He leaned forward and grabbed the cigarette packet. He crumpled it in his fist and hurled it at the wall. He needed to hit someone. Desperately.

4

The old woman was asleep in the chair, a thread of dribble hanging from her broken lips. Her face was scarred with age, her thin hair revealing a red-patched dome. Her head hung heavily on her chest and a snarl curled her lips occasionally as age and pain tore into her.

Bony arms rested on a bolster, fingers clawing into the material as though she were ready to pounce. It was an illusory pose.

Before her, the hysterical roar of a television game show went on unheeded. A middle-aged woman came into the room and looked at the figure in the chair before dropping a bundle of chopsticks in the centre of the table. She left the room.

In a little den next door, lit by a desk lamp and the glow of a computer screen, sat Wilson Chan. He flicked off the monitor and reached into a drawer for the manual. It was as thick as a telephone directory and its weight reassured him. He wanted to know everything about this new model; it was a challenge finding new functions and abilities and committing them to memory. Only a few years earlier he had been using an electric typewriter. Useless, stupid, inefficient things. Business was so much easier with the new tools.

He listened to the clatter of his wife taking in the food, and checked his watch. Dinner was earlier than he anticipated and would disrupt the rest of his work that evening. Everything he did was in boxes of time. He sighed and closed the manual.

As he stood, he peered at the sole decoration in the ascetic room: a postcard from Vancouver. It had been taped to the wall by the window for a year and its corners were turned and discoloured. It was from his eldest son, Ka-fei, or Charlie as he insisted on calling himself in his desperate transition to Western model and unknowing or uncaring that his name would be a joke in his new home. In a few days, Chan Ka-fei would no longer exist. He would be a Canadian citizen, living with his American wife in a spacious, split-level suburban home, driving to the office in a Cadillac or something, drinking Martinis after work, playing baseball and camping in the woods over summer weekends. His home-life would be alien.

It could be different for Wilson, too, but he had chosen not to go. He could afford the official bribe to persuade the Canadian government that he would be worth adopting as a citizen; he had the business experience, the drive, the understanding of the language and the willingness to be a component of that great machine over there.

But he also had his mother. He knelt by the old woman asleep in the chair. She had just returned from hospital and seemed little stronger than when she went in. He stroked her wispy hair and examined her face, a soft smile on his lips.

She woke, startled, and he soothed her. "How's my favourite girl?" he said, stroking her hands.

In a whisper, she asked him what she had missed while she was asleep, a ritual cue for him to entertain her and make her forget her pain. Chuckling, he related a court story he had read in that day's newspaper about two triad members who had been sentenced for extortion. They had threatened a building site foreman and demanded protection money. He had said he had none and asked them to leave their names and phone number so he could get back to them. They did.

"So it was the police who went collecting," he concluded with a slight flourish as though telling a fairy story. Her thin lips cracked into a smile.

"Smiling makes you look even younger."

Her eyes closed again. How long has she got? he mused,

standing, a thought that had frightened him a thousand times. He did not know. The doctors did not know. And she no longer cared. She wanted simply an end to the pain, relief for herself and her doting son who crouched by her every evening as though she were an icon.

"Will you wake her?" It was his wife; he shook his head.

"Ka-fei is late. And so is Bobo," she tutted, using the baby name for their 23-year-old daughter.

"I am not hungry yet. We'll give them another 15 minutes." And he looked back at his mother. A spasm ran behind her eyes and she let out a soft gasp before settling back into sleep.

He took the remote control from her lap and changed channels. The news had just started. The lead story was about another heavy-handed threat from the bullies in Beijing, the faceless tyrants he so despised. This is what we want; this is what we do, said the report. There was barely an attempt to conceal the intent beneath diplomatic language.

"They should leave their names and phone number," he said to the TV screen.

He sighed. Their daily dictats were wearing. They were bad for business and bad for morale. He hated the incoming landlords, that group of contradictory old men who sat in their big halls 1,000 miles to the north, fiddling with the lease and rental agreement. They seemed intent on frightening their remaining tenants into submission, tenants who had tasted a measure of freedom for too long and stood to lose much of that freedom.

But Wilson would not run from them. Quite apart from his loyalty to his dying mother, he felt loyal to the place that had given him so much opportunity. Though he would stand, he would not fight. He was a pragmatist.

Whatever happened, he knew that he and his wife had to stay. He could not accept that his mother might be dead by the time of the handover and that there would then be nothing to stop him leaving. While she was alive, wheezing those feeble breaths and struggling to walk across a room, she would always be alive. And his responsibility. He had shown how far he would go to measure up to that sense of responsibility when his father had died and he had spirited her out of the mainland into the protective womb of her last remaining family. The question of existence without her he would never allow into his head.

The doorbell rang. His mother's eyes flickered open; she looked at her son as though he were a stranger. He returned to her side and muttered a few comforting words.

"Hi mom," boomed a voice.

Ka-fei strode into the room and marched towards him. They hugged.

"How you doing?" he said in his careless voice. It was loud and false, but most jarring for Wilson was that it was no longer Cantonese. Ka-fei had spent most of his developing years in the States and had grown into the accent naturally but to Wilson, in the family home, it felt like a betrayal. It was a rejection in as definite a way as if Ka-fei had run away. He knew he was being irrational.

"I am well, son. And yourself?"

"Fine," he said, moving to his grandmother and taking her hands in his.

"Where is Karen?"

"Oh, she can't make it. Sorry." He kept his eyes away from his father and pretended to fuss with the old woman.

Again, Wilson felt a jump of anger. This shrug-shoulder unconcern in his son – and the absent daughter-in-law – was becoming too frequent. There was no attempt at explanation or apology, no regret, no respect even. Something was done, or usually not done, and that was the end of it. College education and life abroad had done this to Ka-fei. It had changed him for the worse, as Wilson saw it; made him selfish, self-seeking, inconsiderate.

"Why not?" he said.

"Oh, just things. You know."

"Your mother will not be happy. She has cooked for five."

'Whoops. Bobo's not coming, either."

Mrs Chan set the tureen of superfluous rice in the centre of the table and went back to the kitchen. She stole a glance at the two men in her life, sensing the early swordplay and hoping that it would not ruin their last dinner together.

"You are all ready then, son?" she said.

"Sure am," he replied, stretching his arms out over the

back of the chair as though he were taking an encore. "This time tomorrow we'll be on the plane. Move into the house on Wednesday; start the job next Monday. It's all happened so quick."

"I wish you luck."

"Sure."

Dad. Mom. Sure. What sort of language was this? It was the childish vocabulary of a boy immersed in the movies, in the American dream and the great open spaces of myth. It was a denial of his heritage and culture and a slap in the face to his parents, almost a sneer that they were staying behind while this place – what would he say? – went down the toobs.

Wilson's wife, Ying, seated herself at the table and spooned rice and cabbage into her bowl. A small motif of a red dragon broke its monotonous white glaze. She gestured to the other two to start.

"They pay you well, this new company?" he said, staring down at the meat in his bowl and thinking of a huge ribeyed steak.

"A fortune. I can't believe what a good deal I've landed," his son replied through mouthfuls of food.

"That is good," said Ying, out of pride rather than encouragement.

"And Karen will be working too. Only part-time and only until the baby but that should give us plenty in the bank to fall back on."

"Are you expecting problems? Don't call them down. You haven't started yet and already you're being pessimistic. I thought there was no such thing in America."

"Not pessimistic, dad. Realistic. You know, it's a different ball game. Anything could go wrong. I don't think it will, but we've got to be prepared. This is a risk. An adventure. I still say you should come out, too."

"We have discussed this many times. We cannot leave."

"Not yet, maybe. But ..." His mother shot him a warning glance and he switched attention to his food, pouring tea and dabbing his mouth with a paper napkin.

"You think you're going to be okay here?" Something like genuine concern entered Ka-fei's voice for the first time that evening.

Wilson nodded but said nothing.

"What could go wrong?" said Ying. "The eyes of the world will be on us."

"That is beginning to sound like a wise old saying, passed down through the generations," said Wilson.

"The only eyes will be on the TV," Ka-fei rejoined and the two men exchanged brief smiles.

An airline advertisement was showing and his attention was arrested. "That's who we're going with. This time tomorrow."

"You sound keen to get away," said Ying, stooping to clear the table.

"Well, yeah, I am, of course, but I'm going to miss you. And Bobo. And even that silly, good-for-nothing husband of hers with his madcap schemes and that pile of scrap he dares to call an automobile. But you've got to keep moving. You mustn't let anything hold you back. You taught me that."

"You will end up rootless."

"No. Not true. Where are my roots here?"

"With us." Wilson's voice had maintained the same level throughout the conversation but it now carried a hard, uncompromising edge.

"I'm sorry. I didn't mean that." His tone suggested that he did not mean anything.

"This will always be your home," said his mother.

"I know. Of course it will."

"You can always come back to us. If there are too many troubles in Canada, if you cannot settle, you can always come back home. To us."

He grinned and shrugged in embarrassment. Dad reached for the brandy.

5

Heads turned in knots of people as they entered the room. There were perhaps two dozen guests clustered in units, most of them near the main door where two hostesses stood behind a table, ticking off names and handing out raffle tickets. Waiters in white jackets balanced over-burdened trays as they weaved from group to group. Although the sun was still shining, the dark wood panelling of the room sucked in the light through high windows on two sides. Sprays of flowers flaunted themselves around the walls. By each spray was a long table of alcohol and buffet food. A mirrorball floated overhead.

"Ridiculous," said Phil, pulling at his collar. Carol tapped his hand away and began fussing with the lapels of his dinner jacket. She loved him looking like this; the suit gave him the power of suggested wealth and his grave, hooded eyes invested him with potential danger. There was a quality to his confidence far more attractive to her than that he tried to build with barbed observations and drink, yesterday's charms.

"You look lovely," he said, touching her waist. She was wearing a low-cut dress in flame red, adorned with a single white carnation below the shoulder.

"So do you." He flashed her a sarcastic grin.

A waiter popped between them and they ordered drinks,

casually surveying the congregation. The ostentation of the dress and the glitter of gold on necks and wrists was breathtaking and, in a few cases, risible in its desperation.

"Looks like an explosion in a jewellery shop," said Phil pointing carelessly at an elderly woman draped in gold. Even her blonde hair was false and in an attempt to return to the beauty of her adolescence, she had missed the stop and regressed to childhood. She was wearing a black and white checked Little Bo Peep outfit that flared from the thighs. It only exaggerated her age. By her was a man in a crimson tuxedo, a multicoloured bowtie and white trousers who looked ready to give a funny turn at a seaside holiday camp.

They were all strangers, gathered for the annual ball of the company Carol had just started working for. Alice had kept her word of a month earlier. As a newcomer to the firm, Carol had been invited out of form; nobody had known her long enough to judge her or to know whether it would appeal. But she had wanted to come and had persuaded her boyfriend to join her in her endless quest of meeting new people and experiencing every facet of life in this strange, intoxicating place. He had protested and they had argued again but without drink behind it there had been no vehemence in him and it quickly abated.

She drank in the spectacle as she meandered to the toilet. The knots of people thickened, the volume increased; there was a growing density and anticipation in the atmosphere. He was leaning against the edge of a table when she returned, his legs crossed at the ankles, hands in pockets, appraising everybody in the room with a dispassionate calm.

"My king of cool," she said, stroking his arm.

"So who do you know then?" he said, guiding her by the elbow past black-clad backs to a corner.

She glanced around at the animated faces, lit by rushed cocktails.

"Not that many. I recognise a few people but can't remember any names."

"Can they?"

She gave him a nervous glance. "You'll enjoy it," she whispered.

"I intend to."

She touched his cheek gratefully. This gentle determination of his moved her. There was a helplessness to it. Only when he fought against that, turning against himself and against her, did she harden to him. He blushed slightly and signalled to a waiter.

The room continued to fill. Isolated parties of people were merging, bumps were exchanged as long-lost friends, opposite numbers from other companies and former colleagues who had not spoken for a fortnight spotted each other and manoeuvred to convenient spots. The waiters no longer bobbed through the throng but stood against the walls as if they were waiting to be asked to dance.

A short man in a shiny, braided bolero jacket eased through the room, tapping a gold bell on a salver with gentle respect. Guests slowly disengaged themselves from their chat and their cocktails, gathered around the table plan pinned to a board and glided into the dining room.

Phil and Carol found themselves in the company of strangers at a table on the corner of the dance floor. After the scraped chairs, flicked napkins and quiet greetings, a blanket of self-consciousness settled over the group. Only one person among the dozen tried to lift it. A compressed man who was going bald, he thrust his arm around the table like a fairground carousel, desperately grabbing flesh and barking his name. When the hand-shaking was over, he flopped back into his chair and began chatting to anyone who caught his eye, but it was dull and self-referential chat, the one-handed dialogue of the chronically lonely.

Only after the third course was cleared, the fourth round of drinks poured and the band opened with a clumsy rendition of a 1960s rock standard did the tension fade. The egoist began talking to his partner for the first time that evening.

The band, too, lost their initial awkwardness as more people took to the floor and the growing liquor-loosened volume from the tables demanded competition. Phil was tapping out a paradiddle on his chair and gazing bemusedly at the drummer who seemed content with a simplistic four-four rhythm. Phil became suddenly aware of Carol staring at him. They grabbed hands and moved to the dancefloor, crowded now as an old Stones number unlocked the most rigid of limbs.

The band played three more numbers before finishing and the couple, exhausted and gasping for air, pushed through the crowd with the cymbal finale clanging in their ears.

"Hello my dear," boomed a laughing urbane voice. "Isn't this fun?"

It was a different George Bradshaw to the one she had got to know in the two weeks at her new job. What little she had seen of Bradshaw, her boss, had left her with the impression that he was a driven man, decisive, committed and serious. He appeared almost obsessed, she had thought with something like admiration. He devoted himself to that business and his energy and enthusiasm drove his team, a feeling that excited her as she gradually became part of it. He seemed to live for nothing else. And because he took the business so seriously, whenever he laughed or joked it was disconcerting. It did not jar as false but it did not fit; in his office persona he relaxed into amusement as if with an effort, an effort that could be better used. To see him out of the office for the first time, in a tuxedo, greeting her frivolously and jocular for its own sake, deviated from her inchoate perception of him.

His forehead was glowing and his eyes squinted against the sweat. She smiled and unconsciously reached out to touch him. The crowd thinned around them.

"And you are?" he said, flicking his blazing eyes to Phil who was grinning stupidly simply from the exertion of dancing.

'Phil," he said, sticking out his hand.

"This is my boyfriend," she added uselessly as the two men shook hands. Bradshaw was pleased to feel a firm grip, even though the hand holding his was thin and boyish.

He invited the couple to his table, careless of the formality he exhibited in the office. His wife, Alice, was sitting alone. The other guests were standing, eager not to let the liberating impetus of the dancing subside and ready to throw themselves back on to the parquet before the second bar of the next set had been reached.

She stood as the trio approached. She was tall and bronzed and warmed when she recognised Carol. She was pleased to see her, but not surprised: the members of this tight community were always bumping into each other. They were like passengers on an ocean liner. Sooner or later, you would meet every other passenger.

The women dominated the conversation with talk about Carol's new job and the incident with the boat children and general comments about the people who passed around them. Bradshaw was happy to settle back into a reverie, occasionally asking Phil a question. Bradshaw offered a cigar which Phil took and puffed at uncertainly, breaking into a violent cough when he swallowed the smoke.

"You were very brave," Bradshaw suddenly announced, turning away from Phil and tuning into the conversation of the women. "Alice told me all about it."

"In my normal selfish way, of course. I spent more time talking about what I was feeling. I stood there like a stuffed dummy. Useless."

'What do you do for a living?" Phil interrupted. Her disquiet was loud in his ears.

"I am I suppose what you would call a tai tai. A kept woman." A bitter, resigned smile ran across her lips. "Horrible phrase."

"You're not being fair on yourself, Alice," said Bradshaw. "It is a horrible phrase. Demeaning. Spoilt people with nothing to do all day but spend money. Though, I have to admit, some of our best friends are tai tais. In fact they all are. But you're not one of them, my dear," he added hastily, with mock graciousness.

"Don't be silly. I think you've had too much to drink."

"Oh well." He looked at Phil for support against her complaint. There was none.

"I am a dollar widow, just like most of the women here. Of course, it can be fun. But it does get boring. Some people enjoy the shallowness of it all. I don't any longer. Don't be tempted." She leant over to Carol and tapped her on the hand.

"No risk of that. I enjoy working too much. It's great experience here."

"Of course it is," said Bradshaw. He turned to Phil, irked suddenly by his supercilious expression. "What is it you do?"

"Teach English." He shrugged. "I wouldn't mind being a

kept man." Polite bubbles of laughter popped around him. Carol found herself staring at Bradshaw to see how he reacted.

The conversation sauntered on, oblivious to the fresh attack of the band and the growing hysteria in the room. All the elegance and the civility of the early part of the evening had been stripped away. The dancing was frenzied; the noise intense. A woman was being sick in a corner; a man, half-stripped, jigged spastically on a table. Most of the waiters went home. The night was accelerating towards madness and release. It would be the same in another ballroom the following night and in another hotel the night after that and in every other bar on the street. And on the Monday morning, the wreckage would be swept away and work would resume with an equal hunger.

"Oh, I do run on sometimes," Bradshaw was saying. "But you know I'm right. You know what I'm saying, don't you, Carol?" He grinned and she was excited by that grin, almost grateful for it. And she half-acknowledged something else, too. Greed, greed for that face. She realised with a start that she was damp with the slow-drip thrill of sexual arousal. The smooth voice, the intense face, the physical presence of this man, in possession of everything around him, excited her. And he was old enough to be her father. She glanced down quickly and coughed and squeezed her eyes to shut out the embarrassment.

A drumroll throbbed through the room and ended in a clash of brass. Carol looked over her shoulder in relief.

"Fancy another dance?" she said to Phil who was swaying slightly in his seat.

"Not just yet. I'll sit this one out." He looked from her to Bradshaw. "You run the whole company?"

"Only this end of it. It's based in London."

"Aren't they all?"

Bradshaw let out a breath of laugh. It sounded like a throwaway statement, clumsy, and he could think of no reply.

"It's all outsiders running this place." Phil was slurring heavily, hunched on his elbows, deep among the debris of food and crockery, his head sunk but staring hard across the table.

"I think you'll find that's not true."

"It is. It is. Ultimately, it all goes back to London or New York or Beijing or somewhere else. The money is made here, then spirited off. It's all a front, that's all this place is."

"Nonsense. Look at our currency reserves, at the wealth out there."

"And look at the people sleeping under flyovers and look at the slums. And look at the difference in salary a white boy would get and a local bloke would get. Yeah, it's out there – in bits. The rest is taken away, nicked."

"I find that rather offensive." He glared at Phil who locked on to that glare in silent, savage challenge. Carol pulled him out of his seat and led him away, the eyes of Bradshaw burning into his back.

PART 2

I have learned a lot about myself over the last year and I don't like any of it. I had been certain of so many things – of everything, really – from a very early age but I know now that that certainty was just arrogance, a deliberate blindness. There were never doubts; I would not allow them because they would have held me back. Now, I am full of them. This last year of extremes has seen me do so many things I would once not even have conceived of doing. They did not fit in with the plan I thought I was following. I question myself for the first time.

I question why I threw away the plan. When I did so I lost everything. My guide, my map, if you would, kept me on course. I suppose it shows a paucity of imagination but if that protected me from myself for so long then all well and good. It is tragic – if I may be allowed to use that word with regards to myself – that just when I was beginning to feel at peace and believed that I really had achieved everything I set out to, that I could start to sit back and enjoy the fruits of my labour, I threw it all away. I hijacked myself.

Since arriving here, I have wondered often if circumstances changed the man I was, if the environment altered my basic character. The natural urge to blame something else for our own misfortunes. In the West, it has *allegedly reached such a pitch that it has been identified as some sort of social phenomenon: the victim complex. But I am not a victim; I cannot blame my environment, I keep telling myself. I can only blame me. My character was moulded by the time I became a teenager. Circumstances changed fundamentally and frequently over the years and I adapted to them each time, all the while retaining the true Me, the same Me that was there as a spotty youth. I was strengthened by experience, I learned, I grew. I always believed that. Even here, even now.*

Maybe that means that I took myself for granted; I did not know myself. I did not look hard enough. But there was no need to, you see, circumstances did not require it; what I did know of myself was enough. I knew where I was going.

And when things did start to go wrong, they were set in motion by me, not by where I lived, or how I lived, or by anybody else. By me. And my motivations and reactions were natural for me, too; I had just not learned that they were there, always there; they were strangers but they were as natural to me as the colour of my eyes. Greed, an ability to betray, a self-destructive guilt. This place did not make me greedy or selfish. It did not make me hurtful. That I could so utterly destroy somebody was innate, not acquired. I always had the capacity to do those things. Always. They were not grafted on by outside influences. I cannot blame the place. I don't want to.

So many people do, of course. Especially here. I have seen so many casualties and not one of them had the courage or the insight to say that what happened to them was their own fault. They defend their actions – those that are still capable of speech or self-analysis – by saying that they have changed since they arrived here, that they became a different person in response to their surroundings and what was happening. In all the cases in my experience, bar one – the one – I always believed that to be nonsense. And I tell myself rather glibly that that one case is the exception that proves the rule.

Of all the cities I have lived in, in all their various personae, not one imprinted itself so strongly on me that I changed to fit it. That was what I believed, so firmly. The situation I am now in could have happened in London or

Rome or New York. It did not. It happened here. Mere chance.

Before I left London for my first assignment abroad I became quite chummy with a man from Scotland. He was a very shy young man, a single child who had grown up in a lonely farmhouse with his two elderly parents in some remote part of the northwest. We became friends because I soon learned to respect his quick-thinking professionalism and his diligence. We seemed to be on the same wavelength.

I also felt a paternal need to protect him, though he was only a few years younger than me. He seemed so lost in the big city, so awkwardly transplanted from the ringing quiet of the empty moorlands to the brash, claustrophobic urban sprawl, that I felt if I did not keep an eye on him he would go astray.

London in those days seemed to be gagging with its first breaths of freedom after the austere postwar years. It was an exciting time, an exciting place. Anything seemed possible. There were clubs and women and booze and an exciting new music coming out of America. For a young man it was a heaven of a place.

My friend seemed to make an effort to enjoy the dancing and the parties but away from the comforting discipline of office routine he was lost. Nothing could loosen the chains of his lonely upbringing and he was shy and awkward and, frankly, embarrassing on many social occasions. I wanted him to enjoy himself without falling into the clutches of the wrong sort. So, while trying to satisfy my own need for fun – this was at weekends only, of course; I had stopped drinking during the working week – I felt that he needed bringing out of himself so I would make the effort and we would barge around the West End from pub to club to party.

It never worked for him. He could not relax, he would not come out of his shell no matter how much he had to drink. He exhibited an infuriating docility in social company. When introduced to someone he would stammer and mutter. If it was a girl, he would blush. I'm told that that is an endearing quality in a young man these days but then it was laughable. He would only react, while everybody else was acting. I decided I was fighting a losing battle and my initial encouragement began to wane.

Then one night we stumbled into a poker game somewhere around the back streets of Soho. After his usual display of reticence, he was persuaded by a very pretty young lady to join the game. This time, I stood back, but only out of pragmatism. I had barely enough money for a drink and the bus fare home. I watched, uneasy and helpless, as he was drawn into the game by a group of obvious sharks.

As I watched, he seemed transformed. A self-confidence I had never seen outside work manifested itself as he got into the swing of the cards. He began to relax, unaware of the trap that was being laid around him. I watched in growing bewilderment and horror. His unusual jocularity and flamboyant gestures started to give way to anger as he realised he was being chiselled. He started shouting at the girl who had invited him to the table and calling her names. The dealer jumped to her defence and my friend slapped him. Everybody was suddenly on their feet and trying to grab him but he pushed me away and ran up the stairs, disappearing into the night.

They gave chase but could not find him. It was raining heavily and the street lighting was atrocious. Luckily, I got off lightly. I assumed that I was in the presence of the London underworld and that those gangsters would take out their frustrations on me. But they let me go with a few insults.

He did not show up at work the next day. The police did. They said he was wanted in connection with a vicious attack on a young woman as she left a poker game in the early hours of the morning. A maniac had slashed her face with a knife several times and she was in danger of losing an eye. The police had tracked him to me because in the melee his wallet had fallen out and in it was his work telephone number. The head of department had pointed me out as his closest, indeed his only, friend.

I told them what I knew, which was not much, and they went away. I walked around in a daze for days. I could not believe what had happened. I had seen him drunk so many times before but that just made him more introspective. I had never witnessed the animation of that evening or believed him capable of the violence that was alleged.

To my eye, he had become a completely different person. I

blamed London. This simple country boy had been unable to cope with city life and had cracked. His new home had sent him off the deep end.

The police found him before long and he was taken to court. A previous conviction was mentioned during the hearing. It transpired that that was for a similar knife attack in the area around the farm where he had grown up. The victim had lost the use of his right arm after my friend had severed the nerves. The details were hazy but the attack had happened in a tiny, remote village, near the place where he had spent his whole life. It was similarly unprovoked. My friend had not been changed by his environment at all. He was capable of such a horrible act wherever he was. It was nobody else's fault and where he lived could not be blamed.

But if I really believe that, why am I here?

1

"Still no improvement then?" said Bradshaw, smiling down at Alice as he pulled out his chair at the breakfast table. She followed his quick glance around the room and tittered.

"It beats me why these people come on holiday. I've seen more good cheer in a dentist's waiting room."

The gloomy breakfasters in the open-sided room offended him and he had to turn it into a joke. Young, fit, bronzed couples poked at their food and hardly spoke to one another. It did not make sense to Bradshaw. They were not doing what they should be doing – enjoying themselves. That was what holidays were for and that was what he had been trying to do, whether by swimming, or reading, or poking fun at easy targets to make his wife laugh and induce the holiday atmosphere. It was not easy for Bradshaw to relax here, time dragged and felt wasted, there was an oppressive monotony to it all, despite the beauty of their surroundings and the sunshine. But he was determined. She needed a holiday, she needed a change. He did not.

"They need a damn good talking to, some of these people. Smile, for God's sake!"

Alice smiled as she patted the napkin into her lap, glad that he was trying. He was misplaced here; in his quiet moments when she glanced at him, on the verandah of their beachside villa, walking through the sand alongside her, he had that distracted air as though he would rather be somewhere else. She knew where that was. And he would realise that he was being preoccupied, neglectful, and compensate – or overcompensate – in his typical fashion by making silly observations, desperate to make her laugh, to show that he was relaxing and not taking things seriously.

But it had been a lovely fortnight, she thought. The exotic vegetation framing the golden beach, the sea shimmering to a hazy horizon, the low cliffs at either corner of the bay, the sunsets and the insect-chirruping, black, black nights had all drawn her down lovingly into a sort of half-slumber of satisfaction.

They looked up at the sound of scraping chairs. A blond man and a dark-haired woman, both tall and slight; were moving away from their table. Their expressions were glazed.

"More happy campers," said Bradshaw. "Mr and Mrs Glum, I presume." The couple passed by and nodded curtly. Bradshaw returned a huge, disarming grin. They ignored him.

He sighed and carried on dissecting his breakfast, a huge, greasy plate of eggs and fried meat. It was settling uncomfortably on his stomach but he loved the taste and the texture and relished the liberating irresponsibility of ignoring his doctor's advice. It was another way of reminding himself that he was away from it all.

He wiped egg yolk from the ends of his moustache. "I found this," he said suddenly, leaning sideways and scrabbling in the pocket of his slacks. He pulled out a pink-brown object, smaller than the heel of his thumb. "I bought it for you weeks ago and forgot all about it. Then I found it again, and packed it for the holiday and forgot it again. Came across it this morning."

Alice took the tiny Buddha pendant. "It's lovely," she whispered, turning it between her fingers. "Thank you, George." She leaned across the table and gave him a light kiss.

"Don't know what came over me. I had a sudden urge to buy you a present and I came across that. Nothing really." He took it from her and made a play of examining it.

"It is very pretty."

"Wasn't sure you'd like it. Thought it might cheer you up at the time. Sorry I forgot to give it to you then."

"It doesn't matter. It's the thought."

She held it by its chain below her throat and looked at him for approval. He nodded.

"It really is very lovely indeed," she said, dropping it into her purse with a slow smile.

"Time for my dip. Are you going to read by the pool?" She said yes. He kissed her on the cheek and she watched him walk towards the beach, parting palm leaves like stage curtains. Around her, the quiet stillness seemed to thicken. She was the last guest in the dining hall. The staff floated around her, clearing and relaying tables for lunch in their endless somnambulant routine. Her eyes were locked on the little spot of beach she could see through the bushes. The glow above the sea hypnotised her.

Tomorrow, they would fly home and all this, all this peace and quiet and beauty, would be locked away in the memory drawer. Work would reclaim George and chip away at the calmness that had settled uncertainly on him; she would return to the hollow shell of her luxury life. They would draw apart again, only occasionally finding ways to cross the gulf to each other.

She was convinced that their unsettled life was to blame. As soon as she felt she had put down roots, he would suggest pulling them up and transplanting them, as if in need of fresh nourishment. She had only really been happy in England until those last few terrifying months. Although he was often away in the early days of their marriage he would always return as if to home-base, carrying trophies of sales and deals and settling down for a while before venturing out again on the hunt. But when he was again given a position abroad and home was wherever they could find it, she slowly started to feel left behind, left out. Even though he had done it for her. She knew that.

She wondered if his first wife had felt the same contradiction of wanting to be with him while he wanted to be somewhere else. It must have been very difficult for Joyce, the first Mrs Bradshaw. She wanted to possess him. On her deathbed, George said, she told him: "I give up. Now you can go."

Alice did not want to possess anybody, nor be possessed. But she felt she had been.

She opened her purse, pulled out the Buddha and put it round her neck then ambled to the pool. She did not stay long. The sight of those prone oily bodies on the white wooden loungers fatigued her; the exaggerated activity in the blue water exhausted her. She returned to the villa for a sleep.

Bobbing in the sea, 100 metres offshore, Bradshaw could see her shrunken figure slip into the gloom of the verandah. He rolled on to his back and floated, staring at the glaring sheen of the sky. The blue had been washed out by an angry sun. He felt the pricking of burn on his toes as they poked through the water and he thought about work. He was keen to return. There was nothing to beat it, not even this, lying on his back in the Andaman Sea under a furnace sky with nothing to do.

He swam ashore and jogged on the spot as he dried himself on the slope outside his villa. He knocked on the door and entered. Her back was to him in the half-light.

"Alice?" he whispered. She replied with a groan.

"I feel like going for a walk. Don't suppose you do?" Her hand appeared above the sheet and waved with regal indolence. "You get a good rest, I'll see you later in Ta's bar, if you like"

She muttered something and he left. A chipwood path led from the villa through the resort, winding around boulders and clumps of trees and other villas, all based on an alleged ethnic design in bamboo and nipa, all the temporary homes of the rich. Past the pool, where the growing heat of the day had stupefied even the most active, the path joined a grit-littered road and he followed that for 500 metres to a collection of open bars under a single corrugated tin roof.

He hitched himself up on to a stool and greeted the barmaid.

"Mr George," she said, reaching automatically for the frame of a Connect4 game and a pile of red and yellow counters. She pushed the frame towards him. He shook his head.

"Not today, thank you. Just a lime juice." He took a long noisy gulp as she put a dish of pineapple chunks by his elbow.

"It's even hotter today," he said, wiping his lips and pushing the glass back to her for a refill.

"Where is Mrs George?"

"She's a bit tired. She's having a lie-down."

"Is she not well?"

He laughed. "No. You know how it is at the end of a holiday. All your energy is gone."

Ta nodded sagely. "But not yours?"

"Not mine, good gracious, no. I'm a driven man," he boasted. She responded with a teasing smile.

A second woman glided behind the bar and Ta moved away to busy herself with the tape deck.

"Hello, On."

"Good morning," she said, affecting a formality she thought appealed to him. Her coquettish eyes ranged over his face and he felt a surge of vanity.

"This is early for you." And she sat opposite, heavily, in mute challenge. He had to be forced to acknowledge she was there, as a person, as a presence, not just as something that chatted and served drinks. She looked directly into his eyes and her big mouth melted into a smile. He shifted on his stool, Her round brown arms girdled his vision.

"This is your last day here?'

He nodded. "Afraid so. Back to the grind tomorrow. We'll have to pack soon." "Where is your wife? In the sea?" she asked softly.

"Having a rest."

"And you are here alone?"

He gave a short snort.

"Did you have a good swim this morning?"

"Yes, thank you?"

"And your wife?"

"She's not a keen swimmer. Never has been. Now she's resting, so I thought I'd have a couple of quiet drinks and a bit of time to myself."

"You must be lonely."

"Not at all."

"What is your room number?" she said abruptly, bending

imperceptibly towards him. His gaze shifted to Ta, then back to On and his eyes locked on the brown triangle of flesh of her throat.

"I can't tell you that," he tried to say lightly. "Mrs George is there."

On nodded, eyes still on his. He felt his temples burning. He made a clumsy rush for his glass and finished the drink.

"You won't tell me your room number. Why? Have you forgotten it?"

"Now, now, On," he said. "That's enough of that." He stood, flustered, smiling weakly in a feeble attempt to cover his embarrassment.

"Why don't you tell me?" she pleaded, mockingly, toying with the counters from the game. "I would like to see it. Maybe when your wife goes out for a walk. It must be very lovely."

"It is. Now I must be going. Thanks for the drink." He dropped coins on the bar top. "Another time, eh? We leave tomorrow. We'll see you before we go. Mrs George and me."

She put on her best look of petulance as he hurried from the bar.

As the shock of daylight hit him he stumbled. What had started as easy flirtatious banter had slipped just as easily into a blatant offer and he had felt tempted suddenly and had panicked. He tried to laugh it off, to laugh at himself and his stuffy, almost pompous, reaction. It was just a bit of suggestive banter, that's all, he told himself. It didn't matter. But it did: her calm assurance and his nervous rush to leave the bar humiliated him, made him feel naïve, unworldly, stupid. He had been in similar situations in bars all around Asia dozens of times and he had laughed them off or ignored them. He just dealt with them and moved on. But the image of On's soft, brown arms and wide smile and that fierce challenge in her eyes echoed again and again in his head. He felt strangely guilty.

2

On the coffee table by his side stood a near-full bottle of water with an empty bottle lying beside it. He never felt thirsty, except when his gasping throat woke him in the still of the night after too much beer, but he made a point of drinking three bottles of water a day. The heat sucked out the body's fluids, dried the skin, desiccated the organs, stretched the eyes. Tea, coffee and alcohol were no good. It had to be the pure stuff, racked in the fridge in plastic litre bottles, poured down his throat at regular intervals and always readily in supply.

The television hissed. It was the last tape from home and he would have to wait at least a month before his next fix. He had watched the videos twice over – little flickering windows on the life he had left behind. They were essential anchors to home, whole and unspoilt; Western programmes and films imported by local TV stations were hijacked by advertisers with their glib, shiny showcases of brandy, watches, cars and expensive department stores. Every 15 minutes, midway through a scene the commercial break would burst through. Rutger Hauer's hardware was worthless against it.

He switched off the set and leaned back, a wave of tiredness dragging him down. It had been a long, wearing day. All days were. The travelling, buffeted by crowds, squeezed into trains and buses, walking hard, greasy streets with the heat seeping up through his feet, tired him before he got to the school. Then there were the demands of the principal, the long hours of extreme concentration and frustration, the boredom, the routine and the snatched lunch in a nearby dai pai dong, reeking of fat, overripe fruit and beancurd, always crowded.

Back on the chain gang, he hummed to himself.

He stopped and listened to the silence. It was seducing him to sleep. It was 8.30pm and he desperately wanted to lie down. Just for a few minutes. But he pulled himself up with a shrug. He needed some music, something loud and aggressive and driven by drums, layered in guitars and a wall-of-sound production. He bent by the CD cabinet and fingered out a plastic box, turning it in his palm to read, again, the scant information on the back. This would do, this frightening noise would keep him awake. The speakers shook as the first bassline broke the air.

He sat down again, facing the stereo and feeling the music in his head, his chest and his loins like a physical force. He tapped in time on the table as the invitation to violence shouted again and again in his ears.

He did not hear the door open.

"You can hear that in the lobby," said Carol, easing her bag from drooping shoulders to the floor.

"Maybe they'll reduce the rent."

"We're not paying it, remember? Do you have to have it so loud?"

"I'm turning it down. I thought you were coming home early."

"I couldn't. I tried."

"You wanted to go to this party."

"I know." She eased off her shoes and yawned, stretching her fingertips towards the ceiling. "There was a late job needed doing."

"Again?"

"Again."

"Do you still want to go."

"I suppose so."

"They're your friends."

It was another leaving-do. There seemed to be one every weekend, even in Phil and Carol's small, embryonic circle. It was as though everybody were trying to escape this transitory place. No sooner had you made friends, said Phil, than they left for the other side of the world. I'm going to wake up one morning with no drinking partners, he joked.

There was no solidity here, no consistency, no permanence. It was a place for passing through, a facsimile of home. Early-stage expats like Phil and Carol went through their lives pretending but never penetrating and were rarely able to scratch below the skin of their borrowed existence. Like the people they knew, they were skimming the surface of an alien culture, always aware that it was temporary and therefore did not really matter. And, by implication, nothing here mattered, not even friendship. Nothing was to be taken seriously. Instant gratification was the only thing to seek.

Carol sat on the edge of the bed, trying to calm herself with deep-breathing exercises. In. Out. In. Hold. Out. Deeper she drifted to blot out the impinging images of the day. Flashes of events, snatches of conversations, things to do, things done, things not done. She pushed them all away.

"We need to go. It's my last chance to see Jenny and Jim," she said, returning to the lounge. "Try not to drink too much tonight, eh?"

"We're going to a party, aren't we?"

"Yeah, but you don't have to get sloshed, you know."

"I enjoy it sometimes."

"But it doesn't enjoy you. You know how you get."

"No. How?"

"You know."

He turned off the stereo. "You are drinking too much, you know," she said.

"I know," then repeating in a quieter voice: "I know."

"Why?"

"Don't know. It's just easier here."

"There's nothing wrong?"

"No."

"Sure?"

"Yes," he hissed. "Now, can we go?"

The party was only a few blocks from their apartment. They stepped into the communal garden and felt a lacklustre tug of wind breathe warm air. The lawn and the bushes were lit in pools of ground-lights. The garden was enclosed on all sides by towers.

The noise was at hysteria pitch when they entered. Grinning faces and shouts greeted them from those nearest the door.

"Carol!" shouted someone.

"Jenny!" Carol shouted back, hugging her. Jenny pulled herself away and eyed Phil. "Hi," she said calmly. He smiled hello and looked over her head towards a gang of people blocking a doorway, all strangers. Already, he was beginning to feel uncomfortable, trapped.

Jenny dragged Carol to a window-seat, leaving Phil alone, looking around for familiar faces.

Most of the people were Westerners. British, American, French, German. A lone Armenian stood in a corner, unknown to everybody. The rest congealed in clots: in this room as they did throughout the city. They came together to live, to work, to party and to fuck as though afraid to be absorbed by their hosts, all strangers with the same home address. They ignored, in the main, Chinese bars and drank in their expat pubs where frequently the only true Hongkongers were staff. Eating Cantonese was still a special event for many. Only one of them had ever been in a Chinese family apartment. The lines were drawn and rarely for crossing. These people found their middleclass ghettoes in Mid-Levels, Discovery Bay, Happy Valley, Shek-O and Sai Kung, spacious and rarefied, and were granted just fleeting glimpses of the real life below. They were economic migrants from crumbling empires and the majority had drawn a line of their own choice. They knew where they were and who they were and tried to keep both in separate areas, maintaining an uneasy symbiosis with their surroundings.

Phil said hello to two guests as he reached around them for a winebox. They grinned back and returned to their conversation.

He continued his survey. The United Nations, he snorted to himself. But it was really a United West – Americans and Europeans gathered in their clans as if trying to forge an outpost in the new empire of the next century. In a decade, they would be close to irrelevant as the world turned to spin on the axis of China.

"Hi! I'm Tad!" a man shouted into his face. Phil put his hand out warily. The large man in front of him had a stone-cut face and tiny round glasses. On his features, they looked like they belonged to someone else.

They slipped into the standard conversational routine, incuriously batting questions and answers to each other. Tad drifted away.

Carol watched from the window seat, watched his tangible shyness and how often he refilled his glass and the little indifferent forays into conversation he made with those near or passing. It was not his scene. There were too many people packed into that room. She kept a cigarette cupped in her hand and hidden between her knees and took sly puffs, blowing smoke towards the floor.

"Jim's job sounds exciting," she said, turning back to Jenny.

"We're really pleased. We've been here too long. Three years. Can't wait to get back to New York. Have you settled?"

"Think so. Once we get a proper apartment sorted, anyway. I love this place. It's so alive. It makes me feel alive, every day."

"And Phil?"

She shrugged. "Sometimes. I think. You know what he's like. Restless. Never satisfied, really. The only time I've seen him really happy is when we're travelling, on the move. Now we're in one place, he's gone back to all his grumpiness."

"Homesick, maybe?"

"Yes and no. You can never tell what he's thinking. I ask him now and again but it's like getting blood out of a stone." She looked up and caught a glimpse of him between bobbing heads and bodies. He was talking to someone with quiet animation. Occasionally, his mouth would break into a toothy grin.

"So everything's packed?"

"Sure is. Spent all week on it. I'm exhausted."

"I'll miss you. We'll all miss you. Lots," Carol replied, biting her bottom lip. They fell into a tight hug, holding each other until Jim broke in and gently prised his wife into his jealous arms. Carol stepped back, an almost maternal smile on her face as she watched them through softening eyes.

Jim pulled back from the kiss and looked over his wife's shoulder at Carol. "Just had Dirk on the phone," he said. "He and Philippe are coming back early. Germany's not worked out. He said sorry but they're going to need the flat back earlier than expected. Next week, in fact."

"Oh, shit, why didn't he tell me?" Carol groaned.

"He tried, he said. Could never get hold of you. Guessed we'd be seeing you before we left so just rung me here. Lucky."

"Yeah." Carol felt suddenly deflated. They had been spoilt looking after their friends' flat. It was luxury compared to their poky little rented walk-up in Wan Chai, its buckled and tarnished steel front door, the old, tired furniture, the grimy and sweating walls, the gasping, box-like airlessness of the place. Here, in the newtown calm of Discovery Bay, the rooms were large, the lines were clean, the walls white and shiny, the parquet floors unscuffed. Everything was showroom new, even the views: steep green hills glowing in the sunshine through one huge picture window and the sparkling waters of the bay through the other. She smiled thinly: they would get this. One day. It was achievable.

But not yet.

"Back to Claustrophobia Towers," said Jenny.

"God, that rotten apartment" said Carol. "That place – urghh! I hate it. We've got to see if we can break the lease. We've got to find somewhere better quickly. It'll drive me mad, going back there. It'll drive him mad, too. We can do better."

"That's great," laughed Jim. "You're beginning to sound like the spoilt gweilo already. Only the best is good enough. Welcome aboard."

3

There was a churchlike quiet in the office when he entered. The late-morning lull, as regular as staff sleeping at their desks during lunchtime and the six o'clock panic as the junior clerks and secretaries rushed to the lifts, was something he had got used to. Bradshaw had come from a culture of manifest industry where success was measured in decibels and burnt calories. He had been accustomed to screaming phones and scurrying activity in the workplace; and this genteel decorum had unsettled him with its seeming apathy and made him think that the company was losing money. It had to be. But a look at the monthly figures belied his fears. He became aware that what he had seen as inaction masked a quiet and determined approach to making money. It was something that should be done quietly, respectably and sensibly. There was no need for show.

He nodded at his secretary and hung his jacket on the bentwood coatstand outside his office. The jacket was his flag, alerting staff to his presence. When he was in his office the door was always shut and he hardly shouted on the phone; without the jacket there would be no sign that he was on the premises. He wanted his presence felt in a subtle way, distanced somewhat from his underlings, although his initial mistrust of the diligence and reliability of them had long since evaporated. He still wanted them to know that he was there, that he was in control.

He pulled the business newspaper from his briefcase and began circling stories he had noticed in the front page digest while on his way to work. He called his secretary to deliver them to Wilson's In-tray, and only then did he set about the task of sifting through the accumulated data of the preceding fortnight.

Wilson received the newspaper with a glow of satisfaction, almost of gratitude. It reassured him, this renewed stamp of authority after the holiday absence. He never doubted his own ability and he no longer saw deputising as a challenge but he was glad that Bradshaw was back, glad of that firm sense of direction and refusal to be deflected. The man was a true pro.

He had been looking through the papers to cull more amusing stories to tell his mother but pushed them aside as soon as the secretary closed the door. The first red-felt circle made him smile. Here, again, was confirmation of the vision of that man. It was steadying, it renewed his sense of purpose when every other indication of the past few days seemed to say that it was all futile, all coming to an end. His mother, who had begun frothing at the mouth over breakfast that morning like a rabid dog. His son, unheard of since returning to Canada. His family, in fact. And maybe even his job, he thought, as he fingered the faxed memo again. He gazed through the window and the view said nothing. Those vessels aimlessly plying back and forth through the water, the container ships, the ferries, the tankers, the launches and the sampans drawing meaningless white lines. He had to remind himself that their apparent purposelessness, slowed and confused by his lofty distance from the harbour, was deceptive. They did have an aim. They were doing business, making money. And he, too, had a purpose.

"Wilson!" called Bradshaw, framed in the doorway. "What's new?"

He strode to the chair opposite his No 2 and yanked it from under the desk. The two men swapped pleasantries; queries about the office, questions about the holiday. They enjoyed each other's company, like old lovers.

"Mr Fraser has called several times from London," Wilson

was saying. "It was important, he said, but not enough to disrupt your holiday. Then, this morning, came this." He passed the memo into Bradshaw's butcher-like hand.

He scanned it and his brow furrowed. "Not much information there. Any clues?"

"No. London hasn't told me anything."

Bradshaw left the room, clutching the paper, and called his secretary into his office. His jacket swung on the coatstand as the door closed.

The jacket hung undisturbed all day. The door opened once, for his secretary to emerge, her pad bristling with new inscriptions. Wilson left to make calls after lunch and was aware of a subtle unease in the atmosphere. Nothing had been said, but a feeling seeped through the partitioned rooms, desk by desk. There was a tension that nobody could put their finger on. Furtive glances flicked to the jacket as though waiting for it to give a signal.

The London clock read 9.10am. It had taken an agonisingly long time to reach, though Bradshaw had busied himself with numerous tasks throughout the day, stealing glances up at the clock between phone calls, and orders, and memos, and e-mails, and reading, and messages, and arranging appointments and arguing with distributors and checking figures. Now it was time.

He pushed the pile of papers to the corner of his desk, took a diary and a small pad from his drawer and, drawing invisible lines on the blotter with his still-hooded fountain pen, picked up the phone and dialled the number direct.

"Fraser!" barked a voice. It was terse, business-like and intimidating. And it worked.

"Peter. It's George Bradshaw, Hong Kong."

Some of the stiff formality at the other end of the line softened as they exchanged greetings and small talk. But, at an invisible signal, some strict, unforgiving body-clock that allotted only a tiny amount of time for trivia, the voice clicked back to its brusque barking commands. His staff called him the Colonel behind his back. They sneered at his pomposity and rudeness and even his most impressive achievements were undermined by their contempt for him. He was overbearing and took himself too seriously. If he had known, he would not have cared. He just carried on, pushing ahead, trampling over anything in his way: opposition, rivals, people, sensibilities. He had no time for sentiment. He did not like Bradshaw, but he was impressed by him.

"Right!" he snapped. "Shame you were away. We would have valued your input. This is going to sound like a fait accompli."

"What is?"

"We are relocating after all. Your office will be downgraded. We're going to rationalise the whole Far East division, with Singapore as the new axis."

"Why?"

"Obvious reasons. The uncertainty et cetera, et cetera. You know it's been on the cards for six months. Our reading of the situation post-Handover next year is not encouraging."

"What about my reading of the situation."

"Appreciated. Useful. Local. But from the global perspective – which is the approach we need to take, obviously – we have a more pessimistic outlook. We have to be cautious and cover ourselves. Uncharted waters and all that."

"It will send out the wrong signals. Orders may be jeopardised."

"Only in the short term. We're making allowances. Don't worry about that."

"I could have done with more warning. Will the board reconsider, or delay? What sort of timeframe are we talking about here?"

"No, the board will not reconsider. Those early reports you submitted have been taken into account, of course. But this is the way ahead."

"So what happens to this office?"

"It will still function. Its role will be vital."

Bradshaw sighed and pushed the cap from his pen. It clattered on his desk and fell to the floor. He felt a tic in the corner of his mouth.

"And me?" he said in a rush of breath.

Fraser responded with one of his hearty laughs, one of those empty, jeering sounds he used as another tool to patronise.

"You'll be okay, of course. We were hoping you'd take on Singapore. Get it up and running. You can stay where you are if you like. Of course, you're retiring soon."

"Not for a year."

"Fine. Singapore would be ideal then."

"I wasn't planning any more moves."

"No, of course not. You're on the home stretch. The choice is yours."

"Redundancies?"

"Naturally."

"We could be talking about 25 people."

"They'll easily find work."

"We can't take that for granted."

"Well, that's their look-out."

"It's more difficult these days."

"Oh, George, come on. Are you getting soft in your old age? Your people should thank their lucky stars they're not over here."

Bradshaw held the receiver at arm's length and let out a groan. This smug inverted boasting highlighted the things he hated most at home. It was a sort of perverted stoicism, a self-pitying enjoyment of their own misfortune.

"Anyway, I'm sending Chris Dulwich over for a chat. He'll be working alongside you to oversee the operation. Let us know soon what you want to do about your future. Bye." The line went dead.

Bradshaw slammed down the phone and looked back up at the clock. He had been bypassed and he was angry. A decision had been reached without consulting him and it was a decision he did not agree with. He had set out all the arguments against it months ago and he was frustrated that those arguments had failed. Had they even bothered to read his report? His impotence, shown so baldly in the conversation with Fraser, nagged him. He needed to regain control. He reached for the pile of folders and set to work.

Carol was passing by his door when he emerged hours later. She gave him a bland smile of encouragement, aware that there was trouble brewing and that he alone was carrying it. But he grunted at her and brushed behind her back on the way to the lift lobby. She watched him jab at the lift button and thought that his frostiness was her fault in some way. Maybe he blamed her for Phil's rudeness towards him at the ball; his absence from the office had effaced her memory of that incident until now. She sighed and rubbed her face, feeling grit and grease and a growing sense of disgust. Just a couple of words, exchanged weeks ago, and yet this man still bore a grudge. Why did men have such low self-esteem?

She switched off her computer and clicked shut her bag. Bradshaw called to her, his tone light, amiable.

"Looks like you've had a wearing day too," he said.

She nodded a mute affirmative, slightly sulky.

"I'm going with Mr Chan for a drink. Trevor's coming too. It's been a long day for all of us. Would you like to come along?" As he cooled towards his bosses, he warmed towards his staff.

She hesitated. What she really needed was her bed. But the long trip home, to an almost certainly deserted flat, stalled her. Okay, she said.

The companionship she had hoped for was not there as the three men spoke seriously and exclusively in the bar. She was an adjunct to their group. Now and again, they would ask her opinion but she felt that that was out of politeness more than anything else. She was still new to the job, she was inexperienced and she was female. However much they would deny it, that last would always be at the backs of their minds, she felt.

Bradshaw was rebelling at what he perceived as shoddy treatment. He did not care about the sensitive nature of Fraser's revelations and his normal shield of secrecy was lowered as a gesture of defiance against head office. These people had a right to know anyway. It was their future. He pronounced confidently that none of the team would lose their job. Carol and Trevor accepted that at face value.

When the cycle of discussion had spun for the third time there seemed to be nothing left to say. Trevor got up, wobbling drunkenly, and suggested going to a girlie bar. Carol smiled patronisingly and Bradshaw was suddenly aware of her eyes as they flashed. They were a clear grey, translucent almost as if lit from within. He waved Trevor away and found himself drawn towards her, his big elbows hunched on his knees, crouching forward, pushing himself into her space. He was single-mindedly attentive. She had seen that pose in men many times before and was not convinced. She moved back slightly.

"You've not had much to say this evening," he said as if it were her fault. She winced at the wave of whisky breath.

His glowing face, so near, made her suddenly bashful. This was her boss and yet she felt attracted to him. His moustache seemed to invite stroking.

He looked over her shoulder at Wilson, almost it seemed to her, conspiratorially. But Wilson was looking in another direction.

Bradshaw cleared his throat and focused again on her. "I don't think you should worry," he said.

"I won't worry," she said breezily.

"Good. Anyway, I've had too much to drink. I must go home." He seemed to suddenly realise that he was looking too hard at her and made an effort to pull back.

The city was sweating as they stepped outside. Wilson belched and the three set off in silence, wading through the crowds and the thick air, heavy with aromas: shit, sick and sweat; petrol, cooking oil and food; the greasy wake of the harbour; the clagging breath of a million bodies.

4

The police had come for George and Alice's amah as she was getting off the bus. Standing on the corner, Abril Flores had wiped the sweat from her eyes, bent down to pick up the groceries and, as she straightened, four men in military green uniforms marched towards her.

An officer had demanded her ID and as she rifled through her purse, flustered, she could feel the contemptuous stares boring into the top of her head. Then she realised that the card was in her other purse, the little pink one with gold thread that she always took to church on Sunday. She had forgotten to transfer the laminated plastic that bore her photograph, her name and a seemingly arbitrary number that gave her the right to live and work here. Without it she was an alien, undesirable, probably an illegal immigrant.

They had taken her to the station and questioned her. The voices had snapped like dogs but they were not angry or hostile, just bored. They went through this dulling routine hundreds of times a month and it was only with the smell of success, a likely bust, that interest flickered through their words. They were wasting their time and her time and they knew it but the law was the law. They waved her away. She was free to go.

She laughed bitterly as she waited to cross the road. Their

law. It was the law of the colonisers, the white man, and his collaborators. It was a law with a soft skin and a hard heart. It was a law drawn up by pirates to keep out other pirates. And anybody else who was not born here or came from the master race.

She was just a hired slave, brought in for two years to clean up rich folks' shit and they made sure she knew her place. She knew they expected her to be grateful, that her desperate position at home made her a willing accomplice in her own feudal subordination. Their law protected her with a job and a home and a set wage but it also made it clear that she could be kicked out for any minor transgression. She wondered if not carrying around her identity in her purse was one such transgression. She knew her bosses never carried their cards with them; they were always left on the side table in full, flaunted display. Why should they carry them? It was their law and their county.

She sighed as she dragged her bags across the road and again felt that worrying twinge in the pit of her stomach. The pain, slight but nagging, was growing more frequent. She imagined a little animal in her belly, eating away at the edges. It always came out to feed when she was worried, when she had done something wrong and was fearful of reprimand, when she felt overwhelmed by her troubles, when her husband failed to write to her and tell her about the kids and his latest job. He had had three already in the four months she had been here.

She was so alone. Her only company was the little animal gnawing away at her insides. She knew that when she got back to the apartment she would burst into tears and spend hours on her bed sobbing, the shopping still unpacked, the chores undone, time building up like water behind a dam. It made her bitter, the unfairness of what had happened, her weakness in dealing with it, her loneliness and the impending complaints from her boss when she saw the bags on the kitchen floor and a sink full of washing-up.

Life was never this hard at home. There was poverty, yes, but there was unity and comfort, too. There was always the knowledge that she belonged to something. Here, she belonged to nothing and day by day that picked at her like the imaginary animal in her stomach.

She would try to be strong. She would try to put away her bitter thoughts and get on with her life. She would try to strengthen her good heart. But her shoulders drooped as she looked up the steep empty hill towards home. A proud block, phallic and remote, stood at the top of the hill. She had no physical strength to reach it and no spiritual strength to fight her misery. She needed the Virgin Mary but she needed to hold the image in her hand, not her head. And that little picture of the Virgin was in the same purse that had caused all her trouble that afternoon.

The smart buildings on either side of the road added to her burden. She barely registered the expensive stone, the high freshly painted spiked fences, the security guards behind the gates, the bragging cars in their bays, the manicured gardens, the small sounds of peaceful wellbeing, but she absorbed their presence every day she passed. This is us and that is you, they said smugly.

In the first weeks here, that boastful indifference had impressed her. A simple girl from a poor county, she thought she was, and this ostentation and physical wealth had awed her. She was almost pleased that people could have so much money and that they took pride in displaying it. She never kidded herself that she would one day be the same. It was just good to see so many nice things, the things that money could buy. In this high altitude there was no want and no desperation. She had been pleased for these invisible people in their grand, high towers.

But as the reality of work and her isolation seeped into her and the exhortations of the church seemed more remote from her real life, she began to find fault with this other world. Why did they have this, and not she? Why could they have nice homes, nice cars, nice food, nice clothes, while she had to leave her family behind to find work, just to make sure they ate one meal a day?

Her brother had tried to politicise her when they were growing up as teenagers. She loved him but she closed her ears to his diatribes. They were the thrashing thoughts of a boy who would soon grow up and find there was no time for such foolish opinions. She felt older than him; she knew. He would have to work and raise a family and all these beliefs would be left behind on a shelf to grow dusty. It was always the same.

Now his declamations came ringing back to life. His tirades had been in a vacuum, ghostly responses to things outside her experience, bitter complaints about the lives of the rich and poor picked up from newspapers and television programmes and the silly chat of drunken men in bars.

With a smile she pictured him here, screaming with anger as he stood outside the gates of these rich peoples' homes. He would raise his fist and shout. And she, perhaps, would join him.

But these were idle thoughts. She had work to do. She keyed in the entry code and let herself into the apartment block.

The peace of the place soothed her. Now she was inside the walls, the envy disappeared. She kicked off her shoes and glided over the thick, soft rug in the centre of the floor. She fingered the furnishings, the lamps, the hard wood and gilt frames of the pictures. She was alone in the flat and it felt like her own. While she was alone, she could believe that it was hers, all hers. But the whimsy was short-lived. This comfort was not hers, it was borrowed. She realised that it was an empty possession. Her stomach ached. And, with a click in her throat she wandered ghostlike to her room and lowered herself on to her bed and sobbed herself to sleep.

She slept through the door slamming behind Alice Bradshaw. Hours had passed since Abril had returned home but the bags still sat on the lounge floor, the coffee cups still marked the glass-topped table, the dinner things from the night before were still marshalled in the dishwasher and scattered in the sink and over the draining board.

With a whispered curse, Alice put her own bags next to the others. It looked like a pile of rubbish, waiting to be collected. The whole room looked like a tip.

"Abril?" she snapped. There was no reply. The only sound was the hum of the aircon, a noise she normally liked because it reminded her of the sound of an aircraft on a long flight, at night, possibly going home. Even when it was cool, she kept the airconditioner on to help her sleep.

But now its hum irritated her. She snapped it off and sat down, brooding and unmoving until she pulled her bags over and slowly began to empty them, holding out each item before her, pulling it towards her face, clipping off the price tag and then laying the item on the seat next to her.

"Abril," she called again when she had finished. She marched to the amah's room, gave a curt knock and went in. The girl was curled up on her bed, her long black hair cascading to the parquet floor.

"Abril. Wake up. What's been going on?"

Abril turned slowly on her bed, drowsily regarding Alice, and pushed herself up to rest against the headboard.

"Are you unwell"

"Yes, mum. It is my stomach"

'I've told you before to go and see a doctor. Have you been sick all day?"

"No. But I was delayed with the shopping. The police took me away because I did not have my identity card."

"Oh, for heaven's sake. It's one excuse after another. You haven't done a stroke of work."

"The shopping, mum."

Alice left the room. Abril followed and took the bags into the kitchen, slowly unpacking them. The rustle and the crackling, the opening and shutting of doors seemed like a goad to Alice as she sat in the other room. She picked up a magazine to take her mind off things. But the stories and pictures irritated her further – vacuous buggers Mr and Mrs Nobody at some dull party, this ridiculous, impractical car, that hideaway holiday spot so well concealed it was impossible to get to, these nasty pieces of fashion jewellery. It was all such a tiring sham.

I shouldn't be like this, she told herself. I've just come back from holiday, a wonderful holiday. And the thought of that calm and that beauty and the rare company of a husband who tried mocked her. Post-holiday depression had hit quickly and hard.

She flicked the magazine away and leaned towards the table to adjust a picture frame. It was a laminated photograph of herself and her husband, beaming at the camera with a yacht in the background and a stunning blue sky overhead.

She studied their faces closely. She was not one of those people who feigned embarrassment at images of herself. I was a very good good-looking woman, and I still am – for 55, she thought with a curl of the lip. The crow's feet were now permanent imprints around her eyes, the grey was becoming more pronounced in her hair, there was a deep line at the corner of her mouth that looked like a cut.

What nagged her more than the slow loss of looks was the picture as a whole. The two of them, happy and glowing against that glorious sky, did not look real. It was a photograph of a dream. Where was the equivalent picture from their life in this city?

There wasn't one.

Even their most recent holiday, the memories of which were just a couple of days old, seemed such a long while ago now. For nothing had changed, nothing had fundamentally changed. She had returned, refreshed and relaxed, and fallen immediately back into the rut. At 8.30 on that first Monday morning he was at his desk, the holiday man another persona hanging up in the wardrobe until the next time.

The rut stretched before her. He would come home each evening, tired, worried, stressed, maybe with a few drinks on his breath, maybe not, and he would flop into a chair, pull his briefcase on to his lap, pull out some papers and get on with more work. She could be bright, or chatty, depressed or anxious – it made no difference. He responded with short grunts and warning monosyllables while he scored marks on the paper. Shortly after dinner, often spent in near silence, she would get up to go to bed. As she announced that he would suddenly brighten and he would kiss her and mutter something kind and he would smile. She would drift out of the room and turn to see him hunched over the documents again, unaware that any conversation had taken place between them just seconds earlier. He would be locked back in his own aloof world.

"Would you like a cup of coffee, mum?" Abril asked. She had been watching Alice in her reverie, her eyes staring blandly at the photograph with no expression in her face. It had frightened Abril until she felt she had to break the silence. She read a strange kinship in that lost expression.

"So will you go and see a doctor?" Alice said as the cup was handed to her. "For my sake."

"I will go at the weekend, if you like."

"It's not what I like, Abril. Really, you shouldn't be so cavalier about your health. We'll help pay, if that's what's worrying you."

And she began talking about health and Abril responded with shy comments, unsure of her position. For the mistress of the house to treat her as anything other than a domestic machine was a rarity: she was uncomfortable. But Alice talked on, dispensing advice, retelling anecdotes. So that when the call came from her brother in England, telling of her sister's serious illness, it felt to both women as though they had willed this bad fortune, as though talking about bad health had brought it down.

"They say she has a liver disorder," she addressed the table in a quiet voice with Abril hovering uncertainly at her side. "They make it sound as though it's behaving badly and needs a good telling off. If only. My brother says it's much more serious. Much more." She brushed her eyes.

She wandered around in a restless daze until the need to do something forced her to the telephone. She managed to get a flight home on the following day. Weakened by anxiety, she went to bed soon after and was sound asleep when Bradshaw came home. She had hoped to see him, to share her misery and to feel his support; to hear words of comfort from someone who meant something. It was at times like this that they could talk, that he would notice she existed, that he would listen, with the long empty night before them and no external demands to deflect him. She felt incapable of dealing with it alone. He would put it into perspective and help her to face it. The only other person she went to in times of crisis was the very sister who was sick in a hospital bed on the other side of the world. She called his name twice as she lay down and fell straight into sleep. She was not conscious of him coming into the room and did not hear him undress, did not feel his hard back touching hers when he got into bed.

He knew nothing of the crisis until she told him the following morning. He allowed himself an extra 10 minutes' delay so that they could talk. She was disappointed when he left; the conversation seemed half-finished. Even though it was going around in circles and there really was not much to say, she wanted more words. But for him, there were more pressing demands at the office.

PART 3

Lee brought me a dog-eared paperback today. In the back of the book, neatly folded, I found a centrefold from a girlie magazine. He had designed that I found it by accident. It is typical of his furtive nature.

The book, and the picture, are just the latest in a series of gifts he produces whenever he stops by. They are his way of showing friendship and, I suppose, of making me reciprocate some sort of affinity. This is a lonely place and some sort of alliance is probably necessary. But he is not the sort of man I would have chosen to ally myself with. There is about him a degree of obsequiousness that I find offensive; although his grasp of the language is excellent, his grasp of the intellect is not and I find that frustrating. But he wants friendship, he needs it. And more and more, I need some sort of listener, no matter how passive and unsatisfactory. He listens and he responds although with little more imagination than an autocue. But, still, he listens.

I tried to rebuff his advances early on. They were unwelcome. I wanted to stew in my own juice. I have always maintained a distance from all but the closest associates but that option has become too stark. He gradually whittled down my defences.

It started when he brought me a packet of cigarettes. I had noticed, with increasing annoyance, his sly but silent little overtures towards me. Whenever we passed, he would nod and smile as though we shared a secret. He seemed eager to ingratiate himself with me and my defences went up immediately. I took to ignoring him altogether.

Then one day he dropped by with a crumpled packet of cigarettes. I had stopped returning his nods, had looked away from his smiles, and thought that he understood our positions. I was certainly in no mood for him on this particular day and I was brooding deeply. I thought I had made it plain that I wanted nothing to do with him. But he was oblivious to my rudeness and persisted in that quiet, determined way of his.

He knocked at the open door and peered round the jamb, grinning, his eyes hidden behind glasses made opaque in the dimness. Interrupted from my negative reveries I was prepared to put him down once and for all.

I brought you some cigarettes, he whispered in that irritating voice of his.

Slowly, I put down the ancient magazine I had been reading and removed my glasses.

I. Don't. Smoke. Cigarettes. I said it with a level of menace perceivable even to him. I have told you that a hundred times, I continued, relishing his growing discomfort. Why do you keep bothering me?

He looked crestfallen, like a naughty child, and that angered me even more.

Now will you leave me in peace? I don't want your cigarettes and I certainly don't want to see you hanging around any more. Please get lost.

But they're for you, he said. And the "you" seemed to echo in my head and I suddenly realised that in my self-absorption I had over-reacted. I had made him lose face and all he had done was to show an act of kindness. And I remembered again the thought that went round and round in my head – that my churlish disregard for other people's feelings was what led to my downfall in the first place. I still did not like the man, but I became mortified. So I took the packet and in an attempt to lighten the atmosphere said, with an exaggerated laugh, that I preferred panatellas. Two days later he brought me a packet. I was genuinely grateful this time. And he took that gratitude as a signal, the all-clear that he could finally attach himself to me.

So we became uneasy acquaintances. He told me his story. I told him mine. He continued bringing little presents, while asking nothing in return. And this latest present obviously is a sign that he thinks he has my full confidence, that he knows me well enough to presume to bring me a picture of a naked girl lying on a bed of ferns.

It doesn't arouse me – nothing does any more. But after he had gone I sat and stared at it for hours and thought of what the imagery meant, what it held. And when he returned, supposedly just stopping by on his way to somewhere or other, I called him in and thanked him for the picture and started to tell him about the women in my life, because the face of the girl in the photograph vaguely reminded me of one of them. I thought he was going to have an orgasm on the spot, so obviously excited was he that I would finally reciprocate his gifts. Not that mine was a particularly exciting or erotic history. Though maybe to him it was. All things are relative, aren't they?

Still, I managed to disappoint him. Because I took a metaphysical approach, rather than recount lurid incidents. I saw the sex on the page but I thought of the things behind it. I thought of women in the abstract. I thought of relationships – that ugly modern word – and desire and love. He must have wanted specifics but I was trying to concentrate on the whole. Love can turn to hate can turn to war so quickly, I began rather pompously and he nodded happily. It was a quality introduction to what he presumed would be a tale of sleaze.

And where are the lines that separate them? I said. Yes, where are the lines that separate them? They are fragile states that can slip one to another without notice. The shift does not need a major event to force it. It can be subtle, unnoticed: a gesture, a word, a realisation. Only the bravest try to deal with the new state, try to get back what was or break away from what is. The rest of us put up with it, or award ourselves consolation prizes, or become cynical about the whole thing. Most of us aren't even aware it's happening.

It is easier just to accept. I remember a young reporter from my local paper telling me about his job once. One of his main tasks was to interview golden wedding couples. He sneered at it, he seemed to think it demeaned his calling. But it still fascinated him, meeting these tired, sad and faded husbands and wives and listening to the fumbled, potted or edited versions of their lives together. What always struck him, always, was not what they had been through, not their triumphs and misfortunes, but the basic fact, the reason that he was sitting there chatting to them over a cup of tea or a glass of sherry in a quiet front room. He could never come to terms with the fact that these two people had spent 50 years living together. Fifty years. He, a young man with no experience of life and love, was impressed and a little frightened. He refused to believe it was possible.

He said that on rare occasions there would be an obvious love still alive between the couple. But that was seldom. Usually, the strongest vibration in that room would be one of affection. At other times it would be a barely patient tolerance or in their words would be resignation, complacency, occasionally outright hostility.

Every report he wrote would read the same. The subjects would be different but there was a depressing similarity about each story. These people, these couples, were cartoon characters, never alive on the page. But he had met them and he knew different.

And he wondered, when he was with them, when he left them, when he typed up the story on his bulky old Remington, and when he saw it in the paper: how have they managed to stay together for half a century? Are they lying to each other, or to themselves?

I paused and looked at Lee. He was nodding sagely as though he had given the same thing a great deal of thought, the fraudulent bugger.

The reporter said that nine times out of 10 it was as though the couples had given up on each other, that they were just going through the motions, I continued. That was what frightened him most: that one day he would be 75 years old and there would be a knock on the door and a cub reporter would invade his house and ask him and his wife about their 50 golden years together. And they would put together a story, and might realise as they were doing it that the feeling that *had brought them together had died long ago. It had died a natural death but they had been unaware or unable to do anything about it.*

He did not comprehend the underlying cynicism of his thoughts. He was too young for that. I was, too. But I can see that the cynicism was there within me, albeit asleep, waiting to be roused by experience and circumstance. It was a bitter thing to come to terms with: this inbuilt knowledge that each one of us is alone.

Lee was staring at me as I looked up again. He was hunched on the stool towards me, his glasses clasped in his cut and battered hands. Yes, he said dreamily. That is true. I had been talking, but to myself really; he had been listening but it was as though his thoughts were being manifested through my disembodied voice. And for the first time in our short relationship I felt an empathy towards him. He understood after all.

And you were still alone? Even when you had ... women? Your wife? Your girlfriends? he said in a whispered, tentative voice. You were still alone when you were in love?

I can count a handful of women in my life, I replied. A few were love. They were genuine, yet they did not last, they could not last because deep deep down I was alone. At the time, of course, I believed they would last. I might even have daydreamed about being interviewed on my golden wedding anniversary. What happened with them? I don't know. There was no single event that ended the affair each time. Until the last one, that is. Just an imperceptible, fluid shift in emotion, from love to hate, from hate to war. Sometimes on her side, sometimes on mine. Sometimes on both.

It was love that brought me here, in its way. Love and my blind destruction of it. Because something inside of me could not accept it. So I destroyed it, not consciously, I don't think, but I destroyed it, killed it.

What? What do you mean? said Lee, grinning stupidly. You fucked her to death?

I was shocked, so shocked I almost laughed. But he was grinning stupidly at his crass bravado and there was a nasty expression of lasciviousness on his rat-like features.

No, I said coldly. That's not what I meant at all.

He apologised and asked me to go on. I refused, aware suddenly that my anxieties, once articulated, were nothing but cheap titillation. He left shortly afterwards and I lay down, hands behind my head, staring at nothing. Maybe, in his clumsy way, he had been right.

1

Phil had a clumsy way of rolling a joint. He pulled three cigarette papers from the cardboard pack, licked along the line of glue on one and stuck it to a companion sheet. He laid the third across the top of the first two and rolled the construction into a half tube. He split a cigarette and sprinkled the tobacco along the length of the tube, rolling it as he did so. Then he played his lighter flame against a corner of the hard lump of dope, breaking powdery fragments into the tobacco. A bit more rolling, packing the ingredients in tight, and, with a final lick, he sealed the tube, twisted one end and inserted a tiny cardboard column in the other, open, end.

The spliff was dented, uneven and soft, with a slight bend near its centre and leaking tobacco. But it would do. It did the job. He lit it and sucked in a deep breath, holding the caustic smoke in his throat and lungs and finally releasing it with a satisfied breath. He wondered if cigarette smokers got the same pleasure from their unadulterated tobacco. He knew they did not. What, then, was the point?

He looked around at the dark, undefined shapes and the thick shadows thrown by the night and the glare of office windows and neon behind him. He was sitting on a bench on the waterfront, staring idly across at the lights and the silhouette of hills on the far side as he took slow, long gasps on the cigarette and dragged the smoke sensuously into his lungs.

The night was still around him. The occasional thump of traffic noise crossed the torpid air; the chug of a launch in the harbour impinged on the silence. He felt as if he had been deserted.

Polar city, he thought. Crowded and dense by day, screaming with activity and bustle, yet at night sleeping, at rest. The fabulous wealth built up in tiers behind his back and the indigent curled asleep on the bench opposite. The dirt and the degradation around his feet and scattered over the grimy concrete walkway, yet the clean, serene beauty of the hills in the far distance.

It had been a good evening, truncated, but that did not bother him. He was at his happiest when he was alone. He flicked the expired joint towards a bin with a smile and walked to a corner for a piss. He returned to his seat and rolled a second.

The drinking had ended early, for once. The Gang of Four, they called themselves, four European teachers at that poxy school, who, nearly every night, would wash away the woes of the working day in beer and vodka. The rule to avoid shop-talk was broken every time as the alcohol took hold and they dissected the day's events.

But tonight there was a flatness about the affair; the bar had been quiet and all but Phil had other places to go – one to football practice, one to the cinema with his girlfriend, the third to meet someone at the airport. So there had been a weight of restraint on the gathering and the chat had been listless. Pleasant, a laugh, but going nowhere, except to the knowledge that they could not get smashed that night.

They had talked about work, each one of them proclaiming a determination to find a better job. They had talked about football and sex, eyeing up a barmaid, leering at an actress on a television set over the jukebox. They had talked about music with the attention to detail of a convention of trainspotters. Dates, names, numbers poured out with a breathless, puerile enthusiasm for the facts. They had not talked about anything that mattered – there was not enough drink in their systems to do that.

Through their idle chitchat ran the thread of work. The conversation always came back to the dramas of the day, the laughable little adventures of humdrum lives. In early days, they had worried that their complaints about the principal and jibes about other staff had racist overtones. But these days they no longer cared about that. There was such a bitter enjoyment in criticism.

In that company on that evening Phil's story was the most exciting. How he had arrived 35 minutes late for work and had been pulled up by Wang, the odious, pompous principal they all shared a hatred for. How Wang had almost manhandled him into his office, barely managing to keep his voice from rising to a shout as he berated Phil – for his time-keeping, for his attire, for his attitude – that damning, all-encompassing word that usually signalled an end to a job.

And then, as Phil stood silently in the centre of the room, not invited to sit down like an adult, Wang had hinted that he thought Phil was drinking and that that was affecting his work. Phil's idle posture as he stood listening to the complaints took on a hard, defensive shell as the sly suggestions began to anger him.

It felt like the opportunity he had been waiting for. It felt like the chance to vent his fury at this man and this job, going out in a blaze of glory with an unforgiving crushing burst of righteous auger. Stuff it, then, you incompetent little wanker. What do you know, you greedy, grabbing, time-serving, little piece of shit? The speech formulated in his head as the principal took tiny stabs at his self-esteem. But the script stayed unspoken. He fought to keep it in his head, holding his voice, stifling the anger, and merely pursing his lips and twisting the silver stud in his earlobe in a slow, almost menacing gesture.

A sense of responsibility, and of fear, kept Phil in check. Walking out of a job was stupid, foolhardy, no matter the provocation. Carol would be upset. She would lose faith in him, that already fragile faith he knew she had to refresh each morning she awoke.

He did not doubt that he would find another job quickly

enough; he had the assurance and the arrogance to believe that. But she would not be so certain. She had seen him unwind over this last year, she had watched him shuck off the layers of convention, skin by skin, and as he got closer to his tormented centre she became more afraid.

He could not let her down, not without letting her go. That, too, was an occasional scenario that played to favourable reviews in his mind, but he always turned away from it. His desire for liberation, for a life of solitude, was dishonest and impractical. He needed her just as she thought she needed him.

And he was aware, painfully, of how much he let her down, how much of his short measures she put up with. With barely a complaint. The occasional outburst, yes, when he was drunk too often, or missed something, or failed to do something, or when his stone wall of surliness and silence became too oppressive. But she gave him a huge degree of freedom and space which he would not have been able to cope with by himself

He lit a third joint and crumpled the empty cigarette packet, flinging it along the concourse and into the sea. His eyes rolled in his head as he pushed it back and stared at the sky, burnt orange at the bottom and seeping into black. He felt a swooping sensation, fast floating away from his body as the third, biggest, hit of cannabis took hold.

He looked abruptly at the ground again, his eyes swimming. Mellow now, mellow. Thoughts of Carol added to the feeling warm. He thought of her body, her face, her eyes, and her voice. The way she walked, that sexy slowness, the gestures. And yet he almost treated her as an intruder.

He pictured their flat the night before. How he had been listening to music and felt a nip of resentment when she had come in from work, breaking into his solitude and his selfness. How he had dried up her flood of words about work with his silent, threatening dam. How she too had lapsed into silence and they had been enclosed in music like two strangers on a bench. And how, when the music had bored him and the silence had made him uncomfortable, he felt the need to provoke, using real words and real feelings.

That cold, hard anger had congealed in him again. With an almost vicious enjoyment he had announced that he wanted to return to the United Kingdom. She had heard all his complaints about Hong Kong before and she let his tirade have its run. And then, when he had finished, she had quietly said, "But we've just got here. We're just getting settled."

"Exactly."

And she had gone quiet again and he could feel himself immovable, could feel her feel his stubborn, shiftless weight.

Almost with a sense of formality she had let that weight settle, had let him feel he had ended the discussion, and then she had said, quietly, with a small, manipulative plea in her voice, "At least let's give it six months."

He pondered. Then he had said "Okay." And after another pause, "Six months."

Relief had come to them both, he knew. She did not want to go; he did not want to stay. Yet the thought of separating scared him and, he thought, her. He shuffled to his feet. He wanted her now. She was not an intruder, a stranger or an enemy. Now, he wanted her.

2

She was not home when he got there. She was in a bar a kilometre from where he had been sitting on the bench, halfway to drunkenness, enjoying a night out with the girls. With the girls – and Trevor, who had tagged along when he had heard there were to be six women and as much drink as he could handle. It was yet another leaving party and Trevor as ever, was in a party mood.

"Did you know?" he slurred, leaning across towards Carol and Corrine, the petite Chinese girl from the office with the twisted smile and the frightened eyes. They backed away from him. Even sober, his presence would be an intrusion. This was supposed to be a girls' night out..

"Did you know?" he repeated, circling the rim of a glass with his finger. "That the Chinese have never been properly acknowledged for their one great invention?"

Corrine grimaced. How easily these gweilos, particularly drunken ones, insulted her culture, turned it into a cheap joke because they could not see it for what it really was and could not understand the native pride in it. Carol decided to humour him.

"Gunpowder?" she said, a smile on her lips. He was a likeable man, a silly, show-off idiot, who compensated for his lack of confidence by playing to the gallery. It was an endearing quality.

"No, no. This is something far more important. Something that altered the course of history and for which they have never been properly thanked. The whole world should be grateful. Gunpowder? Who cares about gunpowder?"

Despite Corrine's growing discomfort, Carol carried on with the game. She listed inventions and discoveries, remembered from school. Paper and porcelain. Silk, she said unsurely. He laughed her down showily, spurred by her willingness and Corrine's disapproval.

"Corrine?"

"I don't know. Something stupid, I suppose. But you think it's funny."

"I'll tell you then." He paused for effect. "It was the wheelbarrow."

"The wheelbarrow?" Carol spluttered into a short laugh.

He liked the way she laughed and the fact that he had made her laugh. He did not care about Corrine's reaction. "Strange but true," he intoned, pushing on with drunken insensibility. "Strange but incredibly dull. Not a lot of people know that." He reached for his drink and emptied the glass, signalling to a waitress for a refill, pleased with himself.

The waitress came over with a bright, hungry look in her eyes and stooped towards him. Here was another chance.

"Bet you didn't know the Chinese invented the wheelbarrow, did you?"

No, she did not.

"Couldn't give a toss, could you?" She smiled and hesitated. Then: "No, I couldn't actually. Did you want another drink?"

"What are you offering?"

"Anything you can handle, buster," she cried in her Australian twang. He gave an exaggerated whoop and beamed at Carol and Corrine. Carol smiled back, despite his almost desperate display of vaudeville, a sense of humour she had never understood in England because it was so cheap and obvious. But still she liked him. His boyishness was refreshing.

She liked it like this. It was fun. It was college days in the

States, aliveness and youth and noise and enthusiasm, not the slow dead hand she remembered in Britain. Inhibitions had been cast on the floor with the dog-ends and the spilt drink. She looked around at the crowded bar, at permanent party time, at the twentysomethings having a good time. Huge smiles and barking voices and bright eyes in a rush of hysteria. No worries, no anxieties, just a loud, raucous determination to have fun. She felt her nerves tingle with excitement, Every night she went out it was like this, a well-earned celebration of liberation that reminded her so much of her youth.

A splintering crash made her turn her attention back to the table. Trevor, trying to perform some trick for the entertainment of an indifferent Corrine, had knocked over a glass.

"Sorry," he said, unapologetically.

Corrine turned and pulled a pack of tissues from her bag, wiping at the dripping liquid on the edge of the table.

"You're pissed again, Trevor," said a woman at the next table. "You're always pissed." But she gave him an indulgent smile.

"Stress, flower, stress," he said.

"Bollocks. You just can't handle it."

"Dee, my lover, I can handle everything."

"You couldn't last night." And the women with her laughed. He swelled under the glow of their attention.

House music was booming and spastic dances of intoxication were taking over the small, cluttered floor between the tables. Dee wanted to dance and challenged Trevor to join her. He rose and grabbed her hand and lumbered after her, bouncing off other couples and muttering unfelt apologies.

The tempo was fast but they fell into a clinch, licking each other's face, hands gliding over each other, fingers prodding. Their month of passion was almost over, it would fizzle out as quickly as it had started. And they would pick up other lovers in other bars. And neither of them would worry about it.

Corrine, drowning and bruised in the waterfall of noise, excused herself to go home and left with the three other girls. Carol watched her friends now bobbing stupidly on the floor and felt the need for a dance. A man with gelled hair and stubble grabbed for her in the chair and she relented easily.

When the music died she heard another of Dee's bellows. She was arguing with Trevor, the alcohol exaggerating his minor misdemeanour. The couple pushed each other from the floor; Trevor toppled into his seat and Dee grabbed her bag and fled. Carol was distracted by her dance partner but ducked away from him through the slow-moving crowd back to her table.

Trevor was slumped awkwardly on the chair, his head resting on its back, and gazed lugubriously through befuddled eyes at the ceiling.

"Now what's happened?" said Carol, sitting along from him.

He muttered something incoherent and pushed himself upright. His hand flopped towards Carol and grabbed her knee. It was not a sexual move, it was a plea for support. He felt sorry for himself. She pushed it away.

"Women," he gasped. "Can't live with 'em, can't bury 'em in the garden." He gave a weak smile, suddenly ashamed through the haze that he might have offended her.

She was not offended. It was another of his familiar silly cracks, a line she had already heard countless times. Repetition was one of his tools of humour. Sometimes it worked and sometimes it did not. She liked his little lines, and his little-boy-lost, that sweet, irresponsible behaviour that made everything such fun. He never seemed to take anything seriously, as serious and miserable as he now looked. Manana, he would say at every chance. Who gives a fuck? It was the mantra of the city.

She stroked his hand fleetingly and got a sickly smile in return.

"You're alright, though," he said.

"Thanks a lot."

The table jarred as somebody bumped into it. She looked from the intruder back to Trevor, uncomfortable that he was still staring at her. The warning light came on in her head. Going out and having a good time and flirting were all great fun. But there were lines not to be crossed.

"Dee's such a tease," he moaned. "One minute, she's up for it and the next she gets all haughty and freezes up as though I'm trying to rape her. Christ, I haven't even stuck my tongue down her throat this evening. Some hope."

"Perhaps you should go after someone else."

"She's great in bed when she does get going, though."

"Trevor..."

"Sorry," he said.

"There's more to it than just bed. Surely. You two have got nothing in common. You don't even seem to like each other very much. Yeah, you should both find somebody else. You should find a girl more on your level, someone you can talk to and not just... you know."

His eyes narrowed. "What? You, you mean?"

"No! Course I didn't mean that. I'm spoken for, Trevor." She paused, then added: "I think so, anyway," with a nervous laugh.

"What?"

"Nothing, nothing. Doesn't matter."

"What if you are spoken for? What if you're not?"

"Look, there are plenty of other women here. It shouldn't be too difficult for someone like you."

"No. I suppose not," he said, brushing his hand through his hair in a well-practised gesture.

"She's a bit of alright," he continued, nodding over at someone walking away from the bar.

"Go on then. Talk to her."

He squeezed past her knees and weaved towards the woman. He tapped her on the shoulder and Carol watched, fascinated and amused, as they exchanged words. She saw him wave at the bar and the girl nod and the two of them push through a crowd and order drinks. Then he escorted her to a far corner and was lost from view. Carol picked up her bag and slowly climbed the stairs to the street, a small sense of victory buoying her. How can such a nice guy be lonely? she thought. He does not know his own potential. How can anybody be lonely in this place?

3

"So you think your purse was stolen?"

"I don't think. I know." Alice was chagrined by the hiss of her reply but it felt justified. This policeman, trying to present an old head on young shoulders, a world-weary, knowing, tired scepticism, irritated her. It was false and it was obnoxious. And it was not helping her, she who felt an unwelcome vulnerability in this suddenly unfamiliar place.

The officer bit the inside of his cheek and waved the pencil like a wand he was unsure how to use. He gave her a slow, appraising stare.

"You don't think you might have just lost it?"

"No. I'm sure of that."

He let out a stage sigh and bent over the record sheet. She noticed the baby tonsure in the centre of his grey-flecked hair and suppressed a smile. He looked up suddenly, self-consciously.

The station door burst open, letting in the strained sounds of crawling lunchtime London traffic. He nodded at two men as they entered and clicked numbers into a security lock, pushing through a metal door with a clang and disappearing upstairs.

"I think I was followed by two young men while I was shopping around Haymarket. They came closer when I went into the tube – that was at Piccadilly Circus – and one of them bumped into me while I was waiting on the platform. Then they just sauntered away."

"It's a crowded station, Mrs Bradshaw. People get bumped all the time." He laid the pencil on the counter.

"Yes, but it was after that I noticed my purse was missing. I had it when I went to buy my ticket, obviously. It had disappeared between then and the time I got off the train five minutes later. It must have been those boys. They stole it."

"Hmmm," he said, with a slight edge of conviction and picking up the pencil again.

"They were black," she cried.

"Of course they were," he said sarcastically and frowned down at the page.

She left the interview with dissatisfaction in her heart and a few pound coins in her hand. They had given her just the bus fare to her friend's house; the sergeant's refusal to give her enough money for a taxi had seemed like more deliberate awkwardness. Were they trained for it, these people? she wondered. The thought of the long journey back to North London on public transport wearied her.

Everything this day had wearied her. Or scared her. Or disillusioned her. Only the weather was pleasant, a watery sun throwing a cool mantle over the streets. The shabbiness of this part of the city was relieved slightly by a few sickly saplings in midsummer bloom. She sat down in a park, her back to black Victorian railings, and checked her shopping again to occupy herself. In the bottom of a bag was her purse.

She bit her top lip and smiled broadly in a great rush of relief. Not just over the purse but over everything she had seen and done since she got back to England. Rediscovering the purse put everything back into perspective, a perspective that had been warped out of all recognition.

So quick to jump to conclusions, so ready to assume the worst. And feeling out of place ever since she had stepped off the plane. She began to sense that she was emerging from something, that she had dragged her negative thoughts with her from Hong Kong and laid them over this place without giving it a chance, without looking at it, but now she was starting to see.

It had depressed her straight away. Because it had disappointed her. In her ache to return, even before her sister's sickness had forced her hand, she had painted a false picture of London. It had been a place of fond memories where life had meant something, where everything had a purpose. Telescoped in view from her luxurious but empty high-rise apartment in a hot land, it was a place where all the streets had trees on them and everything was ordered and made sense.

Instead, she had been confronted by steel mesh shutters on the shops closed for the half day, a litter bin with its skirt of trash on the ground, a blocked drain, a car that looked abandoned on a corner and an almost deadening atmosphere. There was no vitality to redeem it, no lust for life, just a surly despondency, a tired defeatism.

She had wondered if it had always been like this and could not remember. She had been protected from it by the sweeping lawns, leaded windows and big, clean roads of her middle class enclave. She and George often joked when they watched current affairs programmes about some worrying aspect of life in Britain that they may as well have been watching a wildlife documentary.

They were screened from it, remote, safe. And returning to it after four years, back in the thick of it, she had felt unsafe, a disturbing sensation after the complacency of her Hong Kong home. There she could walk anywhere by herself in the middle of the night without fear. Here she felt vulnerable in broad daylight.

It was not the ambling crowd or the humble streets. It was the loiterers, the beggars, the young people with time on their hands and callous disregard on their faces, the packs and the tribes. She crossed the road when she caught sight of a group of travellers, in dirty rags and with patches of skin glistening through the grime on their faces, laughing and talking loudly outside a launderette. She crossed again when a beggar lurched towards her, waving his hat like a weapon and spitting incoherent words. On the train into town that morning, she had been frightened by a group of young men whose rowdiness grew as the cans of Special Brew hit home before hitting the tracks. There was a barely suppressed violence in the air. They had been at the far end of the nearly unoccupied carriage, self-contained in their spiteful joy, unaware of her quivering presence. She had been too paralysed to move to another carriage, as if a sudden movement would alert them and they would pounce. Her imagination was stronger than they were.

These pictures of tribalism sat uncomfortably with her memories of her life in Britain and with the illusory homogeneity of the city she had left a few days earlier. She skated the surface of life there and everything below looked the same. In this street, she was beneath the surface and felt trapped and threatened in a place that seemed to be breaking up.

It was the threat of the tribe. This was not a society at ease with itself. Its people were dislocated, alienated, lost, under threat and lashing out. It petrified her. She felt more alone than she ever had and could not establish whether that was unfamiliarity with her surroundings, or shock, or the fact that her blindness had lifted for the first time.

And she had felt suffocated. Long-buried feelings of claustrophobia began to return and with them the fear, that fear that had almost driven her over the edge those few short years ago. When the sporadic anxiety attacks had become one long scream, despite the lawn and the leaded windows. She had been sent away, for tests, for counselling and for convalescence. Gradually, the terror had abated. And then George had been offered the job on the other side of the world. He had wanted it so desperately, but said it was not worth the risk. He needed to know that such a complete change of environment would not endanger her. They needed it to benefit her. Just like the old days, they said.

He had had long discussions with the doctor about the wisdom of it and had returned positive, strong enough to renew her faith. It doesn't matter that it's the most crowded city on God's earth, he had reassured her. It won't be where we're living, I can assure you. And she had believed him. And he had been right. And they had both tried hard, in those first couple of years, to make it work. When it started to come undone, she had been too frightened to tell him. She felt he had sacrificed so much for her that it would not be fair to make more demands. Anyway, this time the feeling was different; it was not the blind terror of before. It was something she could live with. It is not a feeling that will make me crack, she told herself.

She had kept it in check until she had returned to the place she had missed so much. And everything seemed to conspire to bring the terror rushing back.

When she thought her purse had been stolen it was like a confirmation of all that was wrong. She had shed tears, because it all suddenly felt so utterly hopeless. She had wanted this place to revitalise her, after the almost comatose existence she had temporarily escaped. Instead it had just seemed to shout: You don't belong here, either.

Now, with the purse in her hand, things were in perspective. She phoned the police station to apologise and made a detour to The Strand to treat herself to a cream tea in Simpson's. She was celebrating.

Peace of mind was restored amid the polite clink of teacups and the dutiful attention of the waiters. It was civilisation, a restful retreat in the heart of an angry country she could hide herself from.

"I shall write to the station sergeant, of course," she said to her friend Helen two hours later. "He quite restored my faith."

The walnut oak door glided open on polished bronze hinges and the two women entered the house. They piled the bags at the foot of the stairs and went into the living room, both pausing to look through the bay windows and drink in the profusion of colour in the garden. This was what Alice missed most.

"So Josephine is on the road to recovery?" said Helen, easing herself into an armchair by the firegrate, as clean as a display model.

"Yes. We think so. Tom painted his usual blacker than black picture but that was natural – he was very upset. She did look terrible when I saw her. But you know Josephine. A fighter. She perked up quite a bit yesterday and the doctor told me this morning that he is optimistic. There's no guarantee, of course..." she trailed off.

"Yes, she is a fighter. A survivor." And they swapped comforting anecdotes about Josephine to illustrate her spirit. The woman never gave up, they agreed. She was little more than a frail shell at the moment yet inside was a bright fire of determination that age and disease and tragedy could never snuff out. When she had recovered from her mastectomy she had made a joke about her disfigurement, she who was so proud of her body. When she had finished grieving for her first husband she had turned the desire for a more stable, reliable and loveable bedmate into a mission. When two muggers tried to attack her she gave one a black eye and chased the other down the street, waving her umbrella like a deadly weapon.

"Anyway, there's no need to rush back. I'll go as soon as she's alright. It could be a few weeks but I can treat it as something of a holiday."

"When you're not worrying too much."

Alice smiled, her eyes taking on a shine that had been absent for three days.

"I'm not so worried now, after speaking to Dr Standish. And she did look so, so much better when I saw her."

"She's a strong woman. It runs in the family."

"I didn't feel too strong today. I kept thinking I needed George. He wouldn't have put up with half of what I went through."

"Neither would you, there was a time. I thought you'd got over all that. Why didn't you call the ticket collector on the train?"

"But they weren't doing anything."

"They were scaring you, Alice. Whether intentionally or not. Whether they were going to do something or not. They had no right. No right at all. You thought they might. You should have called the collector. You should have done something."

"Jetlag," she joked.

Helen scoffed. "So how is George?" she said.

"George-like. You know. Immersed in his work, uncommunicative in the evenings. Troubled about something, I think."

"He's not told you?"

"Of course not. George never brings his worries home – not vocally, anyway." Helen frowned and moved towards the drinks cabinet, clinking ice into two tumblers and pouring in generous measures of gin.

"Are you enjoying your life out there?" Her tone was cautious.

"George is, certainly. As for me, it's up and down. It can be an interesting place, you remember? There is a buzz, a lot of life. But there does seem to be something missing and I can't quite put my finger on it."

"You're bored."

Alice compressed her lips and looked almost guiltily at her friend but said nothing.

"Aren't you?"

"Extremely." She sipped at her drink. "Maybe it's just age."

"Nonsense. Nonsense, nonsense, nonsense, Alice."

"Well, I don't know, then."

"Of course you do. You must. You're just refusing to face up to things. If you're dissatisfied you must do something about it. You must act before it's too late." She sighed and there was a bitterness about that sigh that humbled Alice. "I can tell you Alice that something is wrong. And it's more than just jetlag. It looks like you've had the stuffing kicked out of you. Again. You don't want to go through all that again, none of us do. But you're so... so timid now. You would always stand up for yourself when you were well. Like your sister; you were two of a kind. What is he doing to you?"

"It's not George's fault."

"Are you sure of that?"

"But he's a good man."

"Nobody is saying otherwise. But you've a right to be happy, a duty. And you're obviously not. And it's even more than the worry about your sister, let alone the horrible gang on the train and you thinking you lost your purse. Something is fundamentally wrong, Alice. A blind man could see that. You're not the same person. You are not happy. You've got to get yourself sorted out. It's no good just dragging yourself through this sort of half-life. I'm worried about you."

Uneasy silence fell between them. But Alice welcomed her friend's diatribe because it articulated her half-buried anxieties. And it showed her that somebody cared, cared enough to look inside whatever they found and to speak honestly about it. Alice could almost have cried with gratitude.

"Do you think George is having an affair?" said Helen. This sort of direct approach had been so hard for her in those bad days. But she had forced herself because she had been told that that was what Alice needed. Pretence was no good. Confront the problem, the psychiatrist said, however hard or callous it may sound. Don't pussyfoot – it does more harm than good. Alice looked at her sharply, drink slopping over the edge of her glass.

"No. Of course not. Why?"

"This indifference of his."

"He's always been a bit remote. You've always said that yourself"

"Yes, I know. But... well. You're sure?"

"Yes, I am. I would be able to tell if he was."

"That's what most women say. I don't."

"Well I do," Alice raised her voice for the first time. Their eyes held on each other.

It was time for safer territory. "Why don't you and Jason come out and see us again?" Alice said quickly when they had snapped out of their mutual hypnosis.

"Fine."

"It will give us a fillip. I'm sure that's all we need."

Helen eyed her curiously, then nodded. It was as though one of her pensioners had asked her for home help. There was a muted cry of desperation in that superficially simple suggestion.

4

"It's going to take a long time. A month. Maybe more."

Dr Standish was squinting up at Alice, his ball-like face compressed. Brutal fluorescent lighting bounced from the dome of his head and the nervous tic in the corner of his mouth distracted her.

"I'll stay until she's over the worst of it, at least."

"I think she is over the worst of it," he said in his characteristic rush of words. "I can't promise anything, there's always a risk of a relapse in a case like this, but I'm confident." He squeezed his mouth into a smile.

"How did she sleep last night?"

"Not well. Not well. She called the nurse several times. It was probably the discomfort of the operation, and the medication, which disturbed her. She should sleep better tonight."

Alice nodded. Standish shifted his weight on his feet and looked at his watch. With a grunt that meant excuse me he moved away, his small figure receding down the bright, white corridor.

Alice re-entered the room and looked at her sister staring weakly back at her. Cologne hung in the air. Alice realised that it was not Josephine's usual perfume; it was much bolder than the fresh, airy scent she habitually used.

"What did Dr Standish say?"

"He said you're making a good recovery," Alice replied, perching herself on the edge of the bed and stroking her sister's arm.

"Fibber."

She had Alice's tumbling hair and wide smile, one which had been out of practice for weeks. Alice was glad to see its shadowy return.

"If you're good, he says there'll be no more operations."

"I'm always good these days."

"When you're better you must come and convalesce with us. The doctor says that when you get through this you'll be fit enough for a long journey and you'll be just in time for the autumn – the best time. All the stickiness has gone then and the days are gorgeous. You could almost believe you're on the Mediterranean. It would be good to have some company."

"That would be nice."

"Helen and Jason may be coming out, too. Perhaps you could all come together."

"Oh, I can't stand that man, He's so full of himself." A conspirators' grin passed between the two.

"You can just imagine it," Josephine continued, warming, and pushing herself up against the mound of pillows against the wall. "He'd have me carted round in a wheelchair by some poor little rickshaw puller, jumping out into the middle of the road and ordering the traffic to stop to let me cross and generally treating me as though I was senile."

"I thought you had a soft spot for the old style of gentleman."

"Not that old."

"He tries."

"He's trying, that's for sure. Tcchh!" She shook her head in mock disgust.

A nurse entered with a trolley and a drip. Steel trays clattered as she manoeuvred the cart.

"Not another jab, please," said Josephine as she watched the nurse pull the plunger on a hypodermic. "I'll look like a pincushion."

"It'll make you sleep."

"I don't need any more sleep."

"Now, don't argue. Dr Standish says you're always picking on him, too."

"It's his own fault for having such a shiny head."

The nurse dabbed the crook of Josephine's elbow and pressed in the needle. The woman in the bed gritted her teeth and Alice looked away, through the window at the parkland receding to the stand of trees. There was not a building in sight. Just a green sweep of lawn and a pale sky and in the middle distance an abandoned wheelbarrow piled with mown grass. A flock of birds scratched a charcoal scribble over the trees. She turned back at a satisfied sigh and exchanged a meaningful look with the nurse.

"It's nice to be back," Alice announced to the room and the nurse nodded non-committally and wheeled her trolley from the room, pulling the door shut with her foot. "This is the first time since I've got here I've been able to say that. It is so nice to be home."

Josephine smiled weakly, the freshly injected drug hanging on her eyelids.

"You do miss this place then?" she said.

"Of course. I always did. I certainly miss this," and she turned slowly back to the window, her arm arcing before her to encompass the view invisible to her sister.

"How long before you do come back? Permanently?"

"George has only got a year left with the company. But he's hinted that he might leave before. Then there will be nothing to stop us."

"Can you wait another whole year? Your letters have been terribly gloomy lately."

"I can wait." A pensive cast fell on her face, faraway, deeply introspective. "I think."

5

Stupid bastard. Stupid childish bastard.

He had been hunched on the sofa, rubbing his eyes in the bright light of early morning, when she had seen the wallet on the table next to him,

"What's this?" she said.

"A wallet"

"It's not your wallet though, is it?"

"No, it's not my wallet;" he replied, putting his hands down by his sides and looking up at her for the first time through watery eyes.

"Then whose is it? What's it doing here?"

"I've no idea whose it is. I stole it," he said drily.

Carol jerked back half a pace as though she had been pushed. Her lips moved soundlessly.

"That's right," said Phil. "I nicked it. Last night."

"What? What? You're joking."

"I'm not joking," he said with a treacherous smile.

"Come on. You are." Her tone was desperate. It seemed surreal, him sitting in the chair calmly announcing that he had stolen something as if it did not matter. To Phil, it did not matter. As the slow shock of realisation dawned on her she felt giddy.

And he explained, step by step, slowly and rationally, as if to a classroom, the theft. How he had been in a bar in Central the previous evening, vaguely angry, glaring at the other customers barking round the tables. Bloody yupps, he said. Tosspots. It was as if he were in London seven years earlier during the final boom of the boom and bust years; it was as if these vacuous bastards had slipped through a timewarp to antagonise him with their loud voices, reactionary opinions, sharp suits, coloured braces and arrogant displays of money and wealth. He hated it. He hated them.

And he wanted to show his anger, wanted to do something to show his disapproval. It nearly came with an accidental nudge from someone making his way to the toilet. Phil had bristled when an elbow hit him in the arm and his beer slopped from the glass to the floor. He was in a black mood, getting blacker, and this seemed like provocation. I almost hit the guy, he said. But the man turned and apologised, serious and genuine, and disappeared into the crowd before Phil could react.

His blind anger did not abate. He felt a growing pressure in his head, a need to scream, to lash out, at these innocent bystanders whose only crime was their presence. The volume of their voices added to the pressure, pushing at his brain. He was consumed with hate. Hate and rage and envy his motivators, always his motivators. He felt momentarily sorry for himself, saddened by his negativity, uncomprehending of this darkness. And then he thought, fuck it.

He saw a jacket hanging on a brass hook under a waist-high shelf and he moved over to it, turned the jacket towards himself and slipped his hand into the inside pocket. He did not look around to see if anybody was watching. He felt alone, suddenly. His hand touched the soft leather of the wallet, fat and smug, and he pulled it out and stared at it. He put his drink on the shelf and walked casually from the bar, the wallet burning his hand.

On the street, a light rain fuzzing the neon, he opened the wallet and exploded into laughter. He felt triumphant as he eyed the bloated sheaf of dollar bills. He felt no remorse, just a vague, satisfying revenge. Still gripping the wallet, he went home.

And that morning, under the interrogation of an

increasingly disturbed girlfriend, there was still no remorse. And that was what sickened her most. The fog of beer had cleared but he still felt the same about his crime. It was funny.

"Why did you do it?" she asked quietly, every word sounding irrelevant.

"I've told you," he said, staring up at her. She was still rooted in the centre of the room.

"That's no reason. This is ridiculous. This is so childish, Phil," she cried in a broken voice. "It's not as if we need the money."

He replied with a callous laugh. She had missed the point entirely.

"You'll have to take it back."

"No."

"It's not yours. You've got to give it back."

"Bollocks."

She felt a rush of words but was unable to speak as she stared at his hard, hunched stubbornness. She wanted to run away, she wanted to stay and argue with him. She wanted to use gentle persuasion, she wanted to scream at him, she wanted to anger and shame him into returning the stolen goods. She wanted to call the police, she wanted to share his twisted moral perspective on his action.

She did nothing but lay the wallet back on the table and leave the apartment.

And now she sat at her desk, the blue glare of the screen hypnotising her, unable to think of anything other than that morning's conversation and to draw confused pictures in her head of Phil in the bar, taking the wallet, opening it, and laughing loudly on the street in the rain. Like a kid. Like an idiot. Like a madman.

She was scared and her hands were trembling against her chin. It was a revelation of character she could not cope with. It was as though the man she had lived with and loved for seven years had been taken over by another personality, changed and absorbed into something different. There was a sick swirl in her stomach.

"Hi," said Trevor, a hint of anxiety behind his smiling eyes. "You okay?"

"Yeah, yeah, sure. How was Guangzhou?"

He sucked in his breath and expelled it in a gush. "Interesting," he said. "Up and down. Bit of a problem I'll have to talk to Chan about. But a couple of sales, so not too bad, I suppose."

"Good," she nodded and looked back at her screen. Trevor moved away with a last worried glance at her.

She forgot immediately that she had been talking to him. Her mind was stalled on one line of thought. She searched back through the years, replaying scenes between herself and Phil, trying to spot clues to his behaviour. An attitude, a statement, something he had let slip, anything that she could now analyse under the microscopic beam of hindsight and say, I should have known. But there was nothing there, nothing that her memory would reveal. Phil was Phil. His honesty and his directness were two of the things that had first attracted her to him. And then he pulls a stunt like this. A thief. A thief who thought his crime was funny, who thought he was teaching someone a lesson, who thought he had done nothing wrong.

What was he trying to prove? she thought, and the words repeated themselves over and over. But he had been too irrational for a sensible question like that to occur to him. And then she thought of something he had said, within weeks of their arrival here. She could not remember why he said it or where they were or what they were discussing. But she remembered the words and her spine tingled as if with a warning. You can do anything here, he had said.

She looked up, woken from her trance. George Bradshaw, holding the lintel of the door to his office, was looking in her direction. He gave her an encouraging smile and she frowned back.

"You don't look well," he said, walking quickly to her desk as though pulled over. "Are you alright, Carol?"

She nodded, but said nothing, her eyes flicking from his face to her blank blue screen.

"I think maybe you ought to go home," he said. "You look very pale." On the desk, inches from her, rested his big, hairy hand. She wanted to stroke it. A wash of gratitude choked the words in her throat and she felt an urgent need to cry. His solicitude was choking her.

"Come on, let's get you home."

She shook her head and looked into his face, blinking.

"I'm okay," she whispered.

'Tm not so sure about that"

"No, really," she began and let out a brittle cough. "I'll be alright. It's nothing to worry about." She forced an unconvincing smile. He stood back, feeling useless.

'If you do decide to go home..." he said. "Anyway, it's up to you." His voice trailed off again and he stepped away from her desk, backing down the office, then turning and walking to his door.

Her eyes followed him and she closed them to hold in the water. Self-pity picked at her. She felt so grateful for his attention and his words. He was a nice man. The image of Phil loomed in her head and with it resentment. Stupid, childish bastard. She was weakened by the thought of him.

She could not put up with this, this uncertainty, this dishonesty. It sickened her. Maybe they should split. She was too drained, too shocked, to shoulder the responsibility for his behaviour. She could no longer keep up with him – with his moods, with his stunts, with that anger. Smug, he would expect her to. Because, up to now, she always had. He would believe unquestioningly that she would stand by him. You can do anything here. Grow up.

She was tired by the circular monotony of her thoughts and stood and stretched. Trevor walked by her with a friendly tap on her shoulder and that boyish grin masking some anxiety of his own. She smiled after him as he walked into Wilson Chan's office.

"I got a problem, Wilson," Trevor said as he eased the door shut behind him. With a wave and a smile, almost as if he had not heard, Wilson motioned at a chair.

"Good trip?" he said.

"Er, yeah, yeah. Er, couple of good sales but there is a problem."

"Tell me," said Wilson, joining his hands in an arch and looking seriously at the young salesman opposite. His tie was not straight but Wilson kept back a reprimand. The boy was worried about something.

"Well...?"

"I, well, it's nothing really." Trevor gazed up at the

ceiling, feeling foolish. His eyes returned to lock on Wilson's. "The circuitry order. It's quite a tight delivery, yes?"

"Extremely," replied Wilson, drawing out the syllables.

"Two Dragons can't meet the deadline. Not a chance, they said."

"Oh."

"However;" Trevor paused and licked his lips, marshalling his words, "the Happiness Electronics Group can. But for a consideration."

"What soft of consideration?"

"A bribe, frankly." Trevor's ears reddened; his voice sounded loud and high-pitched. He squinted at Wilson who seemed unmoved.

"I see," Wilson said slowly and sighed. He reached across his desk for a bowl of mints, pulling one out carefully as if it were a jewel. He pushed the bowl towards Trevor.

Trevor felt a rushed need to explain. "Mr Zhang says the order will be expedited for a 10 per cent consideration fee. Without that fee, he says there is no possibility of getting the stuff to us in time. With the fee – his pocket – we can have it by the end of the month. I don't know what to do about it."

Wilson sighed again, a noise of defeat, as though acknowledging his final failure to protect a favourite child. "This happens so many times," he said. "More and more now, too."

"Well, I'd heard it happened here all the time. Mates at other companies have told me about it. I didn't believe the place was so bent until I started working here"

"It is not purely an Asian thing. That's an insult. It is that old Western sense of superiority that angers me so much. It is not true." He became quieter, embarrassed by raising his voice. "It happens all over the world, in business, not just here. In your country, too. Only a hypocrite would say otherwise and that is something some of your people are so good at being."

"Wilson..."

"It makes me angry. It makes me more angry that I have to accept it. I have to go with the flow. We all do."

"Can't we just forget about it? Tell Zhang to get stuffed?"

"It's too big an order. Too important. It is worth a lot of money."

"I'll go back over and check out some more firms. Maybe we can put off the buyer."

"There is not enough time. We will have to go with this offer. Grin and bear it. It's built in. What can we do? It's not harming anybody."

"I don't like it."

"You are still new," Wilson said kindly. "You will get used to it. If you can't, you should look for another line of work. You will find this anywhere."

"I can't believe that. That's too cynical."

"But that is the image you play on, Trevor. Is that not the real you?"

Trevor grinned like a boy, then checked himself. "What happens if I tell Zhang no but that if he gets the order through in time, there'll be lots more from us? Good for business."

Wilson shrugged. He appreciated the boy's tenacity if not his inexperience.

There was a knock at the door and Bradshaw strolled in.

"Is that all, Trevor?" Wilson smiled. The salesman felt trapped. He strained to protest at this calm disregard. "Just give Mr Zhang what he wants and we can proceed with business. This is a very important order,"

"I'm. I'm not sure," replied Trevor, robotically.

Bradshaw smiled in bafflement and noticed the familiar hardening of Wilson's jaw when he was provoked.

"I'm giving you the okay, Trevor, Now get on with it."

Trevor left the room, shaking his head, as he listened to the muted voices behind him,

He felt naive and was angered by that. Business was business, he thought. The extra cost would be passed on, so what? Nobody would lose out. It was too grey an area for moral judgments. But he baulked at the euphemism, consideration fee, a silly, transparent phrase that dared him to be shocked by it. And it did.

This was business, what was he worrying about? The easy acceptance of it, he supposed. That, and the fact that he felt used, by Zhang and by his boss. He felt used and dirty and then his thoughts switched again to the callous objectivity he knew he should feel, the same pragmatism that drove his friends in London and New York, the same unsentimental drive that made for success all over the business world. What was he making a fuss about? Bradshaw and Chan would be in there now, tittering over his lack of guile and almost puritanical sense of discomfort. He was second-guessing their cynicism and that angered him more. He sat down heavily, two desks from Carol. They were alone in a little pool of angst in a corner of the room.

6

Three days in the company of Chris Dulwich had been enough. Bradshaw had realised that his first impressions, his infallible touchstone, had been wrong.

What had first struck him as confidence was cockiness. The man's drive was desperation; his knowledge was bluster. He was here solely to make an impression and to shove aside a man twice his age and with 10 times his experience. He had taken on the relocation and restructuring of the firm as an opportunity to make his mark, and to move upwards and onwards. He would do well in this city of show and sham. If Bradshaw let him.

What grated most was that guttural London accent, those quickfire, flyboy, barrowboy, keep up or be left behind vocal attacks disguised under a thin layer of humility and humour. It was an accent Bradshaw had left behind years ago, when accent mattered in business, when he did not have a choice.

But Dulwich seemed to take pride in it, seemed to proclaim its humble roots and use it as a challenge, as a statement of new against old, the Cockney in the City, the Bronx boy in Wall Street. Behind his breathless patter was the contemptuous certainty that he knew better because he had worked his way up from the bottom. His class badge said he had the guile of the street that no amount of school ties, university education and lucky breaks could achieve. And that made him a genuine predator, someone with the killer instinct required for the survivalist world of business in the 1990s.

Bradshaw felt threatened. And he did not even know if the accent was genuine.

From the watercooler he watched Dulwich burst into laughter, supported by the wide grins of Carol and Trevor. The man was true scum, thought Bradshaw. He was tricking them into trust, making them like him, making them think he liked them, and all the time he was coldly analysing what they did and said and weighing up their future. One or both of them would be shafted with the move to Singapore, George knew, and this man was stringing them along like puppies.

There was another rattling burst of laughter.

Bradshaw looked again at Carol who nodded and muttered something then returned to her desk where the joyful mask slipped off, she thought unnoticed, and her face was left naked in a sad cast. Her melancholy of the last few days had begun to worry him. Did she think she was going to lose her job? He did not know; her work was still good and showing promise and profit, unaffected by insecurity. She was a true professional in the making he thought.

He found his attention on her growing more specific; as he stared over, propped up by his elbow on the plastic water container, he stopped thinking of her as an impersonal component in the office, a good worker, a real pro, and more as a woman. Everybody else's eyes were on their screens; he had checked involuntarily before indulging himself in this admiring from a distance. He felt a twitch of shame when he realised that he was waiting to see the way the strands of golden hair slipped in slow motion over her ear and hung in front of her brow till she swept it back into place. As if he had willed it, a length of hair slipped forward. He was like a scientist on a field study, waiting for confirmation of a behavioural pattern to prove a point. He held his tongue between his teeth in anticipation and smiled broadly when her fleshy hand rose and unconsciously drew the hair around her ear, the little finger tucking the strands beneath the lobe, unconscious of his appraisal.

He shook his head and looked around, suddenly

embarrassed. Nobody was watching him; in the seconds of suspended staring work had carried on as usual, oblivious of the mental foreplay across the room.

He returned to his room and sat bewildered at his desk. There was blood in his prick and confusing pictures in his head. He was becoming too attentive to that girl. It was unprofessional and potentially destructive. But it held an unfamiliar gratification for him.

With a knock that meant nothing Chris Dulwich tripped into the room.

"Alright, George?" he said casually, spinning the chair and almost jumping into it. "Friday for Singapore then, eh?"

"Yes, it's all in hand, Chris."

"Has your girl typed up that list yet?"

"I've asked for it by the end of the day. We can go through it tomorrow morning and she can line up the meetings with the agents tomorrow afternoon."

"Goodo." He clasped his hands and started tapping out a tattoo on his ribs with erect thumbs. Bradshaw recognised himself in that lost, anxious surplus of energy. And he frowned.

"And the staff list?"

"You've already got that," Bradshaw replied coldly.

"Yeah, I know. I thought we were going to go through it and start marking off the first batch for the cull."

"What's the hurry? It will be months before the move."

"There's a bit of fat here that can go now."

"Is there? Is there, indeed? I thought I'd know that better than you. Wouldn't you?" Dulwich shifted in his seat. He could feel a fight coming on. He liked nothing better.

"Be honest, George," he said with spurious amiability. A wall of ice came between them, Bradshaw's frozen eyes locked on his.

"It is not in your brief to tell me how to run this business,' said Bradshaw, smiling viciously. "You're here to help me make this relocation go as smoothly as possible. That's all. And if you do have doubts about my ability – or, indeed, my honesty – I would appreciate you keeping them to yourself. I'm not interested in your opinions, just your abilities. So if you want them to be heard I suggest you take them back to London."

Dulwich unclasped his hands and coughed. It was the first time the friction between them had been voiced. He warmed to it. "Let's be objective, shall we?" he said. "Eighty per cent of the people here will be out on the streets in a few months. The majority of that 80 per cent we need to keep right up until the move. But there are a few out there we could quite easily lose now without affecting the business. So why hang on to them?"

"Have you anybody particular in mind?"

"Trevor, for one."

"Oh the one you were just laughing and joking with. His figures are increasing month by month."

"Still small-fry."

"He is building some valuable contacts. We'll need them after the move."

"Alright then. Peter Wong."

"You've obviously not studied their sales records in detail"

"He's been off for a month. What's he been up to?"

"He's sick. But he's coming back next week. And his good work will resume. I can assure you of that. Anyway, I want him in Singapore. I've already told you that"

"Mrs Liu, then?"

"Mrs Liu has been with this office for 10 years, long before I got here. She runs the place like clockwork. She's invaluable. And we'll need her more than ever to help organise the relocation."

Chris Dulwich smiled, a slow, sly smile that bared his teeth. He had to hand it to the old git – he fought his corner.

"That Carol girl, then? The new one."

"Look, Chris, you can pick names out of a hat all morning. None of my staff are being made redundant until I'm good and ready. Got that?"

Dulwich eased back in his chair, reflecting on his opponent.

"Yeah, I got it."

"Good. Now perhaps we can get on with some real work. Aren't you going over the border this afternoon? For the factory tours?"

"That's right."

"Well, maybe Simon will have all the stuff ready for you now. All the information. If you'll excuse me, I've got these figures." His bowed head and hunched back were as vocal as any dismissal.

He found it hard to work. The conversation replayed itself through his head over and over throughout the day. Concentration slipped in and out. At 6.30 he decided to call it a day, closed his books, switched off his computer and walked from his office.

Carol was fidgeting with her handbag when he stepped outside. The room was empty apart from a temp secretary screwing up her face at a pile of papers.

"Early night for you, too?" said Bradshaw, moving over to Carol.

"I've got a bit of a headache," she said.

."A shame. I was going to ask you if you wanted to come for a drink." He surprised himself with the sudden invitation and stopped. "There's something we need to discuss. But it can wait till tomorrow if you're not well"

"It sounds important."

"I've worried you now. It's okay – we'll talk about it in the morning."

"No. I could do with a drink anyway."

They walked four blocks to a bar, through streets as bright as day. It was crowded with businessmen and women, gagging hysterically on happy hour drinks as if let off early from school. Bradshaw and Carol found a corner on a raised floor by an opaque window and ordered drinks.

"Something wrong with my work?" asked Carol, taking a careful first sip.

"Nothing at all wrong with your work. Cheers." Their glasses clinked.

She watched him in silence as he went through the motions of lighting a panatella. It seemed to give him strength to carry on.

"You're enjoying your work," he said suddenly between those first few puffs. She was not sure if it was a question or a statement.

"Yes, of course."

"And you're doing well. Very well." He sighed.

She gave him a puzzled glance and looked back at her drink. Discomfort stood between them like a barrier.

"The thing is," he began again, "there are big changes on the horizon, as you know. Despite what I said to you the other evening, though, it may be in your interests to look around for another job now."

"You're sacking me?"

"No. No," he said with a force like a rush of wind. "I'm not sacking you at all." He downed a large mouthful of beer. "We will be letting most of the staff go when we move, of course. For the moment that's between you and me, although anybody with half a brain could work it out. But you're still relatively new and will need more time to resettle. That's why I'm giving you this warning early. To give you time."

"So I definitely can't come with the company when it moves?"

"Would you want to?"

She shrugged.

"I'm afraid you can't. We'll be filling most vacancies with locals when we do go. This office will be drastically shrunk, or downsized as they insist on calling it in London. People above you will have first choice to stay with us. Realistically, I don't think there'll be room for you."

"I see," she said softly. She looked around eagerly and waved at a waiter.

"I've been watching you closely," he said, squirming inwardly at the ambiguity of his words. "You're a very good worker," he continued quickly. "You've slotted into the job very well, you know what you're doing and you've come up with several good sales. If it were within my power you would stay with the firm. You would make a good asset. However..."

"How long have I got?"

"A while yet. But the last thing I wanted was for you to come in one day and be handed your cards without a word of warning. That happens here a lot. Even in my company."

She flashed him a false smile and emptied the tonic water into her double vodka.

"I'll give you a couple of names," he said, reaching into his pocket and pulling out a pen and notebook. "Very good friends of mine. Sound businesses. They may have room for you and I will give you a good reference."

He paused, uncapped pen in the air, at a mysterious glance from her. I am being presumptuous, he thought. Too pushy.

"If you want," he said in what for him was a humble tone.

When she had read the sheet of paper he passed to her, carefully folded it and zipped it into a side pocket of her bag he felt like he had discharged his duty and could relax. But there was a stilted, unreal ambience around their table, an air of uncertainty and unsaid words and unrealised feelings. Silence settled as something tangible.

He looked at his watch conspicuously and seemed to contemplate going home. But he was held to his chair by a vicarious sadness. She nodded yes when he offered another drink.

She took it with a distant, preoccupied look and he felt himself straining to break down this heavy weight of silence between them. He was wary; he thought she might cry, her sombre introspection, once interrupted, might no longer hold back the tears. But anything was better than this strange isolation.

It was she who broke through. "Thank you for the names," she said suddenly. "And the warning." He looked at her bewildered; she seemed to have come through something with the strength and optimism of her first weeks with the company returning to her. Her smile was broader now, stronger.

"I'll ring them tomorrow. You say there's no rush but I might as well."

Conversation came easier as they talked about the companies she should approach and he was quick to encourage and flatter her.

"So how is that boyfriend of yours?" he asked quickly when they had exhausted the topic.

He was not interested, of course, but it was part of the protocol. He was not prepared for the sudden drop of the barrier gate again. She let out a sob, soft yet piercing. "I'm sorry," he protested. He had a generational embarrassment at the sudden show of uncomfortable emotion. Her eyes were glinting. "I'm sorry."

She warmed to his voice, grateful for the apology, for

anything that spoke of simplicity and sincerity. She needed to unburden herself, relieve the misery of the last week, to talk to someone who would listen and understand. At home, life jumped between extremes of silence and screaming.

She started tentatively, shy, pained that she was opening up her hidden personal life to her boss. It was strange, she thought, that to him she was just a worker, someone who made him and the company money. To suddenly reveal her life outside the office would put her out of context. Bradshaw sat nodding, expressionless, carefully nonjudgmental, as she took him through the grubby tale of Phil's twisted impulsive act of the previous week. When she had finished, grinding out yet another cigarette in the cluttered ashtray and looking at him for some sort of acknowledgment, a wave of sympathy pushed him towards her. His hands fell awkwardly on to hers.

He opened his mouth to say something but stopped, aware of how platitudinous it would sound, and moved his hands. He fought a compulsion to lean nearer and brush back a silky drift of hair suspended before her eyes.

"I think we'll split up," she announced. "I feel like I've lost all feeling for him since last week. He's a stranger. I don't think I could forgive him for that. Well, maybe if he was so drunk he didn't know what he was doing. Or if he was sorry about what he did. But he isn't. That's the worst thing."

"The police..?" Bradshaw started to say but trailed off. He nodded, mute now, still uncertain how to respond. The gaps between them seemed to forbid any real empathy with what she was going through. Their ages, their attitudes and the deep pit driven between them by their daily working relationship seemed to keep them apart. But he was desperate for her to understand that her pain moved him. He wanted to cup that soft, round face and slowly pull it into his shoulder. Like a father with a daughter, or lover to lover.

She looked at his hands and smiled softly.

"It had gone stale anyway," she muttered, unwillingly, the vodka pushing her into the relief of the confessional. "It's ...well, you know. I feel like I'm missing out. We've been together a long time now and –"

"How long?"

She paused. "Seven years."

"That's not long," he said with a dismissive air that irked her and made her pull back.

"How long have you been married?"

"Twice that amount of time," he said.

She shrugged. "And...?" It sounded like a challenge; her look demanding honesty. So much truth had passed over that table; why worry about a little more?

"I don't think the length of time is relevant. It's what you do with that time that counts." She was not fooled by his evasiveness.

"Yeah. And me and Phil have done all we can. We're just going through the motions now. I'm beginning to see that. I think he pulled that stunt out of boredom. Maybe he's stifled, maybe he's bored with me. Stealing that money gave him a little buzz of excitement."

"How do you know he's bored with you?"

"I just do."

"How?"

"Oh, nothing I can put my finger on. I don't know. The feeling's different."

"Vague."

"Of course it's vague," she responded angrily. "Things are different. Everything's changed. And I didn't even know till he took that wallet."

"How has it changed?"

She looked up at him from the table top, the fringe of hair curtaining her eyes. His face was very close, too close, they both suddenly realised and he moved back in his seat.

"Lots of ways. All ways," she cried impatiently as though she were being forced to answer against her will. Her voice dropped. "Nothing's the same. Nothing's the same. We don't... we don't, well, you know..." She regretted her sudden coyness, the coded confession to this man but then she felt calm, and glad, that she had exposed herself.

He coughed into his hand. But underneath his embarrassment he, too, felt a strange relief. All evening their conversation had been tightening in circles, closer to an intimate core he would not consciously recognise. What had started as sympathy had hardened into desire, but he kept pushing it away. With those words the desire came rolling back.

"I think I'd like another drink," she said.

More drinks arrived, more large drinks, and then another round quickly after. There was no more talk of Phil, no hints of lack of fulfilment, but his presence hung in the air behind their words. Still the tensions between them evaporated, their chat became easy and there was a deliberate effort on both sides to leaven the mood and regain safer ground. After his warning, and her revelations, and his concern, a bond was being fused between them.

With an effort, he remembered long-forgotten funny stories and she laughed at them, politely at first and then with growing amusement as he became more animated in the telling and she more relaxed in the listening. There was a liberation at work here. Her optimistic view of things came back to life. It was youthful and refreshing to him and he warmed to it. There was an easy flow of talk between them. They felt the closeness of old friends.

And with drink, longing was amplified. He touched her wrist and felt a faint, needful response. Her fingers curled towards his. Shocked, he pulled his hands away, then slowly edged them back, encouraged by a look in her eye, a question. He looked from their clasped fingers furtively around the bar and buried his discomfiture.

Under the shell of laughter she was disappointed, angry, confused, needing some reaffirmation of desirability, some proof of worth, a change, a point to it all. He was weary, sad, hungry, wanting to comfort and to expiate. The blind arrogance of lust worked through the drink and through the words until everything else was forgotten. All that existed was desire; they were a companionship of the troubled, he said, his last words as he pressed his thumb hard into her palm and led her outside to a taxi rank and the short ride to a hotel.

PART 4

The silence lies. There is so much life here, yet no sound. I see life in this room and know that all around me other lives go on. But where are the sounds? Where is the proof?

There are others, like me, in rooms just like this one. But for Lee – and he has been avoiding me since our last discussion – I have rare contact with them. We shun each other and I am left to guess at what they do. They live and breathe but I hear nothing. When I can pull myself out of my self-obsession, I wonder what they do. They must follow silent pursuits: reading, writing, staring blankly at walls. Or they sleep, or they masturbate, muffling their grunts in thin, lumpy pillows. There is no aural evidence of their existence through much of the day, only my blind belief that because I saw them yesterday or this morning, they are here now. I am not alone. Yet that is precisely what I feel. For the first time in my life I am aware of my solitary existence. I have time to feel it.

I have company in this room. Insect life. Repellent, busy, and silent. These shiny carapaces crawl and fly around this airless cell, giving me a sort of companionship. I almost started giving names to the more familiar denizens – the common harvestman spider in the corner by the window, the little colony of termites in the fallen damp plaster around the *bed leg. But I stopped myself naming them. Recognising them with names would be an acceptance, a giving up. It would be the final admission.*

I will not name them, though sometimes I find myself muttering at the spider in the corner, craning my head upwards to look at it in the dim light seeping through the windowpanes. Apart from the odd twitch in its web, it never seems to move. I can rest assured that it will always be there, waiting for me to creep up and start babbling at it.

It has such a tiny body and such long, long legs. I am sure that when the time comes for it to leave its silky nest, when it has had enough of me and wants to look for brighter company elsewhere, it will move very fast. Its minuscule green body will bounce on those telescopic legs like a tiny sedan chair as it runs from this place. I do not know what it is doing here, anyway. Surely it should be in a wood somewhere, nestling in leaf litter, waiting for more varied prey.

Its rarity makes it a more enduring friend, if I can be allowed to anthropomorphise. I am letting my self-discipline disintegrate. Today I am too weary to worry about that. Who can judge me here? That comes later.

I like the spider best of all the arthropod company because it should not be here. Like me. But we have both made a choice. The other cellmates are expected, predictable, boring. The termites soldiering in their pile of broken plaster, the cockroach on the wall by the mirror, the pair of mosquitoes which lazily circle the lightbulb as unaware and uncaring of my presence, only to attack at night. My leg and rump are blotched with their assaults.

I have been too paralysed by shock till now to do anything about them. But one hovers past my face as I stand under the bulb and my hand, still quick, still certain, snatches out and crushes the thing. I look at the body flattened on my palm and brush it off. Its partner is invisible but I will find it. There. But it fades in and out of the light. A sudden exhaustion takes me, a feeble recoil from exertion spreads, and I sit on the bed, trying again not to care. I am hungry and my moaning belly drags the energy from my limbs. But the mosquito taunts me and circles my head and shoulders as I sit hunched looking at the floor. It crosses my field of vision again and then alights on the doorjamb. I slap my hand against the metal, suddenly laughing at the noise in this silent, sombre place.

My eyes rest on the cockroach. It is one of the small ones, its black-barred head pointing downwards. Its long antennae are twitching as I stare. And I am aware of my mass in the mirror below its odious metallic body. It runs a few centimetres and stops at the edge of the glass, then turns and runs back to the spot it had just left. I take off a shoe. The antennae are palpitating but the insect does not heed the warning. I smash it flat against the wall and twist the heel with a spasm of my wrist.

It is time for a clean-out. Such dull, offensive company must be extinguished. I crouch by the bed and worry at the leg but it is bolted to the floor. I pick clumps of loose plaster from the wall and watch the termites scurry as new formations grow on their citadel. Lying on the bed is a bottle of White Flower Embrocation. Such a pretty container for so savage a task, Chinese characters embossed on the glass on either side of the oval green label. I unscrew the lid and pour the thin green liquid on to the termite colony. The insects, already excited by the restructuring of their home, scatter at the burning rain. An astringent scent leaks up from the pile as its occupants thrash under the acid. Tiny bodies curl and legs flick. I empty the bottle and kick and crush the plaster into a pancake with the toe of my shoe. I do not want to stop.

Eventually I pull away. I am pleased. I look around the room. Already it is getting dark. My spider friend is in the corner. It is only fair that he will have to go too. I tear the web from the corner with a single swipe, rousing the harvestman from its cool somnolence. It runs diagonally towards the ceiling with a surprising lack of speed. I crush it with my thumb. Almost casually.

The room is cleared of life. The silence uninterrupted; the same dense quality without life as it is with. Tomorrow, no doubt, new visitors will invade my privacy.

1

The train rumbled into the station, a slowing blur of faces passing the windows, shapes and colours gradually coming into definition. The doors hissed open and Phil pushed through the throng to the platform and struggled to the other side to wait for the connecting train. It was almost an intuitive dance now, getting through a crowd with as little body contact as possible.

This interchange always smelled of puke, he thought. It was the only station in a depressingly uniform line that had something individual about it – and that was its rank aroma. Without that smell he could have been anywhere on the mass transit railway, at any underground station. The pillar blocks, the single colour mosaic tiles lighting the stainless steel bins, the garish back-lit advertisements for Italian fashions, Swiss watches, Japanese cars, American fast food and Thai beach resorts were the same at every point on the line. Only this point had its unique gagging smell.

He was buffeted on to the connecting train and crushed against a support pole in the middle of the carriage. He saw mothers with children, businessmen, office girls in black, labourers in shorts and sandals, people nodding off or sound asleep everywhere, all willing victims of the money god, bits of disconnected body and slices of face. Those eyes that were open were blank.

On the street, a humid weight holding down the smell, he saw the same blank faces. His forebears had called that look enigmatic, a patronising refusal to see beneath. His face, as he glanced up and down the screaming highway, was just as empty.

He picked his way through the strollers, the glare of sunlight refracted by the cluttered mass of huge neon signs, redundant and lost by day, shouting and assertive by night. A double decker bus groaned past, centimetres from his ear, as he stepped over the kerb to bypass a grey-ragged woman. She was heaving a barrow diagonally across the pavement towards him, edging tenaciously through the people who filtered around her like water. Phil kept to the narrow line of the kerb, tightrope-tiptoeing along it with just enough space to his left and his right to move more easily. The traffic streamed past on one side and the slow crosscurrent of people intermingled on the other but he could move along this route unimpeded for a block at a time.

Over bobbing heads he caught glimpses of commodities in windows, brightly lit and showy. There was gold and jade, in all its artificial, plastic-looking glory, black boxes of stereo equipment, a bland homology of casual clothes in shop after shop, glazed pig, and folded ducks and chickens, staring groundward on broken necks like crucified icons.

He turned into a side street. Unsteady fences had been set up around a hole and a workman was jabbing his pneumatic drill into its broken concrete lip. The street ahead was dreary and less crowded than the one he had just left, with shops devoid of ostentation and a poorer, earthier air. The wood and metal frames of stalls jutted into the road from either pavement but it was not clear whether they were being opened up or closed down. In the grease-tracked aisle between them, paper, plastic and rotting vegetation patterned the asphalt.

The woman in the shop ignored him as he walked in, his feet scuffing the bare concrete floor. She was unfolding a newspaper and laying its pages across her dinner table by a bead-curtained doorway. She smoothed the final sheet of paper and looked up at him and smiled. He was a regular customer.

He said hello to her turning back as she reached up to a high shelf pushing aside cans and jars and pulling out a cord of chopsticks which she dropped clattering on the table. Smiling at him again but saying nothing she pushed herself through the beads into the back room, their lazy shuffle diminishing in slow clacks.

He looked at the outspread newspaper, intrigued by the bold multicoloured calligraphy and its arcane messages and the seemingly arbitrary jumble of pictures. Among the bleeding bodies and short-skirted starlets was one of the governor, chubby schoolboy British with a warm grin and the politician's badge of baggy eyes. He was pictured with two suited Chinese men and all three were pretending to share a joke. Did the woman in the shop, this reader, really care what he said or did? Phil wondered as he made futile efforts to decode the lettering next to the photograph. The man in the centre of the picture represented the colonial swansong, as remote from her as the moneymen in the towers on the opposite side of the harbour.

"What do you want?" said the woman, bustling back through the beaded doorway.

"Hi. Just beer," he said, pointing to the chill cabinet, its grimy plastic front half-concealing the cans inside. "Six," he said, holding up his fingers, then repeated the word in Cantonese with a mixture of humility and pride.

She put the cans on the freshly papered table with abrupt, seemingly impatient, movements. He was used to this by now, this apparent brusqueness. It no longer bothered him as it did other expats. In fact, he valued it as a sort of honesty, a refusal to bullshit and follow form, the artificial Western form of politeness and courtesy. Even in this dirty, unwelcoming, sleepy shop, which probably saw less than 20 customers a day, there seemed no time for that sort of nonsense. This woman was always busy.

He thanked her and crushed the plastic bag of beer to his chest. A lorry was nudging backwards into his path as he stepped out of the store and he skirted around its tail, crossed the road and walked into the foyer of his building.

It was an old apartment block, less than 40 years old but antique in this city, 10 storeys high, no lift, a rounded cornice that reminded him of 1930s shopping parades in suburban high streets at home, and a permanently dirty staircase. Its scattered collection of litter, dog ends, dead insects and plastic drink cartons always seemed to change but never to grow. When they had returned here after their stopgap tenancy at Dirk and Philippe's flat, the state of the lobby and the stairs was the first thing Carol had remarked on. She had almost seemed to assume that it would be cleaned up and repainted in their absence, as if by right. He refused to let its shabby condition bother him any more.

He focused on the dull stainless steel of the security door to their flat as he rooted in his pocket for the keys. A double door on every flat he thought. And this was supposed to be one of the safest cities in the world.

Every newcomer here felt that. Another expat urban myth. It felt a lot safer walking round the streets here at 4 o'clock in the morning than it did during the day in some parts of London, they all said. Or Manchester, or Paris, or Sydney or Seattle. They all meant the same place. Not here. Somewhere else.

Yet every day, the papers burst with grim stories of crime; of chopper attacks inside nightclubs, gang fights, vengeful loansharks and blackmail attempts, grisly murders with bits of body washed up in black plastic bin-liners on one of the more remote islands. Safest place in the world? For who?

More bullshit, he muttered, pushing himself into the flat. Was everything about this city lies, fabrication, exaggeration? Never the real story. Or two different stories, depending on who you were.

The flat was in its usual disorder. Her clothes were dumped on chairs in the lounge, her books covered most of the table, her photographs sat stacked in piles on the floor by the television cabinet. He knelt, glancing at the top of each pile. They were not as abandoned as they first looked; she was slowly cataloguing them. That is the pile of temples, there modem architecture, there street life, there water. He smiled affectionately, the first time that day that he had even acknowledged her existence.

He switched on the light and yanked the ringpull from a can. He took a noisy first sip and looked at his reflection in the window, bouncing back from the growing blackness outside the metal frames. He balanced the can on the edge of a table and, instinctively, knelt by the stereo unit and pulled out a compact disc.

He drank and listened until he was ready to go to the pub.

Guilt was still fresh on her, though not visible, as he manoeuvred his way through the packs of standing drinkers and sat at her high-topped table. The noise in the bar was intrusive and intense and neither could think of much to say. They were both elsewhere: she with Bradshaw; Phil with himself.

She tried to push away the memories. George, touching her with surprisingly tender fingers, serenading her with words of uncharacteristic softness, standing before her, lying inside her. It was something to put in a compartment, in a box, something that should not affect her day-to-day living. That was then, this is now. As the roar of conversation around them grew she felt the need to push forward some sort of communication between them. Their desultory chat, punctuated by long silences or daydreaming, was beginning to bother her.

"You're frowning again," she said lightly.

He smiled weakly. "Better?"

"I prefer your smile. Scientists have proved it takes less muscles to smile than to frown, you know."

"I know." His smile was genuine at that; it was a familiar refrain; one of her jokey clichés. "I frown for the exercise. I don't want to get a double chin," he said. "The only people with double chins are the silly bastards who smile all the time, have you noticed?"

He looked past her into the roaring mouth of someone laughing. He was one of three businessmen, sitting at the next table, barking at each other against the volume, their excess chins shaking. Barrages of their conversation were slung at Phil. He glared at them but they were oblivious.

"It's so noisy here tonight," she said. "It's making me tense. I want a cigarette. Do you mind? Phil?"

"No." But he did. He waved his hand casually in a pretence that it did not matter. She could see that anger in him, coiling tighter again, and almost left the cigarettes in her bag but needed to restate her independence. His anger, though, was directed not at her but at the men behind her, bellowing at each other, one of them banging the table at every punchline. A waitress slapped plates on the table between them and even unravelling their cutlery from the napkins and reaching for the condiments could not be done quietly. Then, after the first chips were poked into unstoppable mouths, their loud banter roared up again.

Carol, nervously eyeing Phil, lit a cigarette and let her anxiety seep out with the first puff of smoke.

"Excuse me," said a voice behind her. It was one of the suits, fork suspended in midair as he twisted towards them. "Do you mind not smoking while we're eating?"

Phil leant past Carol, his eyes blazing.

"And do you mind not shouting while we're talking?" he said with quiet menace.

"That's not the same thing," said the man.

"It fucking is, pal," said Phil and he untangled his feet from the barstool rungs to stand.

"Phil..." pleaded Carol. The man turned his back to them and squeezed a joke out to his friends. Their laughter drew Phil to their side.

"Got a problem?"

"Phil! Leave it."

"No problem here. You?"

"Yeah. Your mouth."

There was something in that tight, thin body that made the courage flee from the man. His friends stared at their plates in abashed silence. Phil nodded at them and returned to Carol.

"Did you have to do that?" she hissed. He just looked at her, the frown now stitched to his face, the frown that was no longer a joke.

"What is it with you? What is your problem?"

"Too much testosterone," he sneered.

"I'm getting sick of this. It's that, isn't it," she waved disdainfully at the beer.

"It's fuck-all to do with that. I'm not even pissed. That's always the first thing you think of." The colour had gone from her face. It was iced over with only those shining eyes blazing.

"What is it, then? You've lost me. First the wallet and now picking fights in the pub."

"Those bastards were asking for it. They've got an attitude problem."

"And you haven't?" She laughed bitterly. "I'm sick of this." She grabbed her bag. "I'm going home." She nudged past the men, silently gleeful at their subtle revenge, and pushed past him out of the bar. He shrugged and grabbed his drink and moved to another corner.

She was in bed when he got home. She lay on her back, staring blindly at the ceiling with her hands crossed over her mons, thinking of Phil, thinking of George. The night with him had been a one-off; memorable because it had broken the sealed mould of her experience, and it had acted as a purgative for her despair, something she was subconsciously selfishly aware of wanting in the bar, wanting more than George himself or the oblivion of drink.

It had refreshed her. The occasional twinge of guilt was blocked out by the awareness that she had felt better for it, stronger, fresher. Those two illicit fucks had acted like some sort of medication. Sensibly, objectively, she was gratified by their results.

But her self-satisfaction began to wane as she drifted into sleep, turning on her side with the dense weight of silence enveloping her. On the threshold of sleep, she was startled by the plaintive whisper of a guitar string. She rolled on to her back, her eyes straining upwards through the grey light as she listened to the forgotten sounds of Phil clumsily tuning his guitar and running tentatively through a few neglected chords.

Silence followed, dragging into minutes and she thought, as sleep crept back to her, that he had returned his instrument to its usual corner of abandon. As her eyelids began to seal shut she heard a renewed strumming, soft, almost as if he were experimenting, exploring something unfamiliar. Then there were the slow opening notes of Asturias, a Spanish instrumental, she remembered it saying unhelpfully in the book, that first book she had bought him one Christmas years ago.

Sixteen bars, slowly ascending and descending the scale, mournful and simple. It was one of the first pieces he had learned, something she had not heard for years. It sounded now, whispering through the wall, like a coded message. As it faded into silence, her eyes were running.

He came into the room a few minutes later, shucking off his clothes in the doorway and sliding into bed. He moulded himself against her curled back and bent legs. A hand felt the wetness around her eyes but she gave no answer when he said sorry. The hand glided down to her breast cupping it with pulsing clasps. Still she did not move. Then it slid over her belly and crossed her wrist, lying on her hip, and eased itself under the cheeks of her ass between her legs, the thumb probing until it found the soft flaps of her sex and pushed its way in.

She pushed against him "Not tonight, Josephine," she whispered, and burrowed her head into the pillow. Slowly, he withdrew his hand and curled it around her waist.

2

It was easier when he was not there. Something like equilibrium returned, the disturbance to it boxed away, a fond and burning memory. In that horrible day between his return from Singapore with Chris Dulwich and his flight to Taiwan, Carol had sat and watched his door, unable to concentrate on her work, waiting for another disturbance to confirm whether the first one was real and in an agony of doubt as to how she would react. Even without the jacket on the coatstand she had known he was there, just metres away on the other side of that wall; she could feel his presence as if they were standing next to one another. Throughout that day she was in a state of perpetual stage fright.

He seemed too busy to notice her, blind to the smile quickly shut down, unconscious of the little start she gave when he bustled into the office in the morning, overnight bag and folded plastic suit-carrier clenched in his hand and raincoat over his shoulder, exasperated, with a cooler Dulwich ambling behind. The two men spent most of the day shut up in his office and foremost among her contradictory emotions was relief. There was no chance of meeting, no risk of eye contact, denial or tacit acknowledgement, no words with treacherous undertones.

Yet there was a hollow anxiety still within her. She wanted

acknowledgement after all. But there was not even a furtive glance, not when he slipped into the outer office for a beaker of water, nor when he rushed out to catch the evening flight to Taiwan, barking a general farewell over his shoulder. She felt, with bewildering shock, disappointment and then a sense of violation as Chris Dulwich flashed her an inane grin from the doorway after seeing Bradshaw off. For a second she thought that that grin indicated Dulwich's complicity in the affair, some sort of macho locker room joke of which she was the butt. She brushed away her doubts. He is grinning for the sake of it, she thought. Please, he is grinning for the sake of it. He was.

While Bradshaw was away for the next two days, she was able to regain her composure, freezing the memory of sex in an isolated tableau. She wanted time to seal it. But she was ambushed by a phone call at the end of the week. A tightness gripped her throat even before she heard the voice. Something inside her told her who it was before a word was spoken.

"Is it tomorrow you're leaving?"

"Yes. That's right."

"I won't be able to make your leaving party, I'm afraid. But I did want to say goodbye properly." His voice was still correct, formal, impersonal.

"Oh," she said.

"I'm back from Taiwan. It was easier than I thought so I was able to get away early." He waited on her silence, then went on. "Would you like to meet up this evening? For a drink, maybe something to eat?"

She agreed and put the phone down carefully, staring at her fingers splayed across the receiver.

They met in an Italian restaurant, a short cab ride from the office, a restaurant that did everything it could to pretend to homesick Europeans that they were not in Asia. Low lights, soft classical music and an almost religious respect pervaded the small underground room of shadowy corners and intimate table booths. Prints of Old Masters were spotted around the stucco walls and ornaments and curios were chosen with an obvious attention to expense. The only cheapening effect was the clutter of little red, white and green flags in a vase near the kitchen doorway, put there by a long-forgotten chef. It was the feature she felt most comfortable with as it chimed with her memories of Italian restaurants in Britain – their cheerful lack of pretension and almost sardonic display of plastic gingham tablecloths, high street prints of pouting signorinas, nearly unrecognisable animals in wicker and the ubiquitous plastic garlic hanging from the ceiling.

He was already seated when she finally escaped from her slow-crawling cab and burst into the restaurant. Thin, gold-framed glasses were perched at the end of his nose. She had seen them before, of course, but now they gave him an unwelcome look of age. His moustache was in shadow as he examined the menu with a scholarly air. A psychic warning made him raise his head as she approached and he stood, smiling broadly, as she reached the table.

"Glad you could make it," he said.

"Glad you asked," she replied, surprised by the breezy coquettishness of her words and trying to mask it with a businesslike smile.

"You like Italian?"

"Love it." She took the menu from him, her eyes lingering on his broad fingers and then wide with questions as she looked into his face.

"No, I was very pleased with Taiwan. Particularly after Singapore. Very frustrating," he said, determined to push the conversation in any direction bar the one she wanted. It was too early and he was as confused as she.

"Have you settled on a moving date?" she said.

"Probably not until November. A good way off, I know, but I can't help thinking it will still not give us enough time. There really is so much to do."

"Will you be going?"

"Yes." He noticed a spasm of a frown race across her lips. "Anyway, good news for you," he added quickly. "The new job. Are you starting right away or..?

"Taking a week out. Mr O'Hare says there's no panic. He sends his regards, by the way. And he guesses it's time you two got together again for another round of golf. Says he'll whup your ass." She dropped into an exaggerated version of her native accent on the last word and Bradshaw laughed appreciatively.

"You'll like him."

"He sounds fun."

"He is. You should enjoy it there. Still, I'll be sorry to lose you." He said it in such a casual way, just threw it in like a meaningless formality, that she wanted to swear at him. That dead British monotone was a rejection. But he suddenly grabbed her hand.

"In more ways than one." It came out in an embarrassed whisper, almost sly.

He dropped the hand as quickly as he had taken it and pushed himself back in his chair, waving his hand for service.

"We can still see each other. Friends," she said after the waiter crept away with their order.

"Of course. Friends." It was a disappointing word.

"The other night... it was a one-off?"

"Yes. I think so, too."

"Really?"

"I have a wife. You have a boyfriend. We shouldn't have done it."

"But we did. We're consenting adults."

"Yes, yes, I know, but, well, it was so out of character for me. You're young – you have a different attitude towards these things."

She bristled. "I'm sorry, I'm sorry. I'm so clumsy with this sort of thing. I find it very hard to talk about my feelings. The thing is it's better if it was a one-off. Circumstances, you know. We had both been drinking, you were upset with things, I was in a bad mood. We just..."

Their conversation jumped to easier topics but always came back to the question raised by their encounter in bed and the things that led up to it and what it meant. As course after course arrived and the evening sped by, one or other of them would allude to it, almost unwillingly. They both needed to know. They both hated irresolution. For Carol, particularly, who was drowning in doubts and questions, it was the one thing that should be answered, the one thing she would not let slip away through apathy and confusion as she saw the rest of her personal life doing.

"I've been trying to tell myself it was a one-night stand, too," she said, braver now as she settled into the rhythm of the food and the wine and his company. "But deep down I don't think I want it to be. I've been so confused all week."

"As have I."

"But you didn't just invite me here for a plate of spaghetti and some nice wine, did you? You could have made my leaving-do tomorrow."

"I'm sorry. Am I that obvious?"

"Yup. It's what I like about you."

He looked down at the bowl of fruit as if surprised it was there then began hacking at it with his spoon with that customary excess energy.

"Do you have to go straight home tonight?" he said suddenly.

"Another one-off?"

He smiled. And then nodded.

"I had second thoughts after you called," she said. "But... well, I'm here, aren't I?"

They finished the rest of the meal quickly. At the hotel room, the rush of lust left no room for preliminaries and all shyness was forgotten. With each thrust, her whole torso felt scorched, inside and out. As they moved quicker, him now hanging over her on his elbows, now melded against her slippery skin, the burning intensified, deeper and higher and stronger inside, until her gasping exploded in a sudden deathlike choke, electrifying him into orgasm.

They lay inert, as if killed, their minds separated, adrift. Gradually, they focused on each other again, eyes probing, hands and feet absently stroking random bits of flesh. It was only after rousing from the half-sleep that the traitor of remorse crept back, stronger than before.

3

The radio was twittering to itself. It was a pop station, something Alice would not normally listen to, but she always needed aural company in the morning and the soporific smooth-talk of the lighter radio channels was at odds with her lively mood.

"And here's our winner," said the disc jockey in a breathless squeak. "Well done. You've won some salmon. Are you a big fan of fish?"

With an impatient flick of the wrist, Alice turned off the radio and looked at herself in the big wall mirror. She pulled her new Balmain scarf from its bed of tissue and drew it lovingly between the crook of her thumb and index finger, smiling at the feel of the fine silk and admiring the pretty twisted whorls of the blue and green Paisley pattern.

She looped the scarf around her neck and made small, fussy adjustments to the length hanging between her breasts. She changed her mind and threw both ends over her shoulders. The face in the mirror returned an encouraging grin.

From the jewellery box, she took the tiny wooden Buddha and turned it in her fingers, putting it softly back and then picking up an amber droplet on a chain. She replaced that with a gold crucifix and that with a half globe of lapis lazuli. She dragged her fingertips over the assortments of stones and metal, of textures and colours scattered in the box. Every piece had an association, every item carried a mental picture: of George's smiling face by a stall in a dusty sun-bleached street, of a candlelit table, of torn wrapping paper, of the way he turned from a counter in a shop and his thick fingers pressing the gift into hers.

She picked up the smiling Buddha again. She had recently had it threaded on a fine gold chain, more suitable than the clumsy original, and she raised it to her throat, the comical image dangling in the V of her blouse. She liked the talisman, but it looked cheap. Dressing was a subtle art she was too proud to compromise, no matter the sentimental value, and again she returned the Buddha to the box and selected another, more suitable, piece to hang around her neck.

She turned on the radio and checked the contents of her handbag. The dj was waiting her turn to show off more moronic banter; a song was playing that Alice had never heard before. It sounds quite nice for a pop record, she thought, catching the easy refrain to play to herself throughout the day.

She was humming it as she left the house and started Helen's car for the drive through London's hinterland to the hospital.

Josephine was already waiting for her in the foyer, sitting, her suitcase held lightly between her calves, a dense paperback shutting her off from the world. She looked up as the door squeaked open, and the two women kissed.

"Ready?" said Alice.

"Ready, willing and able."

Alice picked up the suitcase and held the door. Josephine gasped as she stepped on to the gravel and the wide, uncluttered view and fresh air combined in a sensory assault. She had occasionally walked the grounds but this time it was with a sense of freedom. She was going home.

"How are you feeling?" said Alice, unlocking the car.

"I've got a slight twinge but that's all. They want me to come back next week for a check-up and Dr Standish has given me another sackful of medicine but it's only to see me through the first month."

She eased herself into the passenger seat, carefully, still all-too-conscious of her fragility. But she slammed the door.

"So you'll be going home now, will you? Holiday over," she said as they waited for a gap in the traffic on the main road. She spoke abstractedly, distracted by the sights: the black, wrought iron gates and the sandstone gatehouse that spoke of a nobler past, the sunlight picking its way through the plane leaves opposite and dappling the road, the careless hurry of the cars and lorries in front of them. Her incarceration had reduced these mundane images to television pictures, remote and not quite real. She felt a strange thrill as though she had won an unexpected prize.

"When you're ready, Jo. Not before."

"It would be nice if you could stay, now that I'm out of that place and things can get back to normal. But George must be missing you, I suppose."

"He can look after himself. But yes..." She paused. "It would be nice to see the old grump again. He sounded a bit strange on the phone."

"Lonely, probably."

"George is too busy to get lonely. But it's nice to feel he's missing me. Even though he never actually says that."

Josephine tutted and looked out of the window, trying to count the support poles of the grimy central crash barrier as they flicked by.

"He ought to be more demonstrative," she muttered, turning to look at her sister. "It doesn't do a man any harm to whisper the occasional sweet nothings. I'm rather partial to them myself. And so are you." She gave Alice a playful tap on the arm.

"Stop it," said Alice. "I'm getting the same sort of nonsense from Helen. You two ought to know by now what sort of man he is and that it doesn't matter. It does not matter."

"Let's have a drink," Josephine said abruptly.

"What? A drink?" Alice automatically slowed the car.

"Yes, over there. Let's just stop for a quick one." She pointed to a painted sign hanging high from a white pole on the other side of traffic lights. "I feel like we're playing truant from school. Come on, just one. I could murder a bloody Mary."

"But your medicine."

"Oh, come on," Josephine retorted with a flash of her old

no-nonsense impatience. "One won't kill me. Let's celebrate."

The White Bear was an imposing estate pub whose manager tried hard to attract more than just the locals from the council houses round the back. He had grown up in a similar estate himself and now looked on its occupants with a mixture of shame and horror. Big blackboards at the entrance of the fir-fringed car park announced a lavish choice of meals for the passing businessman on the arterial road outside. Bright metal poles formed a small playground to one side. Hanging baskets of fuchsia, primula and lobelia spotted the scrubbed brick facade.

It was Monday lunchtime empty. Two bikers, refugees from the estate, glanced up unsmiling from the pool table as the women passed through the gloomy games room. Alice, step quickened by sudden anxiety, led Josephine back into the hallway and through another door into the red plush lounge.

An elderly couple sat by the fruit machine and a young businessman flashed them a smile from a nearby recessed table. Alice smiled thinly, uncertain; Josephine's response was overloaded with liberation.

"Yes, ladies?" said the barman, pushing the racing form to one side and adjusting a beermat.

"Have you got a garden?" said Josephine.

"We have. Through there." He pointed to a pair of glass-panelled doors through which faint splodges of green could be seen.

"Oh good. We'll sit out there, shall we? I'll have that bloody Mary."

Ornate white chairs were marshalled neatly on a flagged patio, raised from the lawn and the rockery. The pair sat nearest the edge where a sweet floral smell hung in the air.

"This is so lovely," said Alice, sipping her drink.

"Glad I forced you to come then?"

Alice stroked her sister's hand. They fell into an appreciative hush, their conversation lazy with the comfortable feel of a Sunday, unhurried and restful. The solitude seduced them.

They drank slowly and waited with a mild expectancy when their glasses were empty. The barman, proud of his instinctive professionalism, appeared in the doorway after 25 minutes.

"You two ladies okay? Another drink?"

They ordered a lime juice each, its fresh iciness appropriate to the summer holiday feel. The click of ice was the right sound, the faded green of the liquid the right colour. They sipped and looked, occasionally making indolent comments on a flower or a bird. There was no disruption to their languor, no demands, only peace. Alice felt calm for the first time in years, it seemed. If not for her husband, she would gladly have stayed on this patio for the rest of her life, away from that horrible, horrible place and its unceasing pressure.

This was what she wanted. And, she thought, it was her turn to ask for it. How happy she was in this peaceful setting and all that it represented, all that it suggested, and how horrified she felt when she contrasted it with her other life, that life of dislocation and ennui through which she ambled purely because her husband wanted to be there. Each of the women was drifting dreamily along currents of thought and when the barman's body-clock alerted him to their presence again, the spell was broken.

4

In the jostle of Queen's Pier, Trevor was swigging from a can of Double 8. It was, he was fond of announcing to anyone who would listen, the only American beer that had any bite or taste. And, he would add with irrefutable conclusiveness, it was cheap.

The excitement around him was tangible as friends met, lowering their plastic bags of drinks and snacks to the dirty concrete, craning heads to locate their junk bobbing in the jumbled fleet of pleasure boats, buying last-minute packets of cigarettes and watching anxiously for stragglers.

"That's ours," Trevor shouted and quoted the number on a white-painted hull. Corrine winced at his overbearing voice and Dee squeezed his arm excitedly. There was a school playtime feel to the gathering and a liberation bordering on hysteria.

Trevor shoved his way through strangers to the top of the steps, waves patting the jetty wall as the vessels jockeyed for position. With two fingers in his mouth, he let out an old-fashioned piercing whistle and waved frantically at the shadowy figure in the wheelhouse of the junk.

Carol appeared at his side, camera at her chest. She could never quell her disappointment at the almost sacrilegious modernity of the boats huddled before her. She wanted the junk of history, the tourist cliché and photo opportunity, the dark wooden craft with its high poop deck and square, serrated sails. It had a snub-nosed grace and a handcrafted individuality that gave an immediate sense of place at odds with the bland white fibreglass, machine-tooled and anonymous, floating out there.

"Hi!" she shouted up at Trevor. He turned and smiled directly into her translucent eyes. There was a hint of hope in his.

"This is Phil." She signalled over her shoulder, glancing round, and Phil stepped forward, hand outstretched.

"Phil. At last," said Trevor with what sounded like relief. "I thought Carol had made you up."

Phil shook his hand, glad to feel it firm in his. So many of these suits, these Jardine Johnnies, had handshakes like wet fish.

"Our boat's just coming in. Hey!" he shouted suddenly, looking past Phil. "Didn't think you were going to make it."

A small. ginger-haired man widened eyes shot through with red. "Nor did I," he said quietly. A faint whiff of whiskey slipped from his mouth and Carol recoiled, though with a smile fixed to her face.

"I had a shedful last night," he muttered, looking at Phil and Carol but blank to their presence.

"You had the whole bloody garden centre, mate," laughed Trevor. He introduced the newcomer as Jonno who acknowledged them with indifferent insolence. They were less important than what was in his bag. He bowed his body and fished out a can of beer. He looked desperate. With a greedy slurp, he seemed revived

"All aboard then," he commanded and the group shuffled down the steps and lurched on to the deck of their junk, the captain's wife grabbing futilely waving arms as those boarding tried to keep their balance.

"Fhh. She's had a good going-over with the ugly brush," said Jonno, giving a spiteful nod over his shoulder at the woman as he stood swaying in the centre of the covered deck. "Last time I saw a face like that, it had a hook in it." Trevor laughed like a younger brother. His reactions always betrayed his insecurity; he was too quick to laugh, too eager to please, too desperate to be liked.

People staggered on to the boat, filtering out among the decks and attaching themselves to chairs or friends. The vessel cast off and twisted in the water to nose its way through the flotilla into the less-crowded water beyond. Trevor and Jonno climbed to the top deck and sprawled against a low railing, cans of beer and packets of crisps between their legs, while Phil and Carol stood at the stern with a group from her office.

It was her do, a Saturday afternoon junk trip to celebrate leaving the firm, and she was aware of a little glaze of specialness as she chatted.

She ached with the absence of Bradshaw but she was going to focus on the trip and the company and the boyfriend standing beside her. He had his back to her, leaning over the railing and staring into the boat's boiling wake. She felt an urge to stroke that back, but an urge tempered by sadness that something had been lost or broken, never to be found or repaired. She was pulling away but not easily.

He turned and smiled, a light flicker across that dark face, and surveyed the knots of people around them.

"Impressive turnout," he said, stroking her arm. "Didn't realise you were so popular."

"I don't know half these people. This place is full of freeloaders." She followed his glance. "Doesn't matter."

They turned together and leaned on the rails, watching wistfully as the skyline shrank and merged. Buildings shed their angles and softened into trees as the boat slipped eastward past the island. A tug crossed their wake, yanking at a huge container ship. An outgoing plane roared overhead through the gunmetal sky.

As they stood there, lost to the spectacle, Carol felt a renewed warmth for the man by her side. The Incident, as it had become known between them in an attempt to trivialise it, was no longer referred to and receded daily into the past, like the uncharacteristic aberration she wanted it to be. The wallet, its cards and cash untouched, had disappeared one day and when she asked about it he told her he had sent it anonymously to the police station. The subject was dropped.

Yet the nags remained. His anger in the bar, that scaring

threat of blind violence, had unnerved her again. And it was something else they did not talk about.

She had wanted the gulf between them to seal shut but their relationship had moved on to a different footing. She felt an asexual fondness towards Phil, sisterly, and their sporadic love-making was more an act of kindness, not of lust. That she reserved for the middle-aged man with the strokable moustache and the broad, solid chest and the unflinching sense of direction who had lain inside her 12 hours earlier.

In these early days she was able to separate the two men in her life with scientific detachment. Or perhaps she separated herself into two distinct beings with different desires.

A word or a gesture would occasionally bring the two parts clashing together and she would squirm inwardly, preying for strength and a cleansing, embracing decision. But her affection for Phil and her desire for George seemed to balance each other and she was still too paralysed to act.

The boat rocked as a police launch swept past. The sudden lurch seemed to call forward rougher seas as the junk steered into the channel of Lei Yue Mun. The banks of tower blocks to their right had thinned and unspoilt hills rose in steps in fading blues and greys behind them.

"Another drink?" said Phil. His fingers lingered on her chin.

He moved away and two women filled his place, chatting animatedly with Carol, about the trip, the men, the meal they were looking forward to in a famed seafood restaurant on an island to the south.

A ghetto blaster was electrified into life in the main cabin and a drum machine disco beat roared out through the doorway. The sun had melted the overcast sky and glared down on their heads and shoulders. The junk tipped wildly in the rushing water.

"Yeah, I'm an English teacher too," Phil was saying to one of the women. They fell into discussion about their jobs and their futures after the Handover. Carol ducked into the main cabin and caught Dee who was complaining about her inability to get drunk. She spoke with a slur.

The house music was aborted and less alienating pop put on in its place. The wayward rhythm of the vessel tipped dancers on to the floor. As Phil took to the floor with the teacher, Carol mounted the steep stairs to the roof deck. Its treacherous surface slid under her feet as she tried stepping between outspread legs and supine sunning bodies towards Trevor and Jonno who sprawled regally at the front end.

They were unaware that she stood before them, absorbed in talk and drink.

"You know: the big, brassy one," Jonno was saying in his aggressive sneer.

"I think so. The blonde? From Texas?"

"Accrington, actually." Jonno looked up, his eyes resting on Carol. "Howdy," he said in a clumsy mimic. She felt a surge of dislike for him, his arrogance and his sneering, know-all persona, and focused her attention on Trevor who sat cross-legged in the lotus position like a neophyte before the hard, bright wisdom of his master.

But Jonno's hard-shell insensitivity was brittle enough to be cracked by her mute dismissal.

"Oh," he said. "I seem to be suffering from empty-glass syndrome." He waved his can, the ringpull rattling in the bottom, and rested it against the half-dozen depleted tins between his legs. Then he picked it up again and hurled it over the side, grinning and reaching for a can.

"Don't do that," snapped Trevor. Jonno staggered to his feet. "I'm going to get another drink," he announced. He tottered towards the stairs and Carol knelt by Trevor.

"He's alright, really," said Trevor, speaking to the air. "In your face, I know, but a good bloke at heart."

She did not reply.

"So, young Carol," he said. "Are we having a good time?"

She said yes.

"None of the bosses here, either. That's good. Particularly that toerag Chan."

She was startled. "I thought you got on with him."

"Baah." He waved his hand. "Did. But. Oh, it's a long story."

Her puzzled look prompted him.

"He wants me to do a bent deal," he relented. He sighed. "You know the Two Dragons job? Well, they can't do it – not by our deadline, anyway– and it's a big job, as they keep telling me." His voice had a hard and bitter edge. "I found another firm who could do the job but only for a little, you know, baksheesh. Had a row with Chan about it because he doesn't see anything wrong with that. I do. Don't like it. He surprised me, really. I thought he was straight. I'm not comfortable with it, I hate the idea and I've been dragging my heels and dragging my heels." He stopped suddenly.

"So what happened?"

"Time's running out. I reckon I've got a couple more days and then it will be too late and we'll lose the whole bloody order. Chan will go apeshit. So will Buster Bradshaw and I've heard his temper is really scary. But I really don't want to go through with it and I've left it so long it's probably too late now anyway. I don't know what to do, Carol."

Neither did she. She felt useless crouching there, listening intently as he drew out the problem, moved by his anxiety which seemed all the more poignant against his usual carefree attitude.

"Maybe you should have another word with Wilson. Or go straight to George. Mr Bradshaw."

"It's too late, isn't it? If I'd have spoken to Bradshaw a week ago, he could have helped. Or more likely he would have backed Chan and I would have been forced to go through with it or lose my job."

"I doubt it."

"You don't know that. I thought Wilson was straight, but obviously not. Bradshaw's probably the same. But they'd call themselves pragmatists. Oh well, they're probably right. Who am I to be holier than thou?"

"I think you were right to do what you did. I would have done the same."

Gratitude lit up his face. As he looked away, he caught sight of Phil, suspended at the top of the stairs behind her. He had been watching them for a while. Catching Trevor's attention, he walked towards them.

The junk docked and they clambered with the others on to the jetty, a table of concrete built with municipal utilitarianism with no room for fuss and pretension. A toothless woman, her eyes masked by the tissuey black veil of her wide-brimmed Hakka hat, rattled a bag at them for their empty cans. Laughter was loud and sharp as the day-trippers trooped up and along the pitted concrete path to the restaurant which jutted on stilts over a rubbish-smothered beach.

They filtered into orange plastic seats circling the large tables, each with a pot of tea placed on a round dais in the centre. A young girl, enclosed in her own world, absently poured the liquid into porcelain bowls and then returned with paper packets of chopsticks. Foaming beer arrived in jugs, which were passed around the tables, and the food came in relays, delivered by the girl in the same perfunctory manner. For two hours, Carol and her friends worked their way through quickening jugs of lager and the tasty array of garlic prawns, fried squid and garoupa, choi sum, baak choi and broccoli, fried rice and glass noodles.

They were determined to get drunk, to eat until they were stuffed, to talk loud and laugh long. It was their earned release from the grinding routine of work in a strange place.

They were gratified by overfilled stomachs and communal enjoyment. There was still an hour to go before the junk, sitting in the bay with the lowering sun burning crimson behind it, had to leave when the last plate was removed. Carol and Phil wandered off to share a joint in the woods behind the ramshackle restaurant.

With him now sated and again silent and her buoyed by an afternoon of alcohol and camaraderie, she could think of Bradshaw dispassionately, her desire fenced off. Phil made quiet jokes in his sardonic way and she felt close to him again. Her doubts seemed wrong. He ground out the joint and they walked along a neglected path through the dense undergrowth of a hillside. Opposite was the charred debris of a recent fire. They sat on a rock overlooking it.

"It's a shame, isn't it?" she said, pointing at the blackened hill.

"Hmm," he said, almost gagged by the cannabis. She wanted conversation, something to reaffirm their togetherness.

"It's been a great day," she said.

"It's not over yet."

"Maybe we should go dancing when we get back."

"Hmm." He only half heard her through his building wall of self-examination. Yes, it had been a great day. He had felt part of something and wanted it to continue. He was fed up with feeling adrift, in need of an anchor. Something had happened on this trip, some sort of revelation had come to him, vague and unclear at first, but slowly growing and taking form. He turned to her with dream-lost eyes.

"I think we should get married," he said.

5

Abril's belly told her that something was wrong. The niggling discomfort, quiescent for weeks, had returned as she watched Bradshaw bustle around the flat with an unusual aggression. His movements, always pronounced and definite, seemed to be straining more, not with his usual positive determination but with an unfamiliar fury. It frightened her. He should have been happy that his wife was returning. Instead, he seemed worried and angry.

"Not there, not there," he snapped, snatching the vase from her hand. The fresh blood-red carnations and baby's breath quivered in his grasp. She moved back, staring at him, her hands raised before her chest as though she thought he was going to hit her.

He slapped the vase on to a side-table, letting out a sudden noise as he saw he had marked the varnish. He rubbed at the mark with thick fingers, frustrating himself even further.

"I will do that, sir."

"It doesn't matter," he said and hid the stain under the vase.

With a theatrical sigh he threw himself on to the sofa, its too-soft cushions sucking down his big body. He looked up at her, still standing uncertainly in the centre of the room, and bit his lip. Regret softened his features.

"I'm sorry, Abril," he said. "I'm being rather intolerable this morning, aren't I?"

She returned a helpless shrug and an insipid smile.

He looked at his watch and sighed again, though this time the noise was gentler. "I'll take a taxi," he said. "I'm too jittery to drive."

"You are excited, sir."

"I am rather." But his boyish, hopeful smile was false, she could see that.

He asked her for a coffee, then cupped his nose and chin in his hands and gazed solemnly at the floor. His thoughts clashed against each other in a turmoil of contradiction. They had tormented him all week, and had become familiar enemies against which he could find no escape. There was a sense of cynical expediency, a desire for honesty, a need to bury and a need to exhume. None was stronger than any other, none more durable. He was not used to such a range. None of them made any sense, yet in isolation each did. How did I get myself into this mess? he thought.

He had always relied on his wits, on his instinct and his intellect, to clarify options under a hard, bright beam and to be able to select, with certainty. But those guides were wandering all over the place, aimless and hopeless. They could not be relied on. As soon as he made a decision, he would question it, doubt it and dismantle it. There were just two courses open and for the first time in his life he was lost. Neither felt right. Whichever he chose, it was more than just cutting his losses on a business deal or finely balancing a decision about somewhere to live. He was trying to force himself to cut his losses on his life, on his future, and on the life and future of two other people. It was no longer just business. It was personal. Yet he had to make a decision, one, single decision that he could not go back on or water down with compromise.

Listen to your heart, he told himself then laughed a quiet, cynical laugh. What do you want? What do you really want? And the answer came back: useless, craven, denying everything he had ever believed in: For none of this to have happened.

He tried to justify his actions to himself but there was no clarity, only a muddled swirl of images and half-remembered feelings. He had outraged his own solid sense of morality. He beat himself with the labels of his deception: infidelity, greed, lust, selfishness. All despicable crimes in his simple pantheon of emotions.

He took the cup from Abril's hand and sipped at the hot coffee. It burnt a clarity into him. He began to think harder, to concentrate. Despair receded to a manageable distance. Think, he told himself. What are you going to do? What do you want to do?

He had to tell Alice. That was the right thing to do, the right thing after the wrong thing. While she had been away he had made love to another woman. A woman half her age, he would tell her, as if that mattered, as if that made it any more forgivable. He had cast aside his wife and her feelings. Alice was not even a ghost at the party.

And then she would ask him why. And he could not answer that, not easily, not directly, although the truth nagged away at his soul. He forced himself to confront it. He needed to hear himself say it; to articulate it would give it meaning, make it real. Abril was not in the room.

"I did it," he whispered, "not because of opportunity, but because of need. That's all. It was hunger, not greed." That made it sound rational, understandable, acceptable even, as if there were a scientific logic to it that could not be denied. Logic! They would not be talking about something that could be examined scientifically. It was an insult. How could his head speak to her heart when it was not even in touch with his own? How could rationalising it lessen the hurt?

He said the words again and again till they took on a mental echo, a callous mantra of expiation. He cleared his throat and looked guiltily around the bright room as though he had caught himself swearing in church. But I am being honest, he thought. That is what I have always tried to do, by omission if not commission. And for the first time in this short, sorry affair, I've been honest with myself. He knew what he had to do. Because there are layers and layers of honesty and he had only managed to peel back the first few. He would never find the core.

He looked at his watch, drained his coffee and left the flat, pacing the lobby while waiting for the lift, curtly nodding to the security guard on the gate, almost attacking a taxi in his anxiety to get to his destination and his destiny.

As he sat in the restaurant awaiting Alice's delayed flight and found himself paying more attention to his watch and the arrivals board than the newspaper and the snack in front of him, he felt weighed down with a sadness even heavier than the regret he had felt after sex with Carol. It was a melancholy more immovable than the guilt when sensuality had given way to sense. He felt sad for himself – another unfamiliar feeling – but more so for Alice and for their life together, a life he was now going to end with a brutal but ultimately kind honesty. Not because of the fact that he had strayed but because of what it represented. So he persuaded himself.

And then, again, he checked himself. Fifteen years is a lot to throw away in five minutes. But. She won't want it to end; she will want to forgive him out of loyalty to what was and what still could be. But. He had deceived her and could not hide that deceit because it was a cry for help, not a spontaneous act of desire, a cry for help he had been unable to make to her, her who was his best friend, his truest, and who had loved him through it all, he supposed, with a self-sacrifice neither of them spoke about. But. This sudden revelation and seemingly spontaneous destruction of their history and their future could break her. She had been broken before. Not by him, true, but there was a dangerous fragility about her. Could he take responsibility for that? But. He would not allow himself the luxury of such vanity. Her breakdown had been nothing to do with him; it was a reaction to outside abstract forces. The doctors said so. But. They had drifted apart. A relationship cannot be built on guilt, pity or sentimentality, cannot be held together by a fear of the future. But. It had been special. But. It no longer was.

Admit it.

I must take responsibility for my own actions.

His throat tightened as he saw Alice manoeuvre her trolley down the ramp, weaving through knots of slower passengers confused by the blur of faces and cardboard name-signs hemmed around the gate.

"Alice!" he called and ran from the table.

She beamed at him, seemed to collapse with relief and

gratitude, and kissed him clumsily on the cheek, one hand grabbing at his arm.

Throughout the journey home, he was unable to say what he thought he would. He wished for nothing more than delay, a few more minutes, a couple more hours, a sudden reversal of his earlier decision, a chance to put it off forever. As the taxi nosed through traffic on to the manic freeway, he sighed with gratitude as he saw her drift into jetlagged sleep.

She went straight to bed when they got home and he was glad again for the interlude. He rehearsed the exact words and the timing, second-guessing her responses, her words and reactions, and building them into an imaginary conversation. It would be so much easier just to forget it. She would never know. What she did not know could not hurt her. They could carry on as before. But there was more to this than simple betrayal.

His fine, crafted script was discarded after he spluttered out the first sentence that evening when she glided happily into the lounge. Even that was out of his control. He ordered Abril to leave the flat and said to his wife: "We have to talk."

"We do," she said with a disquieting firmness as she looked over from the television and smiled. And the surprise he felt at her reaction made him forget his lines. She, too, had something to say, and that threw him into confusion. He grabbed for the fleeting remnants of his speech and tried to hold on to the image of how the dialogue was supposed to proceed.

"You first," she said.

Only snatches were available to him. He listened to himself as if from another room, aghast that he had lost his grasp on what he wanted to say.

And as the words came tripping and crashing out, devoid of much sense but conveying much more horror in that disarray, she stared at him in disbelief. Then she laughed, hollow and frightened. As her laughter died away and she stared at that bright, red face, squeezed and glomerate and now an object of hate, she understood, accepted the meaning, and sank back in her chair as if she were being pushed into it and held there. She switched off the remote control.

They talked for hours, always in circles. There were times

when there were long, drawn-out silences and others when their words trod over each other. She pleaded and cajoled, questioned and rejected, derided and begged. I don't understand, she kept saying.

"Why didn't you tell me something was wrong? Why didn't you say how you felt?"

"I didn't know. Not until it happened."

"We can try again. Can't we?"

"Would you want to?"

Her mouth fell open but no words came out. She looked at the floor, slowly shaking her head, her eyes held by a detail of pattern in the carpet.

"I don't want us to separate." she said at last, looking up.

"Then what do you want?"

"Are you in love with her?"

"No," he said, a shade indignantly. "Of course not. I hardly know her."

"Should we try again? Try just a bit harder? We can't throw it all away."

"You amaze me. How can you be so forgiving?"

"I'm not being forgiving," she said bitterly. And she started abusing him, blaming him, until the violence of her words convinced him that he was right to leave. And then she stopped suddenly, and softened, spent.

"This would never have happened if things were right between us," he said. "I just didn't realise how wrong they were."

"Things are right between us," she protested, her earlier recriminations mysteriously gone. "It was just a quick bonk with a girl while I was away. Lots of men do it. It didn't mean anything."

"I didn't say that."

They were suddenly battered into submission by the emotional storm. They wanted refuge in each other but too much had been said, too much needed to be absorbed, for that to be possible. She poured them both a whisky and passed one into his hands. Their trembling made her sad. They sat at opposite ends of the sofa and talked about practical things: she offered to move out at the weekend. She was already working at reducing the grief to a manageable size and to him it seemed almost callous; he was astounded by such self-protective pragmatism. It was as if weeks or months had passed since those terrible words had been spoken, not hours; as if the sadness and the anger had been diluted by a long period of time. That was how she had to deal with the pain: by shrinking it as quickly and as quietly as possible. By accepting it as inevitable, after all her protests and her pleading and her recriminations, she had failed. Knowing that hurt him more than the event and the revelation itself. She was burying her grief too quickly for it to rest. So he said that he was the one who had to move out. She had done nothing wrong.

He shuffled from the room, gently closing the bedroom door as if afraid of waking a dying patient. He lay on the bed, his brightly polished shoes glistening in the lamplight at the end of his feet, convinced that he was right, convinced that he was wrong.

PART 5

Control. Essential. My touchstone. I had always kept control – of my emotions, my ambitions, the risks I took, the direction in which I was going. It made for a successful life. It worked for me. All my life, it worked for me. Until this year. This year I lost control, breaking with my character like so many other people here who seemed to fall into a communal madness as hysteria and panic about the future undermined their faith.

I asked Lee f he thought this was true and he nodded with that slow, fraudulent sagacity. Then he shrugged as if denying the nod. After our short period of estrangement, he made coy attempts at returning and I, lonely now, accepted him. Guilt made me give up on the outside life but something stops me jettisoning the life inside. I crave stimulation, even the feeble stimulation of this place. I am no longer allowed to make decisions and that burns me. I have to have something to do and so I grab at every option, limited though they are. I exercise and pace the floor until I am exhausted, I write to stop my mind turning to mush in this oppressive isolation; I also need some sort of human contact, however unsatisfactory. So I invited Lee to return and he did, this time with a small packet of chocolate biscuits and a sly contrition.

He became bolder, as though my asking him back had

turned the balance of power in his favour. He sat on the edge of the bed, without being asked. I walked from wall to door and back again, from door to wall and back, as I talked and he listened.

I talked about the communal madness I could now perceive beyond the walls. It had come earlier than anticipated, I said. There was such a focus on the change of sovereignty, such blinkered concentration on one single, solitary date, that people were blind to what was going on around them, inside them, how they changed as that special date approached.

So? he said. He was born here, had never been away, and for him I was just referring to my people, gweilos who popped in and out to exploit the place without giving any of themselves to it. He was cold to my anxieties.

Many of them have run away, and watch safely from a distance, he added. They had a choice. Many of us do not.

And many have stayed, I said.

But there was never any commitment with any of you. He was unsympathetic, now, hard; for the first time he had begun to emerge from under the stone of his obsequity.

I understood him now. How could they feel loyalty? How could they feel attachment to their adopted home when they had not even felt it for the land of their birth? This was a place of potential, to be used and exploited and then left. It was a giant waiting room for those of us with a choice.

And those who did stay were losing control. Like me. In varying degrees, little by little, rarely dramatic. They take more risks. This place has always had that effect but it had been crystallised by an unconscious awareness of the future, of that date, a fear almost of a last chance. The waiting room may be shut. That pushed people further and faster.

It has only been since reaching here that I have reflected on that. And I can now see, with horror, where I lost control, where I let down a lifelong guard and released that series of events that culminated in a much greater loss of control than mine.

And though I can see the when and how I cannot see the why.

Perhaps I became bored with a lifetime of self-possession, of my supposedly calm rationality. Perhaps I realised that the risks I was taking were not really risks because I had calculated them too neatly. Perhaps I wanted a taste of the unknown and beggar the consequences. Maybe I was reacting to the heady air of adventure and potential that I breathed every day.

I changed the moment I betrayed my wife. I felt an enormous release and that spurred me to greater risks. Something was unburdened, untied, and afterwards, as I lay with my new lover, my soft-skinned release valve, silently in that half-dark room, I was overwhelmed with calm. It was a peace I had never felt before, something I had not known existed.

I got a taste for it but I never found it again. Life got in the way, and rational thought, and circumstance, and guilt. It was never that innocent again. How could it be? Something else took over, first desire, and then love, and I became a different person. I lived two lives. I learned the art of duplicity. In my out-of-control state, I became a master of the art of self-deception. I convinced myself that it was possible to love two people at the same time. Why not? – two people loved me. I thought I was able to split myself into halves, to separate the objects of my desire. I wanted both and they both wanted me; though each wanted me whole, of course. An unknown force drove me along the road to ruin. Here is ruin.

If it was just mine, I could accept it. But others were ruined and though I have taken responsibility it is for the wrong reasons and it is too late. There is nothing left now but emptiness. I lost both loves of my life, two concurrent and contradictory but sustaining forces. I have lost my home and my job, my past and my future. I have lost my life.

You are wrong, Lee said, standing. His voice, an abrupt and impatient hiss, was a shock to me. I thought I had been talking to myself; I had forgotten his frail body crouched on the side of the bed. You did not lose anything, he continued, and moved towards the door, cold contempt seeping off him like radiation. You did not lose anything. You threw it away.

1

He awoke to the sound of sobbing. It was the sharpest pain, the saddest noise, he had ever heard in his life. The resolve of the previous day evaporated instantly with that broken murmur from the pillow. She was still asleep. He felt his throat tighten till he could no longer breathe.

Her bare shoulder twitched and he moved to touch it. His fingertips drew lines along its smooth curve. She did not respond.

He gritted his teeth and squeezed shut his eyes, gripping the pain, holding it in. Her sobbing continued in little gasps, muffled by the bedding and barely audible.

"Alice," he whispered. Cautiously, he leaned over to look into her face. It was a waxy, sweat-faced mask of tragedy, the cheek and nose wet with tears. Her mouth fluttered as though it were searching weakly for breath. Still she slept.

He rolled back and eased himself from the bed, looking back at that prone, quivering form, feeling the stabs of every wounded cry as though they were his own. He could not bear it and left the room. He could not bear her damning misery, its accusatory grief heightened by her unconsciousness.

He sat in the armchair, the newspaper folded neatly on the table in front of him, the ashtray cleaned and sparkling, and gripped his knees as if to break them. His face was taut and his shock-wide eyes stared at nothing.

I cannot do this, he thought. I cannot cause this woman this much pain.

He sat immobile for an hour, unaware of the ghostly presence of Abril as she went about her chores, floating from room to room. Always as she passed she would glance surreptitiously over at him, wanting to say something, wanting to help, but too frightened by that ghastly look on his face and that solid, struck-down mass of unmoving body rigid in the chair.

He suddenly came to life and reached for the phone. He told Wilson he would be taking the day off. Then he froze back into immobility, but this time with his eyes moving, ranging about the flat and following Abril. He watched her pick up the shopping bag and move to the door and nod at him and open her mouth to say something, then quietly slip out into the lobby. Then he picked up the phone again. As he waited for an answer, his breathing quickened. He snatched one last deep inhalation when a voice cut over the ringing tone.

It is over, he told her. And he gave sparse reasons why and cut her questions short, ignoring any emotion in her voice, but saddened and sickened by it all. My wife is back, he said. I thought I wanted to leave her. But I could not. I wanted to leave her, even though I did not know what would happen between you and I. But she is back and I have to stay. Even as he said that, he wanted desperately to see the woman at the other end of the phone, to touch her. But he buried such wants under his reawakened sense of obligation. He had to close down that feeling. He had to be a little less honest within himself, replacing those layers he had so recently stripped away, because that honesty could release a destructive potential. He had to go back to his old self. Sensible.

Then he thanked her, with an almost formal courtesy as though she had given him a nice present, something much less important than her body. And she thanked him. It was an instinctive reaction. When she heard herself say it, she thought she had said it out of mature resignation.

He replaced the receiver hurriedly, burnt by it, and let out a deep breath, his head twitching guiltily to the door to see if Abril had returned.

A paralysing weariness took him. Long-buried feelings had rushed to the surface and battered him into exhaustion. The pain, unknown in its intensity, had drained every last drop of energy. He just wanted to sleep. More than that, he just wanted to die.

He looked in on his wife. The crying had stopped and she lay sleeping peacefully, the colour returning to her face, calm smoothing over her features. He felt another stab of pain and retreated from the room.

Time moved in slow motion until Alice trudged into the lounge. He panicked and lurched from his chair to greet her.

"Sit down," he said. "I'll get you something to drink." She remained mute and standing, with an uncomprehending look momentarily on her face. She sat.

He returned, holding a cup, staring at her. She was silent. She had nothing left to say.

"I can't do it, Alice," he whispered. "If you'll forgive me, I would like to try again."

"What? What?" His words were senseless.

"I know it's confusing. First I say one thing, then I say another. But I've not slept, I've thought about nothing else all night, and I don't want to throw it all away. I can't. If you'll have me back. If you'll give me a second chance. Despite what I have done. I know how deeply I've hurt you and I am very sorry, I always will be sorry, but I want to try again."

He did not tell her that her crying had changed his mind. To acknowledge her unconscious terror, as though he had spied on her, would cheapen them both, he felt.

"I see," she muttered and reached for the cup in his hand, noticing again how it trembled. "Are you sure?" She was sceptical and the bitterness came through, though weakly.

He said yes.

"You seemed so definite. What has changed your mind?" He shrugged in answer. "And maybe you were right at the time. But I have never changed my mind. And I never will. I never wanted us to separate, in spite of your betrayal I need us to stay together. As long as you can promise that it will never happen again. It will be hard to forgive you, and I will never be able to forget, but I want us to stay together. If you are absolutely sure."

"I am," he lied.

"And if there are problems we've got to try to work them through. Honestly. Talk about them. But I'm confused, George. You were adamant about leaving; now you don't want to. It's not like you to be so indecisive."

He forced a little laugh and she frowned at it. "True, I suppose. This whole thing has not been like me."

"What about the girl?"

"That's over." His voice dropped. "Anyway, I've told you: that wasn't the problem." Her look was disbelieving but she quickly masked it. She did not want to ambush their cautious attempts at reconciliation. She did not want to complicate what should be a simple matter. There were other times for that. For now, simple agreement was all that mattered.

"I feel like I've lived a year this last 24 hours," he said. "I never want to go through it again, or to put you through it."

"Thank you. I hope not."

She reached for his hand with a cautious hesitancy. The pact was sealed. She felt as if she had emerged from a long, dark tunnel and could see again. She would forgive him his infidelity, though the bruises would stay for life. She would forgive him because a little part of her had understood why he had done it, although she could never tell him that.

2

In the days that followed, they tried hard to get back what they thought they had lost and buried themselves in each other, isolating themselves from everything else. Romantic, expensive dinners, early to bed, a trip to Macau.

But the casino city across the water jolted them from their tender insularity. It was too hard, too brittle.

"It's lost all its romance, hasn't it?" said Alice, gazing through the spray-misted windows as the jetfoil slowed and tracked towards the dock. She had looked with growing disappointment as the outline of Macau, the other colonial territory tacked on to China and just 80 kilometres from her adopted high-rise home, came into focus. The vessel, its skis tucked back under its hull, bobbed in the water and men in red jackets ran about with ropes. She suddenly wanted to get away. This place, until recently such a sleepy, semi-southern European contrast to her adopted home, had awoken to the power of money. It was now a smaller image of the place she had left an hour ago: incomplete, restless and reinventing itself and she hated that.

"It's not what it was four years ago," he replied as they stood and made their way from the bow of the ship to the gangplank. But his reaction was one of anticipation; he was glad the place had woken up. They paused together on the dock, buffeted by hurrying passengers careless of the view. "Do you remember?"

"I do," she replied fondly and squeezed his arm, a gesture that still felt slightly forced. "It was lovely then. Now look at it. It's one big building site."

Cranes and half-finished buildings reared up wherever they looked. The new bridge arced between the islands over the silt-clouded water. Dredgers moved at a slow, oily pace over the sea. The air was thick with the bellow of construction and clotted with dust.

They fell silent as their passports were stamped and they stepped out into the airy new terminal, glittering shops crowded in tiers around a central well.

"Good lord, this has improved," he said. But she was unmoved by the brash shininess around her; she hated this modem despoliation of a place she associated with smallness and slowness. The improvements, as he regarded them, grated against her as she stared from the window of the taxi on its short ride to the hotel. She ached for the Macau of memory, the Latin somnolence of a place that still echoed with history. She wanted the odd mix of quaint Portuguese buildings and villas, the hidden cobbled courtyards and blue-and-white tiled frontages, the attractive faces of centuries of miscegenation.

Instead, it felt like an ugly new town: big, monotonous buildings, big, empty roads, and everything covered in white dust. It was not until their taxi swung out on to the coastal road of the peninsula, with its gnarled, ancient trees and solid colonial buildings dressed in almost irreverent pastel colours, that her fond memories began to reassert themselves as more than lost dreams. She began to relax.

The hotel was an old fort, built into the rock 400 years earlier. Centuries ago, soldiers had stood watch over those lichen-covered parapets with their muskets at the ready and had trooped up and down the tunnel into the body of the building. Now, lazy guests ambled through the tunnel to look wistfully out over the yellowed Pearl River Delta.

They lay side by side on the brass bed in their room, each lost in thought. When the thoughts ran out, Bradshaw turned to Alice and unbuttoned her blouse with a tentative delicacy. They made love with none of the desperate fire with which they had fought each other in bed over that first week of uncertain steps towards reconciliation. There had been a wildness to that which had shocked them both. It was the love-making of the lost and frightened. Now, they were gaining confidence with each other again, and were grateful, and slipped back into their old, sure patterns. Bradshaw believed he had defeated, so easily, that demon within him.

It was dark when they awoke. The only sound was the slow, rhythmic pounding of a piledriver in the distance. A feeble light was in the room. They dressed without haste and strolled to the hotel restaurant, hand in hand, where they were greeted by the manager and then the showbusiness smiles of a trio of serenaders who danced slow-step with guitars and double bass from table to table. It felt to Alice as if they were on honeymoon and she told him. He grinned, his moustache bristling over his top lip.

Their dream-like enchantment continued for two more days. They went everywhere slowly, did everything at half-pace, savouring each moment, acutely conscious of the presence of each other. They spent time in old churches and took long walks up the steep hill to the guia, the old lighthouse, now barely visible over the tops of the new buildings. They ate in quiet restaurants and drank long cocktails on the balcony of the fort. They swam without effort in the tiny, mosaic-lined pool on the roof. Even the hysterical activity of a casino failed to rouse them from their comfortable languor.

They seemed reconciled to each other, without effort and without shame. It was as though Bradshaw's infidelity had not really happened; it was not alluded to by either of them. They felt right together; at times Bradshaw could hardly believe that he had strayed. But at others there was a nagging acknowledgement that he had, and a sensation, half of fear and half of anticipation, that it could so easily happen again. Sometimes he would stand outside himself and watch the unreal progress of their holiday and their refreshed explorations of each other and wonder. He did not want it to end but he sensed that it would. And he fought against that. He ordered himself not to ambush their new-found joy, not to sabotage it, not to blow up Alice's sacrifice, made for the good of them both. And he would scold his own scepticism and hate himself for a while and turn his attention fully back to her.

When she considered what she was doing, she would do so with disbelief and gratitude. And sometimes a burning fear. This fragile thing between them had been broken once before. She could not face it happening again. Hers was the joie de vivre of the desperate. The terror paralysed her and she would rush to break out of it in a panic to grab Bradshaw or to kiss him or to demand attention from those distracted eyes and slowly bring them back into focus on her.

When the rain came, the spell was broken. On the third morning, the sky was black with cloud and it rained solidly for the day, bouncing the heat off the ground and suffocating them from above and below. The unweakening deluge locked them in the hotel. With their temporary imprisonment, surrounded by the noise of the flood and drained by the oven-warm air, they slipped from peace into ennui. Frustration cornered them. Their silences were no longer of the contented kind; they were silences of boredom and frustration. There seemed nothing left to say without the stimuli of pretty sights, fresh-air walks, sunshine, nice restaurants and other people. The hotel felt like a prison.

Bradshaw buried himself in a newspaper, Alice in a book. When they were tired of reading they would go to the bar and sit opposite each other, polite and attentive but worried inwardly. They listened intently to the clattering of cutlery and the pattering of rain, hoping for a sudden, final end to both and for their happiness to be allowed its freedom.

They were both aware of how much they needed the sunshine like food. Without it, they were hungry.

On their final day, Bradshaw woke to an overwhelming sense of contrition. He could hear nothing outside the room and he looked over the covers to see weedy bars of sunlight falling against the window.

Alice was staring at the ceiling, a strange set to her mouth. He leaned over and kissed her.

"It's stopped, thank God," he said. "Now we can go out again."

"Do you think we have succeeded? That it's working?" Her voice was faint in the stillness.

"Yes."

"You were so quiet yesterday, George. Distracted. I thought you were having second thoughts. I was frightened."

He rolled towards her and clumsily clasped her body. She felt his heat gladly.

"You would tell me if you were having second thoughts, wouldn't you? You wouldn't pretend? For my sake. I'd rather know the truth. However much... however much I didn't like it. It wouldn't be... fair to either of us, otherwise."

"I'm not having second thoughts. I'm not going to have them."

She looked at him for the first time and a weak smile crossed her mouth.

"It is working, Alice. I'm happy again."

He really believed he was. He could not allow himself the choice.

3

"People are giving up on this place too easily," said Trevor.

Chris Dulwich switched his attention from the girl at the bar to the conversation at the table. "You reckon?" he said.

"It won't be easy and there's a lot of nervousness about but, yeah, I reckon."

"You don't think China's going to fuck it all up?" said Dulwich.

"Well..." Trevor reached for his beer, casting his eye around the audience at the cramped table. "There's a risk, obviously. But they won't throw it all away. Too much money involved. They need..." And their argument continued. Trite truisms about China's leading role in the next century were trotted out, how it needed Hong Kong as the starter motor, how the pragmatism of business would help it turn a blind eye to the mainland's authoritarian stamp, how the fledgling democratic movement, despite the increasing daring and vehemence of its protests, would wither on the vine, how swapping one colonial master for another would be met with resignation as long as it did not interfere with the money machine.

At the booth next door, three men sat and shuddered at the conversation, at its glib complacency, but were too weakened to protest. The last time they had made their feelings known, marching through the central spine of the city with 10,000 others to lay wreaths and written demands at the always closed door of Xinhua, the de facto mainland consulate, two of them had had their noses broken in scuffles with police and Beijing goons.

"Depends, doesn't it?" Phil interjected. His tone was lighter than normal. Trevor noted, with something akin to jealousy, that there was a new confidence about him, a fresh clarity. "Depends on Deng, depends on lots of things. You can't say for sure that this place will survive after 97."

"I'm not saying that," Trevor replied. "I'm saying that people have given up already and they shouldn't. This place is too strong. It will manage. And it will be just as good afterwards." He glanced at Carol. She looked remote; there was a blank look about her that could not be explained away merely by the tired repetition of these arguments, the pat philosophy and pretend insight of every expat bar in the territory. What was going on between these two? he thought. It was as if they had switched characters.

"So you think we're wasting our time moving to Singapore then?" said Dulwich, looking back again from the girl who had still not noticed him.

"Would you want to live there? It's like an exceptionally tidy old people's home."

"We're off, anyway," said Phil. "Probably in a few months. That's right, isn't it?" He nudged Carol; she nodded resignedly. Trevor's bewilderment deepened.

"We've done our time, It's time to go back."

"To what? The dole? That place is in such a mess it can't even get its boom-and-bust cycles right any more. It's just one long bust."

"It won't be a problem."

"What do you think, Carol?" said Trevor, trying to drag her from her remote sentry post into the huddle of conversation. He had rarely seen her like this before.

"I don't know. Yeah, we'll go back, I guess."

"I thought you liked it here. I though you were doing alright."

"I was. I am. But Phil…"

"Oi!" he complained.

She responded with a sickly grin and lapsed into silence again. She was bored by this conversation. Nineteen ninety-seven, God! Didn't everybody go on about it? It was just a number, an arbitrary date, it never had any real meaning. There were more important things to think about. Phil's proposal, muttered words out of the blue on that previous Saturday which had seemed to spark him into life yet left her thrashing in confusion. She had not given him an answer yet; in fact, the subject had not been mentioned again. But she knew he was waiting, politely and with complete confidence, and that was what had given him his spark, had breathed life back into those cold, smoking embers of his heart. His patience would give out in a few days, she knew. She did not know the answer to give him.

Because of that phone call from George two mornings ago. Another shock. She was more surprised than hurt. She could see the sense in his decision and in a way admired him for it because it illustrated, once again, that cast-iron controlling grip of his. But it was still a rejection. And it had been almost throwaway. There was something about it that had a slight blur of panic. Yes, he had made a decision, but did he really believe in it himself? And couldn't they just continue as before, without any change in their respective relationships? Was monogamy so necessary? Was a sense of obligation to another person so demanding, even if that other person was completely unaware of the situation?

It came down to possession, she thought. And she realised that that was the state she had been fighting against for the last few months and that was one of the things that had attracted her and George to each other – that refusal to be owned by one person. And now Phil wanted to own her, for all sorts of dubious reasons. But she could not yet tell him No. And maybe she would not, now that her short-lived escape route had been so suddenly sealed. Maybe she, too, would give up. She thought sadly back to her last encounter with George and him welded between her legs and both of them feeling, she was sure, that that was his rightful place. It was ecstasy, even after he had come. And he had just dismissed it, seemingly out of hand, without warning. She still burned with desire.

"Do you mind if I go, Phil?" she said. Phil started, looking from her to Trevor, noticing again that half-formed look of hunger on his face whenever Carol was about.

"Okay. I'll come with you," he said and downed his drink. They stood together. Dulwich returned from wherever he had been and dragged out his chair in theatrical protest.

"Bitch," he hissed. "Bloody dyke." He ignored the couple leaving.

"No luck then?" said Trevor.

"No. Let's move on. You can show me the nightlife. I want something really sleazy. I've been looking but I haven't found it"

"You'll be lucky. The world of Suzie Wong is long gone. If you insist…

"I do. I'm your boss, remember?"

Trevor grinned. They moved eagerly to the street, pushing through the mid-evening surf of hawkers and tourists, shoppers and office workers, to a brightening glow of neon.

"This is one of the better ones," said Trevor, pushing at a thick velvet curtain in a doorway. Dulwich followed into the gloom and his eyes snatched quickly to the girls in bikinis going through desultory moves on a stage behind the bar. They were bored as they writhed around the firemen's poles poking through the stage; out of sync and out of their heads. The thump of disco music was just background noise; the leering faces below just lifeless images.

The bar was a picture of ennui. The tired leering of the handful of besuited clients scattered along the length of the bar mirrored the tedium of the performers. The mamasan, perched by the till in the corner with a couple of resting performers beside her, glanced at the newcomers through cynical eyes. She erected a smile as they approached.

Dulwich ordered beer and whisky and scanned the dancers sleepwalking through their routines. "Lovely," he said.

He was quiet for 10 minutes as he absorbed the show, hypnotised by the serpentine spasms under the arc lights, the flesh, the costumes and the false-promise smiles, and dulled by the synthesiser boom of the music and the womblike red of the bar. Trevor drank quickly, watching him, then ordered two more beers and whisky chasers. The town's casual attitude to money had twisted out of all recognition the cash caution he exercised at home, in England. Here, it was Mickey Mouse money: it was for making and spending. And he was keen to get drunk. And keen to talk.

Their glasses clinked in a toast to getting pissed and laid and they returned their glances to the dancers. A new batch tripped on as tapes were switched. They seemed looser than the first, more interested in the music and the customers.

Dulwich hissed appreciatively as one wound a leg around the stainless steel pole and stared at him with a demanding coquettishness.

"Three grand," said Trevor, puffed up with his knowledge.

"What? You're joking. Three hundred quid?"

"Two-fifty. But worth it. So I'm told." And they shared their braggart's smiles.

Dulwich waved at a barmaid for more drink and called over two part-time hookers, sidling along the bar stool by stool. The night had promise; cheap and loveless but maybe all the more exciting for that.

By midnight, they were drunk. They staggered from bar to bar and it was as if they walked through an interminable set of red drapes into the same cavern of flesh and gloom. The rate of drinking slowed, the conversation now sporadic and circular, subordinate to that stubborn and maddening priapism which promised more than it would ever deliver, teased by interchangeable performers in endless bars.

"Do you know," Trevor slurred through an ugly, twisted mouth, cognisant through the haze of the growing indifference of his partner. "Do you know that that Chan, that bastard Chan, wanted me to bribe someone?"

Dulwich tried to glare back at him through equally unfocused eyes, his head sunk between his rounded shoulders, then slowly looked back at the bar. "No," he said. "So?"

"It's true. It's true." The words fell out of his mouth like gobbets of beer, or blood. "He wants me to bribe some greasy little shit on the mainland just to get an order through. Just so he can line his own pocket with the commission while I take the risk. That's what it's all about. Yeah, that's it. I get it now."

"Yeah?" said Dulwich.

"He wants me," and Trevor's finger tapped the table with each word then slid to the cloth of Dulwich's jacket arm and began poking at that, "he wants me to bung this shit 10 per cent. They must be in it together. Ten per cent. Outrageous."

"So?" Dulwich said again.

"So it's not on. Is it? It will be my name on the books if someone started asking questions. I'd be the one in trouble, not Wilson Bloody Mr Butter Wouldn't Melt Chan Bastard. I don't do backhanders; even if I didn't give a fuck about the company, I still wouldn't do that. If Chan can't do business properly, then fuck him."

The conversation was starting to interest Dulwich, enough for him to drag his eyes away from the girl gyrating before him to look at Trevor, whose head was twisted and looking up as though his back were broken.

"Who's this order with then'?" said Dulwich. "I'll look into it. I'll have words."

"Would you? Would you? Yeah, that'd be great. Great. It's, er, it's Two Dragons. They're the fuckwits who can't meet the deadline but Happiness Electronics or whatever they're called reckon they can. Bollocks."

"Never heard of them. How big's this order?"

"Big. Huge. Massive. So stuff Chan."

Through the fuzz of beer-shorted synapses, Dulwich felt the import of Trevor's words. He smiled viciously. "Don't do it, then," he said. "You're right: stuff Chan. Bradshaw's bound to have put him up to it. I'll sort this out. Don't you worry."

He staggered up and wobbled towards the toilets, hidden in darkness at the back of the bar. Trevor, barely able to see, could just make out his newly heroic companion leaning towards a figure concealed in shadows and the flash of flesh as he pointed at the stage. Trevor got up and left the bar. Behind him, Dulwich was introducing himself to a girl in his own particular style of pissperanto, jumbled words and broken sentences and deep-throated laughter. She smiled condescendingly, still cold, and took his arm.

4

From a dish of polystyrene, Wilson Chan shovelled thin strips of beef and noodles into his mouth. He would pause between every few mouthfuls, to sip from his tepid black tea. He ate quickly as his eyes scanned the data on the glimmering screen before him. He put down the dish and reached blindly for a carton of mango juice, prodding the straw into his mouth without looking, his eyes still dancing over the numbers. He pulled over a pen and paper, again without breaking the link between his eyes and the monitor, and only then did he look away to scribble notes on the pad. Satisfied, he resumed eating, one hand tipping the food into his mouth and the other tapping at the scroll bar, almost in an involuntary spasm, as the information rolled up the page.

How many times had his wife scolded him for this behaviour? he wondered. Ever since they had been married, he told himself, and his face, always serene, was warmed even more with a smile. "You will make yourself ill," she had told him. "When it is time to eat, you must do it away from your desk. You must forget work and concentrate on your food. You must let your stomach relax so that it can do the job properly. When that is finished you can go back to work. Kafei says so. He says you must have screen breaks and you must eat away from your work. Otherwise you will be ill. He is never ill. He eats properly."

He tutted. "Those American ways," he muttered.

But her complaints about his self-neglect were her favourite litany; and his, too. The maternal concern, as though he were her son and not her husband, warmed and amused him. The gentle diatribe about his eating habits would develop into general fears about his health and fitness – how he should take more exercise, but of a more gentle and dignified kind than his manic games of squash, how his life should be more active, less sedentary, how he should not spend most of his evenings at home cooped up in front of a computer. He should learn to relax. He was not young any more, she reminded him.

He knew she was right, though up until now he had done little about it. But that would soon change.

Early retirement. Yes, he had decided. He had the option of moving to Singapore, or staying on in this office, reduced in size and importance, but still valuable. Long into the night for weeks past, he and his wife had discussed the choices and gradually come to realise there was a third. It became more attractive by the day. He was 55 years old and had seen too many people just 10 years his senior work until they dropped dead. That was silly. That was not for him, nor his wife. They would enjoy their days together. They had to. Else what was the point of such hard work, such an insatiable craving after the dollar, such long hours and gaps like gnawing pains when he had missed a child's birthday or a special family event. There had to be a reason for such sacrifice. It was only the impending change of circumstance at work that had made him see that he had been making sacrifices all along and that it was time to call in the debt.

Moving overseas appealed at first but slowly lost its promise. He owed it to his mother to stay. And Chan and his wife were too old for a fresh life. This was home, even under the new landlords, this would be home.

Tonight, over their roast duck dinner in the sprawling restaurant around the corner from their apartment, he would announce his decision to his wife. He pictured her reaction with proud joy and imagined the excited conversation that would follow as they mapped out their future.

There was plenty of money in the bank. His father and mother had taught him the primacy of financial prudence. Though poor, they had managed to save enough to put him through college and that gave him enough education and self-confidence to make a start on the ladder after he crept over the border in 1961. Their thrift taught him a lifelong lesson. Without it, he would be toiling away as a second-rate cadre in some godforsaken prefecture, he liked to tell himself.

He pushed away the debris of his lunch and keyed in the code to reveal his personal account details. His eyes flashed over the figures with satisfaction. There was the proof of his worth, there the recompense for his sacrifice.

And not only for him. For his family, too. First priority would be to invest in his brother's Tin Hau restaurant, a reconciliation so long awaited by the family. With the scratch of his signature on the cheque, the bitter years of recrimination and estrangement would end.

His brother was not a proud man and would willingly take the money and revert to the former amiability that had once been so strong between them. No, pride would not spoil this gift; his brother was a pragmatist. That ran in the family.

He would add the loan to his brother to the clutch of investments he had lodged around the territory, gratified that they, along with his savings, would see him and his wife and his mother through comfortably. They would spend their days together in their home, tending the plants on the roof, maybe buying more. Yes, a forest of plants on the roof – how beautiful it would look. And in the evenings, they would eat out at good restaurants, visit friends, have friends round to entertain. They would discuss families, and markets, and politics, and the future, that looming date, fixed, yet with everything after it uncertain. There would be enough to talk about never to get bored, never to miss the money-fuelled adrenaline rush of business. He could play business as a disinterested observer, still taking risks and making calculations, but in the comforting knowledge that he was protected, that he could walk away.

Corrine entered and knocked. Pregnancy had lightened the dark twist of her mouth. It seemed to Wilson that it was only with a life growing inside her that she had seen how good life could be.

"I'm looking for Mr Dulwich," she said. "He's just had a call from London. They wouldn't speak to anybody else. They want him to call them back."

"I see. It was urgent, then?"

She shrugged, pursing her lips, and left the room.

Mr Dulwich was in the street outside the building, wavering against the heat crawling through his body from the pavement. He was staring through bloodied eyes at a makeshift shrine to one side of the door. A small red-painted tin was filled with sand from which sprouted a handful of incense sticks, glowing softly and breathing thin strands of grey smoke into the air. An orange sat on either side of the tin. On one side of the shrine leaned a tatty picture, almost a postcard, of a strange god. More bloody Buddhist, Taoist, animist, Zenist, ancestor worshipist rubbish, thought Dulwich. He pushed his way into the building.

The corridor on the 15th floor was lifeless and empty and suddenly he was ashamed: he did not want to be seen. He was a mess; he felt brittle and vulnerable in a too-obvious state of drunkenness. He had let himself down. They would take advantage. But then he reminded himself: they would not defeat him because he knew them, he had filed their weaknesses, each and every one, in his mind.

He leaned against the wall by the elevator, insouciant, and adjusted his tie. He wiped his eyes and swept his hands over the polished charcoal grey of his Versace suit. I'll do, he thought. I'll more than do. And he examined his reflection in a mirror over a side-table, futilely placed in the corridor as a pretence to homeliness. With a final appraisal he swept into the outer office, nodding curtly at the receptionist and breezing straight through the main room to Bradshaw's office.

"Shit," he muttered, pulling himself out of the vacant cell and looking around as though there were a conspiracy. His paranoia was always heightened by drink.

"'Where's old Georgie boy," he cried, confronting Wilson in his office

"He's not in yet."

"What? Again? What is this – a rest home? A voluntary

agency, or what? Now of all times. We've got enough to do without him pissing about. First he has to go and pick his missus up from the airport, then he's off sick, then they go for a dirty weekend in Macau that takes up half the week. It was lucky we didn't need him for that deal yesterday after all."

"Yes," said Wilson. "I suppose it was lucky."

"Is he coming in or what? I thought work came first in this place."

"It does."

"Oh, does it? I haven't seen much proof of that."

"Probably because you've just arrived. I've been here since 8.30."

Dulwich's mouth snapped shut. "You..." but he stopped and his mouth twisted into a slow, stupid grin. "Okay, Charlie," he said. "You're a clever man, aren't you? So clever that your staff are running rings around you and you don't even know it. They're disobeying your direct orders and losing this firm lots of money. But you're so clever, you'll be able to explain all that quite clearly to head office when they get to hear about it."

Wilson remained calm throughout the tale as Dulwich unfolded it. And just as calmly, Wilson said he would deal with it and made three phone calls while Dulwich retreated to the outer office. By the time he returned, the problem had been solved. Wilson told him, and pushed towards him the faxed report to head office detailing every aspect of what had gone on. In its unemotional specifics, it read like a scientific experiment, a successful one.

"You've covered your back. Well done," said Dulwich with the bitter taste of defeat in his mouth. "You've saved your job."

"They already knew I was leaving." He smiled.

5

Quiescent now, fear gone and faith restored, she listened to the squeaking of the bats, a sound to her as satisfying as tea being poured from a pot. It was twilight, the time of the mosquitoes. And with them came the bats and she loved to watch their fast flitters across her field of vision, following their dark blurs as they disappeared into the dusk.

The fitful grey shapes moved fast across the deepening blue of the sky and swooped into the shadows soaking up the colours of the foliage on the hillside below her. She counted the bats as they passed. The electric whirr of the cicadas rose up from the bushes and an unknown bird called from the distance.

The air was fresh and cool after the light scattering of afternoon rain and she breathed deeply as she mused, seated on the wicker chair on the balcony, the darkness slowly wrapping itself around her. Just a faint reflection from the lamp in the room behind threw spots of light into her enclosure.

Looking down at the unlit, featureless land beneath, she could believe she was far from the madhouse. The traffic, the buildings, the people unseen, the roar of the city unheard, the stink of its life unsmelt. The hill, untainted, rose steeply up before her, cutting a dark line against the sky. Behind her, in streets a wall or a universe away, was life and activity, the grubby, demanding human kind that frightened her. Below and before her was the more innocent sort of life. The cicadas soothed her; the indistinct shapes and muted tones of the twilight hill lulled her almost to sleep. She wanted to hold on to this peace, to keep it. And although she could find it here, in instants like this, she knew where it would be easier to find, where it would be more reliable. Her stay in England and the renewed hope of Josephine's recovery and the shock on her return and the new pact between herself and her husband had thrown things into perspective. And they had talked about their future and he had listened to what she wanted and had agreed to it, trying to disguise his unwillingness even from himself and agreeing to it as if he were paying off a debt. Debt repaid and hope restored, she felt at peace.

Into this solitary, comforting world crept Bradshaw. He eased himself into the chair beside her and she reached out to grasp his hand. He said nothing. She massaged his palm absent-mindedly.

They sat, self-absorbed and staring at nothing, for an uncounted amount of time. The bats disappeared; the insects quietened. At last, she turned to look at him, the lamplight edging his profile.

"It's so nice to just sit here and not worry about anything," she said.

"That's behind us, I hope."

"Have you made up your mind about Singapore."

"Yes," he replied, drawing out the word. "I'll take it just for those first two months. Get it up and running. I'll bring retirement forward a year. Then we can go home. If you're sure." In his voice, there was a faint echo of hope that she would change her mind but she ignored it.

"I'm sure." She gripped his hand, then let it go.

"So. Off to Singapore. And then home," he said, turning at a shadow falling across the light.

"It is seven o'clock, sir," said Abril, leaning through the doorway.

"We'll go inside, shall we? They'll be here soon."

"No. I'll stay out here a while longer."

He nodded and went into the lounge. But he was restless.

Something was missing. Something was still missing. Occasionally, he would look through the glass doors at her still silhouette. He poured himself a drink and pulled some work from his briefcase, but his mind wandered over ground he could not see clearly. He forced himself to concentrate on his work. But he pushed it aside and found himself absently flicking through his address book.

At "C", he stopped. Among the jumble of half-remembered contacts was a name, or rather two initials, that burned with a demanding intensity. He uncapped his pen to scribble out that memory but stopped himself, the pen arrested by a flood of memories and then the attendant guilt and anxiety. He replaced the pen and sat holding the book between his knees, his fingers jammed in the relevant pages, his eyes blank on the opposite wall. Thinking. This is ridiculous, he chided himself. Ridiculous. But something forced him to stand up, something took over and led him into the bedroom where he picked up the phone and dialled her number. The ringing tone was hollow, accusatory. He looked at his hand as if it were acting independently. What am I doing? he muttered, horrified. He slammed the phone back into the receiver, not angry that she was not there but angry with himself, his weakness, his lack of self-discipline.

He forced himself to resurrect that discipline, not to think about what bothered him. He relied on his sense of honour and his sense of debt. Work distracted him, and plans. But a week later, when his defences were down again, when his own guards against himself and what he regarded as his baser instincts were asleep, he tried to call her again. There was a sudden blinding compulsion to speak to her. He pretended that that was all he wanted but inside himself he had already broken the pretence and made one final, binding decision. Promises meant nothing, his earlier resolution was cast aside. There was a need within him that could not be denied because, however fleetingly, it had been awoken and fed. Rational thought and moral compunction and personal obligation meant nothing when this madness attacked. He acted viscerally, without plan or perimeter. He acted without thought. Because the ache of losing one was stronger than the fear of losing the other.

6

Phil lay naked on the bed, a warming fatigue seducing him. Her back against the wall, her curved and tempting hip just a few centimetres from his face, sat Carol, reading a paperback. He listened intently to her slow breathing and the occasional rustle of a page.

A little murmur of approval escaped her lips as she finished the book and put it down on the side-table. She turned to look at him. His eyes were half-closed and his mouth, under slightly dilated nostrils, was set in a smile of repletion.

"Shouldn't we get up for something to eat?"

"What's the rush?" He nuzzled at her flesh with his nose. He was like a cat. "Mmmm. That was so nice," he said. "Lovely. Love in the afternoon: can't beat it. You're a lucky girl."

"You're a lucky boy," was her pat response but today their little call-and-response routine was not funny or sweet, just irritating. Why not just let it be? Why keep talking about it? It got on her nerves. Usually, she paid little attention to the after-game commentary: it was a boy's thing. But today, with the lights misted against the dirty windows and the hum of traffic floating up from the street and Phil, smug and supine, half in and half out of the bed covers, it was something that grated.

Why was there this constant need with him after sex for

analysis and statement? Why not just accept it for what it was? Why put it into words, him, of all people, who never wasted words on anything else? Why not just enjoy the act? Why judge it, why score it? And why be so desperate as to cheat and never give it a score below seven?

Because that thing they had just finished was way below seven. He had left her high and gasping and rushed to his own orgasm, then pulled away and barely made the effort to continue stroking her. And then he made his silly, self-satisfied statements about how wonderful it had been, acting on just bare assumption that she had enjoyed it as much as he. It was only with sex that he was dishonest.

She worked at her feelings like a crossword clue. The act had been... pleasant. Yes, that was it, that was the description for the slumbering disappointment within her. Pleasant, that damning Sunday-sensible word that meant compromised joy, lazy love. A pleasant walk, a pleasant meal, a pleasant afternoon. A pleasant fuck.

Could she put up with such half-measures for much longer? She knew otherwise; she knew better. With Phil, she had settled for second-best. It had not been like that with George.

She remembered, keenly, what had enlivened her about him. It was passion: there was a tangible animal passion to it that she no longer felt with Phil. There had been a heat and a fire there she no longer experienced with Phil. Familiarity, maybe, had suffocated them. They took it all for granted. Sometimes, it was fun, it was enjoyable. It was pleasant. But there was something missing – urgency, desperation. She needed it.

She pulled her jeans from the floor and dragged them over her legs.

"Bathroom," she said and left him crucified on the rumpled bed.

She returned fully clothed and sat by his feet. He smiled at her and she felt affection for him but something irrational inside wanted her to fight that feeling. It was unfamiliar to her, this waking rage inside. She knew it was something that fuelled him and up to now she had never understood it.

"Do you want to go out?" he said, sensing her unease.

"No." She moved around the bed, lost, uncertain, and pulled another book from a shelf. Lowering herself next to him with a stranger's caution, she opened the book and began reading.

"You read books like other people eat packets of crisps," he said. She snapped the book shut and dropped it on the sidetable.

"What's the matter?" He pushed himself up on one elbow and caressed her arm.

"Nothing. Nothing." She stood up and walked from the room. He padded after her, his feet making an ugly slapping sound against the cold tiled floor, and found her curled up, distracted, in the corner of a chair.

"What is it, Carol?"

She shook her head, mute, and he sat beside her, draping his arm around her shoulder and trying to pull her head, turned away and resistant, towards him.

"Come on," he said. He paused. "Are you worried about getting married? Is that it?"

"A little," she mumbled, glad that her answer was ambiguous. Then she was startled by her easy lapse into dishonesty. It was not her way. She looked at him and was overwhelmed with a rush of love, but it was tainted by pity. She did not want to hurt him with the truth.

"I haven't given you an answer yet."

"I know. It's not cut and dried, is it? I thought it would be – that that was the answer. I've felt a lot better about things since asking you. I don't want to pressure you. But I just wish you'd say yes."

"I'm not sure. I'm not saying no. I'm just not sure."

"Okay, okay." He dropped his arm from her shoulder and moved imperceptibly away. "If you do decide not to..." And she looked at him, a little frightened, a little relieved, the wisps of golden hair curtaining her eyes.

"It just surprised me, that's all."

"It felt like a way of breaking the malaise," he said.

"Oh."

She could feel rather than see him getting angry again. He had opened back on to his core concern of self. He was a loner, yet loneliness terrified him more than anything else. He would do anything to wall back that fear. She felt trapped. The ring of the phone rescued her.

"It's for you," he said. "Sounded like Trevor. Difficult to tell with that racket in the background."

He watched her on the phone, puzzled.

"It was Trevor," she said afterwards. "He wants to meet for a drink."

"Now?"

"Yes. He's in trouble."

"Why does he have to call you?"

"We're friends, that's why. He's been sacked. He wants to meet up at Snaps. Do you want to come?"

"Do you want me to come?"

"Don't be a jerk."

"I thought you didn't want to go out."

"This is different, isn't it?"

"You go. I'll stay." And he moved to the CD cabinet as if she were no longer there.

7

For days after, there was a renewed tension between them, a feeling that something was going to break. Little was said. He retired into that hard shell of his, peering out at her, wondering.

He was in an old-style barber shop, a place he made a point of going to in preference to the brash, modern hairdressers with their production-line process: quick-cut boys and lackadaisical wash-girls, insipid pop blasting from a radio and overpriced styles executed barely competently and always without care. He avoided those places, just as he avoided almost anything that had the feel of packaged youth about it. It was shallow and artificial and it annoyed him.

Here, there was a slow, sure feel of skill. These old men, unhurried, confident, put him at his ease. There was no artifice in this drab and messy room. They did their jobs, day in and day out over all the long years, and nothing changed, nothing disturbed or distracted them. They were a solid echo, built of decades.

He was on his back, staring upwards, his neck resting on a foam pad, while the old man fingered shampoo into his dripping hair. The old boy's an artist, he thought, feeling every prod and stroke of those year-worn fingers into his scalp. The man lifted his head, gently, and rinsed the hair on his neck, dragging his hands through the mass of hair, then pulling it outwards and dragging down again. He sat Phil up and towelled his hair dry, his fingers continuing their work through the cloth, every tip of every digit digging into the bone with a considered firmness.

Phil was led towards the mirror and nylon sheets were draped over his shoulders. He said just the word "Short" and the barber set to work, his little scissors clipping deftly, his hands fluffing up tufts and smoothing them back when shorn.

Phil's scalp still tingled from the massage. His eyes burned into their reflection and he drifted away from where he sat. Today, he would demand an answer. It had been two weeks since he had asked and time was up. If she said no, she said no; he would not argue. He knew that would be her answer. She would have said yes within hours or days.

The barber tapped him on the shoulder and he came out of his reverie. With a nod of approval at his reflection, he slipped from the seat and walked from the shop.

He asked himself, as he stood at the bus stop staring at the traffic swishing through the rain that was too light to break the heat, how he would react if she said no. When she said no, he corrected himself. Be realistic.

It was a question without an answer. They could try to carry on as though nothing had happened, as though nothing had changed. But it would have changed because her refusal to commit to him on paper would mean that she was committed to something else, something that he would never be able to touch.

He could not see what blocked that final step. For him, the idea had come almost as a revelation, an obvious way of settling himself and pushing away forever from the void which daily pulled him in. So why couldn't she make that step? She could see and accept his faults well enough to live with him, so why not enough to want to marry him? There had always been an unspoken understanding between them that one day they would get married. Now, when that understanding was put into words, it was no longer understood. Articulating that faith had seemed to destroy it.

There were no answers, only questions. And as they spun around in his head, that cold anger, that wounded anger of incomprehension and unacknowledged self-hate, started to glow again in his heart.

He got off the bus and pushed through the ambling blocks of tourists to the ferry terminal. He saw Carol, trying to cross a road, face flustered and snapping sharply to left and right as she looked for breaks in the traffic. She carried a thick wad of packages under her arm. He called her name and ran towards her.

They found a coffee shop in the corner of a shopping mall, the staff relaxing in the late-afternoon lull and dilatory when it came to serving. He let out a deep, preparatory breath as they sat down and reached for her hands, crossed on the fat brown envelopes she had been in the process of delivering.

"I think two weeks is long enough, don't you?"

"I still haven't made up my mind."

"Carol. This is torture. Just tell me."

"I'm sorry."

"It's no then, is it?"

"I don't want to hurt you."

"It's hurting me more that you won't tell me."

Her head bobbed like a disturbed flower on a stalk. Her eyes were distant.

"What happens? If I say no?" she said.

He shrugged and let out a long, defeated sigh. The question was as plain as an answer.

"Because we couldn't just carry on as we have been doing," she continued. "You'd be even more dissatisfied. It could come between us."

"Why not say yes, then?"

"Because I can't." Her words seemed to fan that cold anger within him but he tried to ignore it. "Look, I don't see the point. What difference will it make? We're either strong enough together or we're not."

"In the early days, you seemed to be the one who wanted to get married. The way you acted."

"I've changed my mind. I've changed, haven't I? I've grown up."

"What the fuck's that supposed to mean?"

He rattled the spoon inside the cup, stirring the coffee unnecessarily, glad of the noise. She wanted the tension to ease, to go away, and her words were soft and cajoling. But the diffidence of her tone, false and patronising, more the words of a mother than a lover, made his anger flare more.

"This has nothing to do with marriage," he hissed. "Has it?"

"What? What do you mean? Alright: let's get married. If it will make you happy."

"Don't be stupid."

"That's what you want."

"We've both got to want it. Don't try to be funny."

"Terrific," she said. "You won't take no for an answer and you won't take yes for an answer. You don't know what you want. You really don't know. Typical."

He banged the table, oblivious to the jerked heads of the staff suddenly snapped around in their direction.

"I know what it is," he said, his voice low. "There's someone else. You're seeing someone behind my back. And it's not important – because we're not married – so you can have the best of both worlds. But by marrying me... You're a hypocrite, Carol."

"What are you talking about?" She felt the red, treacherous glow of her face and looked down at the table.

"You don't want to be with me but you haven't got the courage to say you want to split. So you go fucking around"

"You're crazy. You're talking trash."

"Am I? I don't think so."

"I am not seeing anybody else."

"Liar. If you weren't we would have got married. You wanted to yourself not that long ago; we both know that's true. Yes, that's the answer"

"It's not. It's not the answer."

"It is," he roared and he slapped the menu card from the table. "You fucking hypocrite." He pushed himself up from the table, his hands pressed against the Formica edge and he hovering over his rigid arms with menace hanging off him like a smell. "You're having it off with someone else," he said in an almost singsong jeer. "It's bloody obvious. All this pussy-footing, all these feeble excuses. And I know who it is. I know the bastard. He's a dead man." He hurled himself from the table, crashing through glass doors on to the street.

8

There was just a scattering of customers left in the cavernous bar. The manager surveyed the remnants, clotted in plush-seated corners and around small tables in the gloom. It had just turned eight and it was almost as if a signal had gone off and alerted most of his customers to the fact that they should be home. Or in another bar, livelier and less reverent than this one.

His was a pub for businessmen. Over lunchtimes and for three hours in the early evenings, its vast interior would be submerged in dense packs of suits, European, American, Chinese, all cloned. There was more variety among the clientele in the pubs he used to run and he pined for them.

But this place certainly brought in the money. Despite the eight o'clock death knell and the sudden clearance of the place and the gradual clicking down, notch by notch, of the volume through the rest of the evening, the money poured in through those busy six hours around noon and early evening. After that, it did not matter. The bar could be deserted every single evening after 8pm and he would still be showing a fat profit to the owners at the end of every month.

His attention wandered to the most vocal group left: a young man and two women welded into their padded seats in the corner between the end of the counter and the teakwood, frosted glass doors, lettered ornately in a style from home. They had been there for hours and the manager knew they would stay until closing time. The man and one of the women were already drunk; the third member of the party seemed afraid to leave them and followed each of their beers with an orange juice, gagging on its monotonous sweetness but unwilling to try alcohol.

Occasionally, the man's voice would reach across the room, snatches of words, loud and angry, would permeate the dense atmosphere. Where earlier it had been an indistinguishable babble in a torrent of words, now it was intrusive and annoying. The manager, fed up with the incessant ranting, retired to the cellar for a soothing joint.

In between lapses into a bewildered self-pity, Trevor was pontificating. It was at these times that the sober girl seemed interested. When he dropped into his sudden rages about his treatment, it was Dee, seated next to him with her hand on his crotch, who gave her attention, sharp and unsympathetic.

"The dynasties never last more than a few hundred years," he was saying. "They always break up. Very messy. And this one looks like it's going to break up any moment. I'd be surprised if it reaches it's fiftieth birthday."

"It's not a dynasty," Dee snapped, taking her hand from his groin to emphasise her impatience with him. "There are no emperors or anything."

"There are. Just because they don't ponce about in palaces doesn't mean they're not emperors. They're as far removed from the people as the old lot. They couldn't care less. And because there are so many of them wannabe emperors, they're going to tear the place apart in the next few years. And it will all come down on us if we're still here."

"You think so?" coaxed the other woman, Frances. Trevor warmed to the attention and nodded sagely.

Frances shuddered. She was trapped here, come what may. She could not join their escape route.

"You're just being pessimistic about everything because of what happened to you," said Dee. "Couple of weeks ago you was singing its praises and knocking down anybody who said different."

"Couple of weeks ago I was a working man. It does

wonders for confidence, that. I can see clearly now." And he sang a few lines from the song.

"Bullshit," she said.

He drained his glass and reached for another beer from a collection of them, flat with neglect.

"You're getting boring, Trevor."

"Boring. I'm not boring. You're just ignorant."

"Shutup, you pratt."

"Keep my mouth shut then."

"Yeah, keep it shut," hissed a stranger's voice.

"Phil!" Dee shouted

He ignored her, his eyes burning into Trevor's face. It had taken him hours to find that face, hours of rushing from bar to bar, with his self-righteous anger primed to explode. "I want a word with you, cunt," he said. Frances moved quickly away from her chair and stood by the door, ready to run.

"Do what?" said Trevor, barely able to see.

"You know why."

"'What are you talking about?"

"Carol."

"What about her? Is she alright?"

"I'm going to get you."

And Trevor laughed, an ugly, frothing snort of expired air. He waved the glass towards his mouth. "You're going to have to put on a few kilos before you can do that, my old mate."

Phil lunged across the table, the back of his hand slapping into Trevor's cheek and knocking the glass spinning through the air to smash against a wood panel. Trevor, dazed, tried to push himself to his feet.

Phil grabbed his collar, yanking him across the table and screaming an incoherent babble of abuse. He thrust him back into the chair, Trevor's sack-like body slapping against the leatherette. Phil scraped the table out of the way and leapt at his drunken enemy, his fists smacking blindly into the other's face. Dee jumped back, frozen except for her raised, quivering hands and her gaping, screaming mouth. Frances ran from the bar.

Blood sprayed from Trevor's face, from his eyes, ears, nose and mouth, as the blows came down one by rapid one. Breath and spit from Phil's mouth were hot on his face.

Suddenly, Trevor seemed to come to life and with a long-buried brute strength he hurled Phil away. He fell against a table, his ankle twisting under him.

Trevor loomed over his half-kneeling body and let out a kick. The crunch as it hit bone drowned their mutual screams and roars.

Phil rolled to one side, gasping out staccato cries of pain as more kicks found their target, and pushed himself to his feet, just missing another black, sweeping arc of boot. He grabbed for the leg and twisted it, then stood unsteadily, everything rushing into fast film, and yanked it in a twist, using it as a lever to stand. He pulled Trevor upright and punched him again, his white-hot knuckles sliding off the jawbone. Trevor grabbed his throat and all sound was lost to Phil, all sound except the bursting pump of blood in his ears and the voice, internal, wanting this violence to last for ever, wanting to hit and kick and gouge and punch until there was nothing left of either of them.

Spastically, they danced across the floor, Dee still screaming in a corner, helpless, the handful of remaining customers aghast on the far side. With a movement that was more like a spasm, Phil was free. His wild, staring eyes saw a glass on a table and he reached for it. He swept it across his opponent's face, the glass shattering on the nose, and Trevor wailed in a long, piercing, primordial scream as he fell. Phil pulled back his leg for a final kick, a concluding, triumphant strike, and felt his arms suddenly locked against his sides and his drained body yanked backwards. The manager spun him around and his hand grabbed Phil's jaw. Phil sagged, spent, unable to make out the words pouring from the manager's mouth. Trevor lay twitching on the floor, blood pumping from his nose into Dee's shaking hands.

Carol moved out of the apartment the following afternoon. Her quivering voice on the phone gained her quick entry back into Dirk and Philippe's flat and she packed hurriedly and carelessly, anxious to get away. Her boyfriend's bloodied body and his furious rendition of the story terrified her. Love turned to hate as if flicked by a switch. When Bradshaw phoned her, she almost wept with gratitude.

PART 6

She drank my semen. Good for the complexion, she said. Keeps the skin soft.
 She did not drink it from the source, but from a glass. She squeezed it from the condom, stirring it into the champagne with her finger, and I watched as the beaded clouds fogged the wine and she drank. She did it as casually as if she were drinking a glass of water. At first, I was a little disgusted but as she drained the concoction and slid the glass on to the table and shyly smiled at me, I realised that that act was an affirmation of what she felt. For me. She wanted to taste every part of me. She wanted every iota of my being. And that shocked me more than her action.

We were in a hotel room, 20 floors up, with a dismal view of backs of buildings: air-conditioner units, metal grilles on windows, grimy glass and patched concrete. We could have stayed somewhere much better, of course, but at least it was clean. We were not really interested in a view and, anyway, she had expressed disquiet early on about me "spoiling" her, as she put it. I loved spending money on her but it made her feel guilty and cheapened. It smacked a little, I suppose, of patriarchy or prostitution. What funny ideas some young women have but rather than let any bad feeling fester, we took *rooms in nondescript hotels. Sometimes, she insisted on paying instead of me.*

A block of blinding sunlight lay acute on the carpet by the chairs in which we sat. We had just made love and sat side by side, half-dressed, comfortable and happy. She was wearing my shirt. That became another ritual: after our love-making she would put on my shirt and wander around in it, as if it belonged to her, as if it was her. It was a sort of reminder, I suppose, even though I was still in the same room. I found that gesture very touching.

On this occasion she had found the champagne in the poorly stocked mini-bar and held it up with a pleading look, almost challenging, over her soft, brown shoulder. Damn the expense, I said, and she poured the drink into two transparent plastic beakers and we toasted one another.

She had left her troublesome boyfriend and had moved in with a couple of homosexual friends. In my ignorance, I made a feeble joke about them and she responded with an ice-cold impatience. It was the closest I had seen her come to anger and I suddenly realised how different we were, not just in age but in terms of outlook, background, culture. It made me feel old and out of touch and even somewhat fraudulent in this relationship.

She called me within days of moving in with her friends. I had already called her when I could no longer bear the separation and kidded myself that a little chat would do no harm.

Her voice was sad and small and there was a barely restrained agitation in it that suggested she had been anxious to speak to me for days; I had been away. I'm not talking about bed, she said, although of course we both were. I just need to talk. I'm so mixed up. I can talk to you, George. That's all I want.

Neither of us just wanted to talk, nice as it was to hear that lilting voice and to share some of her burden. But over-riding my concern and her sadness and the delicious companionship was an urgent, suffocating desire. It was agitated by our inability to do anything about it. We touched hands under the table but we could go no further than that. We wanted to, desperately. I was almost willing to abandon the social constraints, almost ready to throw off the convention keeping us strait-jacketed and make love with her on the restaurant table. Her strange, back-lit eyes seemed to flare with want. But we could do no more than make furtive brushes against each other's skin. Convention kept us in check, after all. I had an appointment and then I was expected home.

So we arranged to see each other when I would not be tied by other obligations and where we could buy a little privacy and that is how it proceeded over the burning months of that summer. We would not see each other for weeks and then be constrained by meeting in a restaurant or a pub; only occasionally fulfilling our passion for one another when I could make a cover story for home and then retreat back there, cowed and somewhat defiled but with a sense almost of defiance that my cover would not be blown.

My resolve never to see her again was just a whispering reminder that seemed to belong somewhere else, that had nothing to do with me. I felt as if I were two people and that these hastily sketched plans for an assignation were perfectly acceptable to one and no business of the other. I was able to divide myself in two and detach the parts. I could still feel love for my wife and lust for the girl. When I did not feel guilty – and that would come in great, drowning waves, unpredictable and unavoidable – I could give myself without stint to either person. It felt completely natural. It was not forced. I was two separate people with two distinct lives.

It was nearly a week after that frustrating lunch in the restaurant that we were able to go to bed together, paradoxically able to explore each other with a freshness and a foreknowledge, and knew that it felt right. We fucked like dogs. Then we had the champagne.

We parted that evening with an infinite sadness. It was the same each time over the months that followed. The joy turned to melancholy like white to black.

It went on for months. And those months had about them a desperation, a hopelessness, because I knew this stolen pleasure was temporary. There was a deadline to it. With the move to Singapore, this dream would be ended. I think that sense of finality absolved me of responsibility. I think that buried at the back of my mind was the idea that this was a final fling which would end, naturally, and with it my double life. I did not want it to end.

And during all that time, my alter ego would love my wife with the same devotion as before. I was hardly aware of the charade. Because to me, it was not a charade, it was an ultimate honesty. I had different desires and I was trying to satisfy them all. What could be dishonest about that? If anything, I was a victim of emotion, of things that for too long had been walled behind my rational, sensible self, my other, dishonest, self. Yes, I would tell myself occasionally, I am being greedy and devious and selfish and cruel. But I am not being dishonest. Not to myself. And ultimately, that is what matters.

Although I had afresh impetus in life, I could not conceive of it without my wife. After that single failed attempt to do the decent thing, I recognised both sides of my character and tried to satisfy them both. And, remorse aside, I succeeded. For months, I succeeded and my wife, looking forward to returning home with me, happier than she had been for years because there was an answer and a promise to end her disillusion, had her horizons set in peaceful anticipation. She was innocent of the knowledge, aware only of a calm and unsullied future with me, and therefore happy. By default, but happy. Only with the knowledge did her self-esteem crumble.

1

So. Off to Singapore. George Bradshaw's words still echoed in Abril's mind but she was happy with them now. Months after he had intoned those words on the half-lit balcony, with the summer dying as if it had finally run out of breath and his wife sitting there in a state of happiness not seen for a long time, they had become a promise. No longer a threat, no longer the words that were to consign her back to uncertainty, of the problems of finding work here or of returning to the Philippines to poverty, worry and danger.

She had feared that so much. She had thought that the sudden termination of her employment would knock her family back to the starting block. Her children's education would suffer because they would no longer be able to afford it. There was no point in paying for the education of hungry children.

She remembered, as she sat in the balcony doorway of the empty flat, savouring the light September breeze, how she had started to write a letter to her husband, struggling over the words, trying to lighten their load, trying to be optimistic. It did not work. Her bosses were leaving and she would be out of a job. How could she make light of that? She feared that she would not be able to find a new position in the short time allowed domestic workers. She craved stability, for things to stay as they had always been until she could return to her family on her own terms. That had been taken away.

And as her pen had made its slow, weary track over the page and her mind focused on Freddie, her husband of 21 years, she felt him calling to her, telling her not to worry, that they would manage, they always had. And with a start she heard the phone ring and it was him. She gasped as she listened to his jovial voice crackling at the other end of the line; it was as though he had heard her fears, had watched over her shoulder as she wrote and had come up with a solution.

"I have won a lot of money," he had said and broke into that squealing, breathless laugh she had not heard for such a long time. His lucky lottery numbers had finally proved themselves, he said, and repeated: lucky, lucky, lucky. She pressed the receiver to her ear as though it were his mouth; she wanted nothing more than to hug him, desperately, gratefully.

She wanted him there in that clean, well-lit room, physically, to make him understand how glad and relieved she was.

As he talked, she looked repeatedly at the ceiling or, rather, through the ceiling. The Virgin Mary was there, smiling, benevolent and sharing their joy. Abril could see her more clearly than anything else.

Freddie Flores, gasping for breath, spluttering and stuttering through his incredulous laughter, told of his plans, ill-considered and unrealistic but with such an infectious enthusiasm that she could believe in them too. She would come home for the children, he would start his own business – a garage, maybe – they would buy that plot of land by the beach and build a resort and from their lucky money would grow security and satisfaction and happiness. There would be no more troubles to face; they would all be bought off. She would no longer have to slave for strangers to keep the family in food and in school. She could do what she loved doing best: looking after him, the home and the children, he said. They could all be together again, together and safe.

Her arms tight around her legs, her black, crinkled hair soaking up the morning sunlight, she almost cried with the memory of that word, togetherness. How soon it would be now. So soon that she could afford to slacken off, to ease back from her chores. The shopping list lay incomplete on the table, the mop stood arrested in a pool of soapy water on the kitchen floor, the crumpled shirts waited by the still burning iron. These repetitive tasks now had no meaning. They were not for her, nor her family. They were for strangers and they were no longer important.

She pushed the French windows full open on to the balcony. Banks of grey cloud were crowding around the hilltop in the east and rolling towards where she stood. She called for it to rain and when the first fat drops came down, she put on her hat and coat and went out.

She felt like an imposter as she ambled through the hissing, glistening streets. She had no business being out here, she thought, but a new carefree lightness drove her on, down towards the city to mingle in the rushing, thickening crowds. She stopped at a store, blocked by people trying to escape the rain, and bought toys and pop posters for her children. She was thrilled by the shock of extravagance. She did not care, as she pushed picture tubes under her arm and clicked shut her purse. It was empty except for a couple of crumpled green notes and some loose change, all that she had until the end of the week. She wanted to share her luck and celebrate its arrival.

Returning towards home, she stopped outside her church. It felt odd to be there on a weekday. The small white building, its European style in sombre contrast to the gaudy, cluttered shops nearby, looked forgotten. On Sundays it was filled with people, Filipino domestics, Chinese executives, European housewives. Today, it was empty. She moved with respectful slowness down the aisle, embarrassed by the almost sacrilegious bright colours of the purchases under her arm, and knelt at the altar, her eyes fixed on the white plaster feet of the icon before her.

She heard a shuffling and turned, vaguely recognising the woman who had entered. Abril nodded and smiled, standing and moving towards the newcomer. They were virtual strangers but Abril wanted to share her good fortune, to spread it over everybody. With a wan smile, the woman moved away to a pew and knelt, her praying hands gripped tightly together.

Abril's gaze rested on the woman, recognising the worn

conflicts on her face, the ever-present troubles, and a surge of pity choked her. She could so easily empathise with suffering. She emptied her purse into the donation box and left the church. She went back to her household chores with a refreshed diligence until late into the evening. I'm going home, she thought, smiling as she dropped into sleep. The animal in her belly went away and never came back.

2

The dogs were barking in the empty night, cracking it like brittle glass. Outside, all was still, the vacant street frozen under the orange halogen glow of the lamps. A few late-night lights shone in windows, picking out squares of yellow in the vague face of the apartment block opposite. Behind the tower rose the hill, dressed in black, the jagged edging of foliage topping it against the lighter sky. The moon was a weak sliver.

Carol perched on the tiled edge of the window recess, pressing her hands against its cool surface, stiff-armed, gazing blindly at the street. The only sound was the spasmodic barking of invisible dogs. The room behind her was tomb-like, grey, hazy shadows slatted across its walls.

She coughed softly into her hand and reached for a cigarette. The ashtray had spilt its debris across a tile and she swept it with her fingertips into a little pile and left it. She stifled a yawn and lit the cigarette. Her eyes felt heavy and bruised but she knew she would not sleep. She had tried for two hours and finally given up, creeping from her borrowed bed into the lounge to stare out of the window and smoke and muse. Circular thoughts, the sort that never allowed sleep.

She looked at her watch. Two months to the day since she had walked out on Phil. Two months since that terrible night when he had staggered home and woken her and stood by the side of the bed, bloodied and triumphant but still angry. And she, not recognising him at all now, had left.

She felt nothing for him now, not even the contempt that had eaten inside her when he boasted of his fight. Phil had helped her by his extreme action. He had cleared a path, cleared her vision, like an unblocked tunnel. She could see a clean, straight future ahead of her and she welcomed it. Her only regret was in wondering why it had taken so long.

Now she could be free to judge him, unbound from love and loyalty, and compare him with what she had found. Because Phil did not matter any more; his feelings were of no consequence; she had no sense of betrayal, no need of respect.

There had always been a certain restraint about him, she realised now, that had always bothered her. His love-making was too gentle, almost a plea, tentative. And it was mean and selfish. He withdrew even more into himself and became distant to the point of non-existence. She was just the silky repository for his torment, merely the medium through which he could reach himself. No matter how excited she became she could see on his face and feel in his movements that they were not together in the act. He was working against her, immersed in his aloneness, thrusting out from the void. Only as he floated down from climax did he recognise that she was there.

How different were the two men. How saddened she was that she had been blinded by what she had assumed was love to the hole in her fulfilment. She loved again now, already and not confessed to, but with a confidence strengthened by previous knowledge.

George was so different. He was in control; he was aware. He shared his power; he borrowed hers. When his face hovered above her, he was looking at her, not through her. He had found what he wanted. He was not looking for something beyond, like Phil.

George felt himself in her and knew what to give and what to take. They both knew, instinctively, what the other wanted. He would push deeper and deeper, trying to merge their two selves, reaching and reaching to grasp her, holding and pulling her with him. It was a journey for the two of them.

He let out a roar when he came: a violent, all-encompassing paroxysm gripped his body. Even that was different; even at climax Phil was silent. He would not even let out a whisper of joy. It was almost as if he were fucking by stealth. Then afterwards he would feel the need to talk about it, like a confession.

She stroked her inner thighs as she thought of George and her guts were scorched with the need for him to be there, by her side, on the window-seat in the grey-washed light, with no sound at all. The image of him, naked, erect, moving rhythmically inside her, was seared on her mind.

A door clicked and she looked around from her watery reflection in the glass. A sidelight came on and Dirk stood in the arched doorway, naked except for a pair of tight pants. A figure stood in shadow behind him, Philippe.

"Could you not sleep?" said Dirk in his deep, steady voice.

"No."

"Neither could I," he said.

"Neither could I," said Philippe behind him. He moved into the lounge and his teeth flashed. "Cup of tea?" he said.

Dirk sat in a dining chair, some distance from her, and Philippe came in with the cups and made a deliberate point of sitting close by her, sensing her unease and automatically offering himself as comforter. He held her firmly round the shoulder.

"Your boyfriend came round this evening," Dirk announced from the middle of the gloom.

"Ex," she said, grimacing. "What did he want?"

"Obvious, I would have thought," Dirk intoned with his usual humourless reproach. "He wanted you back. He doesn't give up."

"Tough luck. He's blown it."

"That's what we told him," said Philippe.

"Did he get angry?"

"He is always angry. And he was drunk, as usual. He is a mess. He is a problem. But he wants everybody else to become involved in his problem."

"I know," she whispered.

"He has an eminently slappable face," Dirk continued.

Philippe smirked.

"What are you going to do about him?"

"Nothing. Forget him."

"I don't want to see him here again. It may get ugly. It seems to be the only thing he understands."

"Be careful," she said. "You know what he can do."

"I know what I can do too. Don't worry. I won't have him bothering us any more. It distracts Philippe from his work. And it is still making you unhappy."

"I'm over him," she said, melting into the warm embrace of Philippe. "Anyway," she continued. "I've found someone else."

"So soon?" said Philippe, pushing himself away from her. His eyes were exaggeratedly wide. "That's shameless."

She giggled and gave him a friendly tap.

"Is that wise?" said Dirk.

"Wise is nothing to do with it. It's what I want and it's making me happy."

"Good for you," cried Philippe and he squeezed himself to her again. "So. Who is he? Anyone we know?"

"No. And I'm not going to tell you anything about it."

"Please. Please, Carol. Just a little snippet of information. Just a little something to work on."

"No. N, 0 spells No."

"You are such a tease."

"He's a little bit older than me, that's all I'll say."

"How much?"

"A bit. Quite a bit, actually. I'm not saying."

"So he's married," Philippe crowed and burst into a whoop of laughter and stared at her through a silly mask of shock. "You naughty girl."

She leaned her head on his shoulder and pushed into his big, bullish neck, and her face was flooded with joy. Everything was going to be alright.

3

The Bank of China Building soared above her as she adjusted the lens of her camera. Its height, its brutal geometry, those sharp and savage lines and angles, the blank walls of glass intersected only by diagonal stripes of concrete, its sheer arrogance, put it above, physically and spiritually, the mass of smaller structures as though it owned this town. One day soon it would.

It was Carol's favourite building in a city of favourite buildings and she was determined to capture its cruel essence on film. She imagined how she would justify its choice in class: its simplicity, its dominance, how it stood as a symbol of potential and achievement, just as earlier buildings had until they were dwarfed by a few hundred metres more of steel as the next new building went up, the need to win shouted across the skyline. It was a non-stop progression of fulfilment. A few arty shots in black and white from ground level would look good blown up into 8 by 10s and scattered around the walls of her room in clip-frames.

The bulk of the tower distracted her as she fiddled with f-stops and she repeatedly lowered the camera to soak in the architectural magnificence unobstructed. It really was an impressive sight, from any angle. Nothing could compete with it. She liked the reverent black marble of the stolid Central

Plaza and the classic New York style of the Entertainment Building and could even, sometimes, forgive the fussy pretension of the Hong Kong Bank. But none of them compared to this.

She raised the camera again, the lens swooping past a beggar hobbling to the tiered arc of steps that funnelled into the heart of the building. The woman's presence did not register. Dressed in black and with a dark, deeply etched face and squinting eyes, she eased herself on to the steps and watched the gweilo girl, her neck thrown back as if broken, straining and craning and shuffling backwards in a greedy attempt to pull in every line of that great structure above her. Carol lowered the camera to her waist, still staring upwards, and the woman rattled her can. She was tiny and invisible and Carol moved towards a flyover for a fresh set of shots.

She clicked off a dozen, the tower diminishing through her lens like an endless road, and then looked around, dazed, as though she had come out of a dream. There was a twinge in her neck and her eyes were filled with too much light. She shook her hand, as if to shake the light away, and caught sight of the beggar, adrift on the wide steps, her rags tarnishing the spotless stone, her stubborn poverty denying the importance of the edifice soaring behind her. Carol's photographer eye focused on spectacle, not incongruity. She had no sense of irony, no sense of the absurd. What she saw was what she got and she was happy not to question it.

The woman grimaced toothlessly at her; Carol dropped a few coins into her can and smiled. The woman nodded and Carol moved away, crossing the road to a square where she sat among resting office staff and shoppers.

A light breeze from the nearby harbour ticked the foliage behind her as she surveyed the constant movement in the square and thought about more pictures. How to capture this endless motion, she wondered. During the day, the city was never still. Its restless energy was fed by the people who lived in it: always moving, always with something to do and somewhere to go. Never at rest. Even sitting in the square had a purpose. It was to recharge the batteries, to take stock, to plan ahead. Time was never wasted.

A figure on the far side of the square caught her eye. The

way it walked was the clue to who it was. Striding over the concrete, encased in that hard, firm set of purpose, was George Bradshaw, moving quickly towards a taxi rank.

He was thinking as furiously as he moved. He was working out, once and for all, this unsolvable puzzle in which he had lost himself. I am tired of this angst, he thought. It is teenage. I love my wife and cannot leave her, yet I can betray her. I need them both. That is what I have chosen to do; I must live with it. I am unable to control it. All the analysing and all the agonising in the world will not change that. As long as she never knows, we can continue as we always have. As long as she never knows.

He looked up at Carol's voice. She stood before him, braked from running, flushed, with the gold in her hair highlighting the red of her face. She swept into an excited babble and grabbed his arm. That touch sent a shock through her. Her belly constricted. She was choking on a surge of craving.

She chattered on: about the coincidence of their meeting, of her recent thoughts, of what she had been doing. Photographing buildings, she said, and her arm swept the gleaming towers into view.

"Very Freudian," he laughed.

"Do you have to rush off?" she asked. "I'm not working today. Lieu day."

"They can spare me for a while," he said, as though he had been merely ambling through the square. "What did you have in mind?"

She grinned. "I'll show you." And she took him by the hand and led him to a taxi, stopping it at a love hotel where rooms were booked by the hour and the bedding was always clean.

Afterwards, her head resting on his pounding chest, he whispered into her hair:

"Please don't fall in love with me, Carol."

She fell asleep listening to his heart.

4

"You are not serious."

"Totally." Chris Dulwich threw himself into a chair and brushed his hand through his hair. His eyes were bloodshot and tight through jetlag and his face was dotted with stubble. Even his suit looked less than immaculate, as though he no longer cared about anything. By his side, his luggage sprawled in an untidy pile, the suit-carrier laying like a corpse over the other bags.

"This is the most unprofessional, irresponsible piece of behaviour I have heard," said Bradshaw, holding the edge of his desk like a support frame. "Just weeks to go and you pull a stunt like this."

"Way to go, George."

"I can't believe it. You've jeopardised everything."

"Fraser took it quite well, actually."

"Did he? Did he now?" Bradshaw paused. "I'll be sure to ring him and see just how well he took it."

"Suit yourself."

"I thought you wanted to run the Singapore operation after I'd set it up. With me and Wilson out of the way you could have done as you pleased. Built up your little empire, just as you wanted."

"So did I." Dulwich crossed his legs and slumped further

down into his chair, smug and unbreachable. "Got a better offer, though, didn't I? Much better offer. Told Fraser you'd be happy to stay on indefinitely to run Singapore."

"What right –"

"You would, though, wouldn't you? Admit it."

"Get out of my office. I want you out of my sight by the end of the day. Understand?"

"Understood, chief." And Dulwich sauntered out, dragging his luggage behind him like a final insult.

Bradshaw threw his pencil against a wall. There was never any certainty here. Every plan, every decision, had to have a back-up. And this time he had slipped, because he had no back-up. Dulwich pulling out of the move switched the responsibility right back on to his shoulders. He would have to extend his time with the company, there was no other choice. It would probably take a year to be on the safe side. Yet his wife was expecting them to return home in three months or so; now she thought they were back together, on course, the recent, damaging past behind them and with a future mapped out to her design and his compromise.

But he had no choice. He would have to deal with it. He lived in a city on the edge, a breathless place occupying a nervous state of not knowing. You had to live on your wits, or you fell.

He would ask Alice for a little more forbearance. It would be hard, he knew, but he did not want to picture how hard. Just a little patience, please Alice, he would say to her, just a little more time. He felt trapped.

The phone rang. Startled, his hand snapped over the handpiece. It was Abril. At first, he was terse, impatient with her complaint, blaming her for burdening him with a petty problem that she should be able to deal with. He felt crushed by the weight of other people's expectancies of him.

But he softened as he heard her tale. He softened towards her and at the same time hardened his anger at a vaguer target. Everything had to be made more difficult than necessary. Half the problems he encountered here, or challenges as they were called in the numerous management courses he attended, were borne of a frustrating stubbornness and lack of imagination, an innate awkwardness at odds with the fiery air of potential they all breathed.

That morning he had given her a cheque for her final pay. She was due to leave in a week and he wanted to give her time to bank her money. He had been generous in the pay-off. But now his generosity had been violated by the intractability of a clerk in a bank.

He had refused to recognise Bradshaw's signature. It did not match the one in the records, he told Abril, and Mr Bradshaw would have to present himself at the bank. The clerk's intransigence was tinged with racist glee. Abril could feel that irrational contempt of her skin colour and her race. She encountered it every day. The poor Filipino, like every one of her compatriots, was from the slum country and was here purely as a tool. She had no rights, she had no future. She was nothing. And her familiarity with that sickening attitude could not prevent her from crying as she slouched, defeated, from the bank with the stares of customers burning into her back.

Bradshaw keyed in the number of the bank, then slammed down the phone. No, he would go round there himself. He would confront the bastards and tear a strip off the clerk who had been so perverse. ,He would shout at the manager with whom he had dealt for years, and threaten action. He would close his account, he would refer the matter to the head office. He would defend his helpless amah, helpless in the face of the smug, fraudulent superiority of a spotty clerk who had nothing better to do than paint a picture of Abril's perceived worthlessness.

The queue in the bank was immobile, glued to the floor from the counters to the door. It straggled, zigzag, between stainless steel posts and red velvet ropes and spilt out into the main area.

Bradshaw glanced at his watch again; counted the number of people in front of him again. A trickle of sweat tracking between his shoulder blades added to his irritation.

The line jerked forward and he made a half-step with it. An old man in a thin grey suit and new white sneakers broke from behind Bradshaw and stood poised to move in front of him. Bradshaw was an obstacle, nothing more.

"Excuse me. There's a queue here," Bradshaw boomed, turning a hot, angry look on the man and jerking his thumb over his shoulder. His voice, cracking the torpid silence, shamed him. It was the familiar tone of the Brit abroad – loud, impatient, superior. How he hated it when he heard it, slow words ringing out as they had done since the earliest days of colonialism. He had constantly to remind himself who he was here and despised those smug supremacists who refused to acknowledge that fact.

The would-be queue-jumper snarled and made a point of not moving. He flashed Bradshaw a challenging look, then ignored him. He said something in rapid Cantonese. But his assumption that the insult would not be understood was wrong. Bradshaw understood enough.

"I don't care whose fucking country it is," he roared. "Everybody else is queuing up. So should you." He added an insult in dialect and the man, stung, slipped back behind him, muttering in stage whispers.

Frustrations mounted throughout the day and Bradshaw's temper was put to the test. By the time he got home, he was bruised and defensive. He felt he had to maintain control, of the situation and of himself, otherwise everything would start to come crashing down. The city on the edge seemed to be tipping him over.

5

Alice pushed aside the sheaf of manifests with a sense of achievement. Every item was now logged, ready to be shipped to Singapore or to England, every possession valued for insurance. Those long lists of furniture and ornaments and clothing and books and jewellery and knickknacks formed one solid, undeniable statement. It was final, irrefutable. It said "Home".

She could now relax again and, picking up her sewing box, moved to the balcony where two lamps burned, one on either side of her chair. Abril was already there, standing awkwardly in a corner, sipping at her fruit juice like a guest who had gone to the wrong party. She was uncomfortable with this sudden generosity, this sudden reversal of all that she meant to the Bradshaws. They were treating her as a human being, no longer as a servant in her last few days with them, and she could not adjust to that easily.

Alice beamed at her and said something about the night air as she crossed her legs in the chair and pulled bits of cloth from the box.

"I will go now mum. I will not be late."

"You take as long as you life. Enjoy yourself."

Bradshaw was entering the apartment as Abril made her hurried exit. He saw the familiar silhouette on the balcony and made straight for it.

She stood to welcome him. "Drink?" she said. It was the easy generosity of the triumphant. He nodded yes and stood leaning over the railing, his hands gripping the cooling metal, and stared into the blackness below. He brushed irritably at a bat as it flew too close.

She gave him the drink with another warm smile, glowing in the dark. He muttered thanks.

"Something's come up at work," he said tightly, after waiting for her to resume her seat. "Not good news."

"What do you mean?"

"Singapore. That irresponsible little shit Dulwich has landed us in it. He's leaving the firm."

"And...?" she said, still with that half-smile on her face.

"And he was supposed to be the one taking over after my initial period there. I'm going to have to stay on longer after setting it up."

"What do you mean?"

He sighed and knelt beside her, contrite and caged and anxious to win this one small fight.

"I can't cut and run after just a few months. I'm going to have to see it through properly."

"But it will be running perfectly well after just a few months. They'll easily find someone to replace that Dulwich, won't they?"

"Not as simple as that," he said, standing again. He could feel the change in mood in her, the cooling enthusiasm and hope, the chill of yet another disappointment.

"Why stay on? They're taking you for granted."

"I know," he muttered in a hopeless tone as though he could do nothing about it. "I've got to. Just for six months; nine at the outside."

"Nine! I thought we were going back to England in three. For good. You promised."

"Alice..."

"George! For God's sake! How much longer have we got to be nomads? I want to go home. You led me to believe we would. Soon. After all I have done for you over all these years,

211

you finally listened to me and were going to do what I wanted for a change. You promised we would go home in just a few months' time. Home. Do you understand?" She brushed past him into the lounge and he stood there looking after her. I have let her down again, he thought. I have put her second again.

But his chagrin was short-lived because she stormed back on to the balcony to throw more argument at him. She was in a fury he had rarely seen, a fury of pent-up frustrations and too many compromises and disappointment, of a stoicism so abused that it was beginning to crack under the strain.

"I have never, ever stood in your way," she blazed. "Have I? Never. I have always put what you wanted first and I, poor, weak, mousy, silly little woman that I must be, have just gone along with it. Then finally, finally, when there is something I want and you begrudgingly – oh, yes, don't think I didn't notice it – you begrudgingly agree to it you go back on your word."

"I did not give you my word."

"What?" she screamed and hurled her glass into a corner. The gesture stunned him. In 15 years, however heated the argument, she had never done anything so violent.

"It will only be for a few months longer than we hoped," he said quietly.

"We hoped? Don't make me laugh."

"You go on ahead, then. Yes, you go on ahead."

She looked baffled by that. She shook her head as though she had misheard him.

"What?" She laughed bitterly. "How can I do that? How can I trust you again?"

He was silent for a moment as her bitter words sank in.

"Oh, that's what this is all about, is it?" He shut his eyes in grief.

"We can't pretend it didn't happen," she said.

And he left the flat. Over the quiet hours that followed, her anger slowly abated until she had almost resigned herself to the change of circumstances. She even felt sorry for some of the things she had said. Yes, it was a disappointment but she would live with it. She would have to, she told herself. She always did. She had over-reacted. Just a few months longer and then everything would be back to normal.

She fell into sleep easily, calmed by her stoicism, but when she awoke with a start and saw the red-lit lines on the clockface flick to 02:00 and felt the emptiness behind her in the bed, anxiety came crawling back in beside her. And when she awoke again, some unknown time later, and felt his bulk push its way under the sheets bringing with it not the smell of alcohol to explain where he had been but the smell of soap, all her terrors burst into view with the sudden clarity of lightning. She bit down hard on her lip, silently, her eyes wide and staring but her body paralysed. She realised that she was alone, utterly alone. Although he was just centimetres from her, he was not with her. She had been cheated back into belief, a deception she had been complicit in, building it up with his help and her desperate hope and pretence. And now that pretence was no longer strong enough. She felt completely alone and terrified by that. Noiselessly, without any movement at all, she sobbed herself to sleep.

6

He looked up slowly and his eyes were watery, though not with tears. "It's something I don't think I'm ever going to resolve," he said. Carol took his hand, which felt limp and unresponsive.

"Why not leave it, then?" she said softly.

He looked at her quickly, then turned away, a peculiar embarrassment about him. It was as though he had been interrupted in his private thoughts, unconscious of her presence.

"You don't understand, Carol," he said, his hand finally coming to life in hers. "For the first time in my life, I don't know what to do."

"Maybe we should stop seeing each other."

He forced a weak smile on her. "I can't not see you."

"And you can't leave your wife?"

"No."

"There's your answer then." She felt bitterness towards him then, a frustrated incomprehension. She thought she had understood, she thought she knew where they both were in this but hearing his answer embittered her.

Yet she did not want him to leave his wife. She wanted this closeness without suffocation; she wanted this freedom. They could hardly live together anyway. The barriers between them, particularly the one of age, could not just be left outside the bedroom door if they were sharing their entire living space.

"I have thought of leaving her. You know I tried once, early on. I couldn't do it then and I can't do it now. She has a tremendous hold on me and I have a great deal of. affection for her. Yet I was an utter bastard to her the other night. And even though she's not speaking to me, we're still together. Neither of us wants to leave the other."

"Are you sure you still want to see me?" she was almost timid as she asked, afraid of the answer yet needing to push him into honesty.

He nodded an affirmative. "I'm a greedy man."

"A hungry man. There's a difference."

"But it's not fair. Not to you, and not to Alice."

"I'm not complaining, George. This is what I want. So long as it's what you want and your wife isn't hurt then really, deep down, we're not doing any harm, are we?"

He snorted. Her words had the ring of truth and commonsense but there was something about them that jarred. They were not complacent, nor glib. They were honest words delivered honestly. Maybe that was all that jarred.

"Anyway, it's academic." She sighed. "Singapore…"

Now she was being complacent. It was not academic.

"I've told myself a hundred times to stop agonising about this," he said.

"So you should."

"Put up, or shut up, eh?"

"That's right."

"It's just that the other night… I think she…" He let out a huge, impatient gasp of breath and fell back in his chair. "Put up or shut up," he said again. "I wish I knew the answer."

7

But the answer never came. Not then, not the next day, nor the weeks after. Bradshaw and Carol would rush towards each other for a few stolen hours, then rush apart. He would return to Alice, to that safe, comfortable existence founded and restored on routine and a seeming trust. She appeared to have forgiven him and she told herself that she had, that she had to. She refused to acknowledge her deep-down core of cold, hard resentment. Occasionally, he would see a blank light in her eyes and he would ask her what was the matter and she would reply, *Nothing*, and flick a weak smile at him and turn away. The flickering palpitations that came upon her out of nowhere and made her heart flutter and clogged her throat with a choking rush of anxiety were unknown to him. The dead weight of sadness that would suddenly fill her in quiet, solitary moments like a dam burst of water was her private torment. He knew nothing. They would sit together on the sofa, the rousing strings of a piece of classical music filling the apartment, and he would think how nice it was, how soothing was this company, this companionship. They would huddle together in bed and he would feel secure. And then he would choke on his own burning desire for Carol and Carol's body and the other half of his psyche would take control.

He was thinking of her now as he stood in the clearing in

the woods, the sky painted grey with fat clouds of rain. He was thinking of her and how soon, how very soon, he would lose her. You got used to loss in this place. You adapted to impermanence. You had to: it was a survival instinct. People came and went, deep friendships and animosities, mutual joy and contempt, were relegated to mere memories. Abril had gone; Dulwich had gone; Wilson was no longer a fixture in the office but just a vague shadow to see now and again when one remembered the other.

They were all figures from the past, losing their outlines. He could cope with that, even with Wilson's fading presence; he was used to that. But to lose Carol to the past he was barely able to reconcile. Being sensible about it, telling himself that a decision had been made for him, a solution imposed from outside, meant nothing. It was a booby prize.

"They're over there," Alice shouted.

He grunted and followed her closely up the path through the trees, skirting the lone banyan with its aerial roots dripping, and took her hand as they topped the ridge and began scuttling down towards another clearing. It was full of people; so strange to see faces and the bright mishmash of clothes in the greens and browns of the woods.

The rain started as Alice tried to introduce her husband to the few people she knew among the crowd of volunteers who were taking the Vietnamese boat children out for the day, out of their prison camp into the freedom of the woods, to picnic, and walk, and play. As the rain intensified, the children were herded towards a large stone hut by the edge of the road. The rain thickened around them, roaring to the ground, drowning Alice's feeble attempts at etiquette.

In a shadowy corner of the hut, hemmed in by children, stood Carol, her face flushed, trying hard not to stare at him. Paralysed by embarrassment, she could move only her eyes which she flicked over the young heads around her. Then they flicked back, at Bradshaw and his wife. Alice smiled back at her; Bradshaw, staring wistfully out at the rain, still did not know she was there.

Carol busied herself with the children, fussing and teasing and talking and pushing herself against their little bodies in that cramped hut.

When the rain stopped, there was a stillness under the watery sun. They trooped out of the shelter: twenty-five children and their adult minders.

The grass was cool on the naked calves of the children as they burst into runs towards the barbecue pits. The volunteers followed at a more leisurely pace, relishing the unusual freshness in the air and the tentative twittering of birds coming back to life after the fury of the storm.

Alice lingered in the doorway of the hut, watching the receding backs of her co-workers and her husband standing at the far corner of the clearing, aloof and alone, staring up at the branches of a tree as if in communication. She swept her gaze slowly around the glade, at the puddles in the red earth, the shining rocks protruding from their rings of water-heavy foliage, the slight bank rising towards the trees. A flock of birds sketched black marks across the sky and she stared after them as they disappeared across the sun which gathered strength by the minute.

Beyond the squeals of the children and the occasional bellow of laughter from an adult, she could hear the sounds of nature restored. The birds, the crackling of twigs under their burdens of raindrops, the rustle of leaves, the mysterious sounds of movements in the undergrowth. She took a deep breath, luxuriating in the sounds and the cool air entering her lungs.

A tiny girl thrust a ragged posy of flowers into her hand and waited, momentarily, for a smile of approval before running back to the main group. Alice, sniffing at the flowers, sauntered towards them. Bradshaw stood uncertainly off to one side.

"Make yourself useful, George," she said.

He made awkward gestures of assistance to the men round the barbecue pit. They took him in and Alice, baffled by his unusual diffidence, went to another group and started chatting. This would be her last day out with the boat children and she forced enjoyment out of every aspect of it. She caught sight of the girl who had given her the flowers, alone again, and Alice felt a kinship and went to her.

"Hello." The girl turned towards her, then looked back at the pile of stones she was playing with.

"Are you building a house?" The girl turned again. Her mouth was set in a frown of concentration and there was a depth to her eyes, a serious, adult depth that was startling in such a young face. She pulled stones from the earth and added to her pile.

"Can I help you build your house?" And Alice leaned over the girl and picked up a pebble to hold before the child's eyes. Warily, the girl reached for the stone and flashed Alice a look, suspicious that this was a game, a trick. She put the stone on top of the pile, still cautious, and suddenly smiled at Alice in shared triumph. The ancient, bruised wisdom in her eyes faded. She edged to one side of her cairn to let the woman closer.

They stayed together through lunch, sitting slightly apart from the others, and again while the children abandoned themselves to their games – football, frisbee-throwing and tag. Alice became lost in the world she and her new friend had created for themselves. They chatted in their distinct languages as if they understood each other.

She looked up suddenly and saw George talking to Carol. There was something in their positioning, rigid and awkward as they faced each other, that made it seem too earnest for idle chitchat. As if by a signal, he looked up and saw his wife looking at them. He walked over.

"Who's she going to rescue today?" Alice joked. Bradshaw responded with an empty smile.

The team leader joined them and said that the group was going for a walk. Up that path there, he said, pointing to a brown trail disappearing into the bushes at the side of the hill. Alice reached for the girl's hand but she ducked away and ran. With a jerk, as the mud slipped from under her, she fell sidewards and smacked into the wet ground. The three adults rushed to her.

The girl was blind to their attention, screaming and absorbed in her pain and pointing to her ripped knee as if it did not belong there. Alice cooed over her, dabbing at the blood with a handkerchief.

"I'll stay here with her," she said, sensing people gathering around her. "You go on, George." She watched them out of the corner of her eye as they disappeared into the vegetation.

George was last in line. He seemed to be holding back, waiting for something. She felt a little snap of impatience with him. Then he waved and the curtain of leaves fell behind him and he was gone.

"Is she alright?" It was Carol, her sudden voice a violation. The child's screams subsided to a shuddering gasp for breath.

"Yes."

"How are you?" Alice stood and looked at her properly for the first time. It had been months since they had met, an entire summer ago, in fact. They exchanged smiles. But Alice noticed there was a tautness to the other woman's face, a pulling back she did not remember from the last time they met. Alice was distracted from the face by something that moved at Carol's throat as she turned away. It was a medallion of some sort, an indistinct brown lump hanging around her neck masked by the floppy material of her shirt.

"You're going to Singapore soon, is that right?"

"Yes. Very soon."

"I'd like to have gone, too, but the company let me go."

"Oh. So are you working now?"

"Yes. Mr Bradshaw fixed me up with a friend of his at another company. Mr O'Hare."

"Did he?" Alice was only half-listening. There was a cold feeling within her, inexplicable.

"Do you know him? I think he plays golf with your husband."

She looked at Carol again and as she did so the child between them burst into a long, racking sob and Carol bent quickly forward to her. The medallion jumped from the open neck of her blouse and hung in the air, swinging imperceptibly before Alice like a hypnotist's watch. It was a wooden Buddha, pinkish-brown, its belly protruding and its arms upraised, the smile on its carved face a sort of sarcastic leer.

Alice shuddered, the skin rippling from her feet to her neck. The cold sensation inside her congealed into ice, choking her. A blur of images rushed before her eyes; she was blind now to all external things. She edged away and stood erect.

"Are you alright?" Carol stood also.

Her words did not make any sense. They came muffled

from far away and Alice could attach no meaning to them. They were like chunks of sound from behind a thick wall. Her head flicked and she stared at the cheap wooden figure again, half-concealed now but clear enough. It was all she could see.

"Mrs Bradshaw? Alice?"

All the clues, ignored, all the doubts, suppressed, came rushing back and amassed into one solid, damning form, screaming the answer, condemning her wilful oblivion. Suddenly, she knew.

Her mouth was open, gaping. One word came out, one long, roared scream of sound burst from her as the block of ice shattered inside her and she exploded into furious life. Carol stumbled back and Alice swept a barbecue fork, as long as an arm, from the ground, her scream bouncing around the grove. Her eyes locked on the twin prongs of the fork as they drew silver lines in the air and then, suddenly, red lines as they slashed into Carol's throat. Alice brought the fork back in an almost graceful swoop and the pointed tips sliced again into the flesh.

Carol fell, gagging, holding her throat, her face frozen in shock. The other woman stood over her and lifted the fork high over her head and plunged it down into the squirming, screaming body. Then she lifted it and thrust it down again, into the face, into the chest, and then again and again, an incomprehensible babble pouring from her mouth like music from hell, and all Bradshaw could see as he raced from the bushes was the flash of silver up and down through the air and the broken sprays of blood from its tail and all he could hear was that cry, that endless animal howl of dislocation.

PART 7

I took the fork from her limp hand. She was not even conscious that she was holding it. She was staring at the body between her legs, that twisted, tragic figure below. I gagged as I saw that face on the ground, a greying mask flecked with blood, red lines wriggling and bubbling through it, the stain of blood seeping through her clothes.

I stood there, paralysed, my wife gasping uncontrollably as she stared at the fork now hanging from my hand. My face was fixed on that death mask on the ground and through my blurred consciousness I believe I cried.

We were both led away, passing through a wall of screams and crying and stuttered outbursts of shock and outrage and horror. We were led away and at some stage we were separated. Not a word passed between us; there was nothing left to say. I believe she never spoke to anyone ever again.

My defence lawyer, desperate to help me when I no longer wanted to help myself, tried to persuade the court that mine was a crime of passion, a simple but tragic loss of control. But the judge and the jury would not accept that. No amount of passion could excuse such inhuman savagery. That was what the judge said. There were no extenuating circumstances, he went on. I was guilty, guilty of murder, of cold-blooded and *calculated murder. He said that and I agreed completely. He confirmed what I had come to accept.*

That was why I put myself in the dock.

I was responsible for Carol's death. Alice did not kill her. I did.

THE END

ABOUT THE AUTHOR

London-born Steve Langley is a journalist and teacher. He lives in Devon, England, with his partner.

Printed in Poland
by Amazon Fulfillment
Poland Sp. z o.o., Wrocław